Praise for the novels of

STEPHANIE
BOND

"The perfect summer read."
—*Romance Reviews Today* on *Sand, Sun...Seduction!*

"[*My Favorite Mistake*] illustrates the author's gift for
weaving original, brilliant romance that readers
find impossible to put down."
—*Wordweaving.com*

"This book is so hot it sizzles."
—*Once Upon a Romance* on
She Did a Bad, Bad Thing

"An author who has
remained on my 'must-buy' list for years."
—*Romance Reviews Today*

"True-to-life, romantic and witty,
as we've come to expect from Ms. Bond."
—*The Best Reviews*

"Stephanie Bond never fails to entertain me
and deserves to be an auto-buy."
—*Romance Reviews Today*

STEPHANIE BOND

Baby,
COME
HOME

MIRA®

MIRA®

Recycling programs
for this product may
not exist in your area.

ISBN-13: 978-0-7783-2994-7

BABY, COME HOME

www.MIRABooks.com

Printed in U.S.A.

This book is dedicated to every person
who has answered the call of going home.

ABOUT THE AUTHOR

Stephanie Bond was raised on a farm
in eastern Kentucky where books—
mostly romance novels—were her number one
form of entertainment, which she credits with
instilling in her "the rhythm of storytelling."
Years later she answered the call back to books
to create her own stories. She sold her first
manuscript in 1995 and soon left her corporate
programming job to write fiction full-time.
Today Stephanie has over fifty titles to
her name, and lives in midtown Atlanta.
Visit www.stephaniebond.com for more information
about the author and her books.

1

"We're way behind schedule," Marcus Armstrong announced.

"That's ridiculous," Porter Armstrong said, smacking his hand on the desk between them. "We're way *ahead* of schedule!"

Kendall Armstrong looked back and forth between his older brother and his younger brother and gritted his teeth, resisting the urge to jump in, like always, to mediate between his stubborn siblings. Serious-minded Marcus had a tendency to be overly cautious, and the more reckless Porter had a predisposition for leaping before he looked—literally. His younger brother had only recently rid himself of the casts on his broken leg *and* broken arm that had kept him hobbled for the whole summer and most of the fall. With the holidays behind them and a new year begun, everyone was feeling the pressure of the one year plus change that remained on the federal deadline to prove their green experiment of rebuilding the mountain town of Sweetness, Georgia, would work.

The brothers had started from nothing—worse than nothing, really. Ten years ago an F5 tornado had flattened their small hometown, sparing human life, but obliterating businesses and homes. The devastation had been the death knell for the tiny town already dwindling in population and economic prosperity. The town council had elected not to reorganize; residents had relocated. When the Armstrongs had arrived a year ago, the roads into Sweetness were choked and overgrown, the land consumed with kudzu vines and littered remains of buildings, vehicles and trees shorn by the twister. Wild animals roamed freely among the rubble. It was as if the outside world had forgotten about Sweetness.

Now, including the two hundred and fifty or so workers the men employed, the hundred or so women who'd come en masse from Broadway, Michigan, in response to an ad the brothers had placed in a local newspaper, looking for women who wanted a fresh start, their children and miscellaneous relatives who had since followed, and various professionals and trade experts who'd come to help them shape the town, the population of Sweetness had grown to— Kendall turned his head to look at the latest number written on the chalkboard by the door—536.

"*Ahead* of schedule?" Marcus said to Porter. "What calendar are you looking at?"

"The same one you're looking at," Porter said, jerking his thumb toward the giant calendar that papered the walls of the office.

"Oh, yeah?"

"Yeah!"

They suddenly stopped and looked over at Kendall, who sat in a chair across the room.

"Aren't you going to weigh in?" Marcus asked.

"You're just going to sit there?" Porter said.

Kendall pursed his mouth and nodded. "That's right." He scooted his seat back against the wall, then made a rolling motion with his hands. "Go ahead, have at each other. Settle this like real men. Porter hasn't been in a cast for a while."

Marcus frowned. "You don't have to be sarcastic."

Porter scowled. "Yeah, it doesn't suit you, brother."

Anger sparked in Kendall's stomach, sending him to his feet. "Really? Because it feels pretty damn good! I'm tired of constantly trying to wrestle you both back to middle ground. You're wearing me *out.* I have half a mind to leave this place and never come back!"

He stopped, surprised but relieved that he'd voiced the thought that had been hovering in the back of his mind for months now. His brothers gaped at him.

"Leave?" Marcus said, sounding alarmed.

"You can't leave," Porter said, his eyes wide. "Not now, not when everything is going so well."

Kendall gave a little laugh—his brother could afford to be cavalier since he'd fallen in love with the town physician, Dr. Nikki Salinger. "Everything is going well for *you,* Porter. You have Nikki and you've started building your own home. You have a reason to stay here." He stopped, before he said too much. Before he revealed the cause of his increasing restlessness.

But from the way the expressions on his brothers' faces changed, he knew he'd tipped his hand.

"This is about Amy Bradshaw," Marcus said.

Porter sighed. "Kendall, why don't you just call Amy and ask her to come back home?"

Kendall fisted his hands. "How many times do I have to tell you? She told me to leave her alone. She doesn't want to have anything to do with me." He exhaled, shaking his head. "I was able to put her out of my mind when I was in the Air Force, but coming back here dredged things up again." He stopped, embarrassed, expecting one of his brothers to step in to rib him.

But they didn't. They just looked at him with such pity, he couldn't bear it. He was pathetic, he conceded. Amy Bradshaw had left Sweetness over twelve years ago, before the tornado had struck. He'd come home from the Air Force to attend her aunt's funeral, and Amy had expected to leave with him. But he wasn't ready to get married. When he'd suggested she stay in Sweetness for a while to give herself time to grieve her aunt's passing, she'd turned cold. Her parting words were branded in his brain.

You think I'm going to sit in this podunk town and wait for you? Forget it. Goodbye, Kendall. And don't ever try to contact me.

She'd left. Climbed into her beater Chevy and drove away without looking back.

He hadn't known where she was for the longest time. She'd left a few distant relatives in Sweetness, but none of them had been close to Amy—or forthcoming about where she'd moved, if they'd known. He'd almost gone mad with worry until a buddy in the Air Force with superior computer skills had tapped into some kind of national database and traced her social security number.

"Broadway, Michigan," the man had announced. "Want her address and particulars?"

Kendall had passed. He hadn't wanted to violate Amy's privacy. And he really didn't want to know if she was living with someone, or perhaps even married and hadn't changed her name. It was enough to know where she'd landed, that she had found a new place to call home. But he'd thought of her every day for the past twelve years.

And when Marcus had charged him with attracting one hundred single women to Sweetness to help them grow the town, he'd reasoned that Broadway, Michigan, had seemed as good a place as any. The economy was depressed, and the unemployment rate was high. It seemed likely that women in a cold climate would find the Southern sun appealing.

And yes, he'd hoped that Amy would see the ad and answer the call to come home to Sweetness.

Come home to him.

But she hadn't. As luck would have it, Amy and

Nikki Salinger had been friends in Broadway. Amy hadn't told Nikki that she'd grown up in Sweetness, but the women had stayed in touch after Nikki had relocated and subsequently decided to stay. Nikki had inadvertently exposed Kendall's strategic placement of the ad when she'd mentioned Amy's name to Porter who had, in turn, confronted Kendall and outed him to Marcus.

Now that his brothers knew why he'd picked that particular town for the ad, Kendall's humiliation was complete.

"It's been a long time," Porter said quietly. "Maybe Amy's changed her mind about you contacting her."

Kendall's temper flared. "Porter, I did contact her! I put a damn ad in the newspaper, didn't I?"

Porter pressed his lips together. "Maybe she's waiting for something more personal. Like a *phone call*."

Marcus grunted. "Since Amy still hasn't told Nikki about her ties to Sweetness, that kind of proves the woman has no intention of ever setting foot here again, doesn't it?"

Kendall's heart bottomed out.

Porter reached over and boxed Marcus's ear.

Marcus pulled back, then looked contrite. "I'm just saying."

"Ignore him," Porter said to Kendall. "He'll get his someday. Look, I know you said you didn't want to know anything about Amy, but Nikki said—"

Kendall held up his hands. "I don't want to know,

Porter, unless Amy tells me herself. I don't need details to obsess over. And I'm not going to stalk her."

"Right," Marcus said drily. "Placing an ad in her local newspaper isn't stalkerish at all."

Porter glared at him. "Shut up already!"

Marcus jammed his hands on his hips. "It needs to be said. I'm sorry, Kendall, but you had your chance with Amy and you blew it. You need to move on with your life. Can we get back to work, please?"

Porter's face reddened in anger, but Kendall held up his hand, then dropped into the chair and sighed. The truth was a bitter pill to swallow. "Marcus is right. I need to let go of this thing with Amy." He looked up, grateful at that moment to have his brothers around. Then he straightened his shoulders. "We have a town to build. What's next?"

"Next," Marcus said without missing a beat, "is having our ducks in a row when the representative from the Department of Energy shows up to file a progress report. The guy's name is Richardson."

"Do we know when to expect him?" Kendall asked, trying to force his mind to the matter at hand.

"*You* should expect him sometime over the next couple of weeks," Marcus said.

Kendall blinked. "Since when did I get voted spokesman?"

Marcus looked at Porter, then raised his hand. "I vote for Kendall to be our spokesman to the D.O.E. rep."

Porter raised his hand. "Ditto."

Marcus turned back to Kendall. "You're in."

Kendall frowned, but knew when he was outnumbered. "I assume this will involve some sort of presentation?"

"And a tour," Marcus said. "Plus lots of schmoozing to make sure we don't lose our grant for being behind schedule."

"We're in good shape," Porter insisted with a sense of casual confidence that Kendall envied. "Our downtown is growing every day. The clinic received Rural Health Clinic certification, the helipad is done, we have a school, a General Store and a post office."

"The post office is *inside* the General Store," Marcus added.

"For now," Porter countered.

"The most important thing is we got our zip code," Kendall said. Since the tiny post office had opened, he'd checked every day for a letter from Amy. So far—nothing.

"Right," Porter said. "Demand for our recycled mulch is growing, the windmill farm is generating power for the town, the community garden is supplying seasonal produce for the dining hall."

Marcus winced. "We'll be in trouble if the representative eats at the dining hall."

Porter nodded. Colonel Molly McIntyre ran a tight ship, but the cuisine wasn't exactly cruise-worthy.

"Maybe we can distract Molly with the Lost and Found webpage, then ask someone else to step in for the day," Kendall suggested.

Porter snapped his fingers. "The D.O.E. rep should see the town's new website. All of our progress is recorded there, with photos."

Kendall nodded, glad to have his mind diverted from…well, there he went again, thinking of Amy. He gave himself a mental shake. "Okay, I'll prepare a presentation. Meanwhile, what's next on our plate?"

"The residents are asking for a church," Porter remarked. "A lot of couples are pairing up."

"But we don't even have a minister," Marcus countered.

"*Because* we don't have a church," Porter said.

Marcus arched an eyebrow. "Are *you* planning to walk down the aisle soon?"

Porter blanched. "N-no. Nikki and I haven't… gotten…that far."

Kendall bit back a smile at his little brother's sudden nervousness. He had no doubt Porter was head over heels for the doctor, but everyone— including Porter—had assumed he'd be a bachelor forever. He was still easing into the idea of being half of a couple.

"For now then," Marcus said pointedly, "we can continue to hold services in the dining hall or in the great room of the boardinghouse. I think we need to shift our focus to rebuilding Evermore Bridge over Timber Creek." Marcus walked over to an aerial map and pointed to a large green section of land.

"This land is within the city limits, but it's cut off from everything else. I think we should relocate the recycling center we're planning to build to this parcel, away from town because of potential noise levels. A new bridge will make this farmland accessible for other projects, too. I received a proposal this week from a scientist who's looking into new uses for kudzu."

Porter snorted. "That vile weed has a use?"

The Japanese vine had been introduced to the state of Georgia as ground cover along the interstates, but had taken on a life of its own, spreading via seed and runners, consuming anything that didn't move. Virulent and aggressive, kudzu was widely considered a nuisance.

"This man thinks it produces a chemical that can treat Alzheimer's."

Kendall wiped his hand over his mouth. There were some moments when the brothers couldn't believe the ramifications of this undertaking—this green experiment was so much bigger than just rebuilding their mountain hometown. "What is he asking for?"

"He has his own grant for a laboratory and staff. He's asking for a half-acre of land for his lab, and twenty-five acres of kudzu."

"Hell, let's give him fifty acres of the stuff," Porter said.

"Okay, this one's yours." Marcus handed him a printed email, then turned back to the map. "I say we rezone this entire parcel for commercial use," Marcus said, "but we have to provide access to it.

That's why I think we need to move the bridge up on our priority list."

"Kendall can build us a new bridge," Porter said.

At his brother's reference to his civil engineering degree, Kendall made a rueful noise. "But I can't design one. We need a structural engineer for that."

Porter held up his finger. "I—"

"Got it covered," Marcus cut in, giving Porter a look that said *he'd* take care of finding a structural engineer. He glanced at Kendall. "That will free you up to get ready for the D.O.E. rep."

Kendall nodded. "I trust your judgment. We're going to need some crackerjack contractors, too, guys who know how to pour concrete in cold temperatures."

"Understood," Marcus said, then he clapped Porter on the back. "While Kendall and I build a bridge, you can get started on a church if you want."

Porter pursed his mouth. "I think you're right— we should hold off for now. I think I'll go scout out the parcel across the creek."

Marcus smiled. "Thought you might."

Porter left and Kendall stood, then reached for his laptop. "Guess I'll head to the media room and get started on that presentation."

Marcus nodded. "Sounds good."

Kendall reached the door, then turned back. "Marcus, about earlier…"

"Yeah, sorry about that, man."

"No...you're right—I need to move on. Thanks for the wake-up call."

"Sure thing," Marcus said, then picked up his phone. "Speaking of calls, I need to make some."

"Right. See you later." Kendall grabbed a jacket, then turned and walked out of the office trailer toward the center of town. The temperature was bracingly cool, just what he needed at the moment to clear his head.

As he approached the crop of buildings that made up the new downtown area, he realized they had much to be proud of. School was letting out, and the sound of children's laughter hung in the air. Pedestrians bustled around and a couple of cars rolled down Main Street. Soon they would have to start thinking about installing a stoplight.

Sweetness had been revived. If he squinted, the scene reminded him of the way the town looked when he was young. Then he sighed. There was only one thing missing.

Amy.

2

Amy Bradshaw pulled out her desk drawer in search of chocolate. Most days she took solace in the surety of the demands of being an engineer—there were no gray areas when it came to CAD drawings and blueprints and per square inch load of reinforced concrete. But going out on her own after being laid off from the state of Michigan's Department of Transportation was another matter.

Her former boss had recommended her for small jobs here and there, but she was waiting to hear if she'd been selected as project leader for a big reservoir project, and the suspense was driving up her stress level. She was qualified for the position, and she'd been told by insiders that the longer it took, the more likely the news would be good—engineers that were out of the running had already been notified.

She had a lot riding on this job.

When her fingers closed around a cellophane wrapped chocolate cupcake in the back of the drawer, she whooped in triumph. She tore open the wrapper and bit into the cake, not caring that it was stale and dry.

While she chewed, momentarily gratified, Amy noticed that underneath the cupcake was an ad she'd cut out of the local newspaper over six months ago. She pulled it out and swallowed, wincing as the hard ball of empty calories scraped down her throat.

The new town of Sweetness, Georgia, welcomes one hundred single women with a pioneering spirit looking for a fresh start!

Sweetness, Georgia…her hometown. Her initial shock at seeing the advertisement for women to help rebuild the small town that had been devastated by a tornado ten years ago was trumped only by the names of the men behind the ad: *Armstrong.*

As in Kendall Armstrong and his brothers Marcus and Porter. As far as she knew, Kendall didn't know where she'd settled after leaving Sweetness. On the other hand, the chance of the ad landing in her local newspaper seven hundred miles away strictly by coincidence seemed a little far-fetched. The first few days after the ad had appeared, she'd been besieged with paranoia, looking over her shoulder and half afraid to answer the phone. But Kendall hadn't appeared on her doorstep and slowly she'd relaxed. Then the group of women, including her friend Dr. Nikki Salinger, had left Broadway to make the trip south to Sweetness. Again, she'd held her breath that Kendall would contact her.

And again, he hadn't.

And then another emotion had crept in—curiosity. Obviously, Kendall knew where she was. So why hadn't he called or…something?

Because she'd told him not to. That last conversation was burned into her memory.

Wait for me, Amy. I'll come back for you.

But Amy had been tired of waiting for Kendall to commit to her, tired of him coming home for a few days of leave from the Air Force for marathon lovemaking, then taking off to another adventure, leaving her behind.

You think I'm going to sit in this podunk town and wait for you? Forget it. Goodbye, Kendall. And don't ever try to contact me.

Amy worked her mouth back and forth. He'd taken her at her word.

Despite her bravado, after leaving Sweetness, she'd spent many long nights crying over Kendall Armstrong. And he'd been heavy on her mind as she'd pursued an engineering degree in night school. Their mutual interest in the science of structure had been one of the things that had drawn them together in the first place.

They'd been an unlikely couple—she was a tomboy and had a tendency to get into scuffles with kids who teased her over her wiry red hair and Goodwill clothes. Kendall was a scholar and an athlete from an upstanding family, with a cloud of beautiful girls around him. One day between classes, he'd pulled her off the back of a boy who'd questioned her sexu-

ality. His blue eyes had twinkled as he explained he'd
been afraid for the boy's life. She'd fallen head over
heels in love with him on the spot. Kendall had been
the smartest and the sexiest boy she'd ever met. He'd
made her feel feminine and pretty. She'd known he
was destined to go out into the world and do great
things—she'd just always assumed he'd take her with
him.

But she'd never shared his adventures. After leaving Sweetness, she'd periodically entered his name
into internet search engines and drank in details of
"Airman Kendall Armstrong" aiding in the El Sal-
vador earthquake recovery, then "Senior Airman
Kendall Armstrong" raising temporary housing in
post-tsunami Indonesia, then "Staff Sergeant Kendall
Armstrong" erecting modular housing for victims of
Hurricane Katrina.

By comparison, she'd been landlocked and rele-
gated to more mundane projects, such as shoring up
aging highway infrastructure and designing parking
garages.

Amy scanned the ad again, conceding a little thrill
at the thought of rebuilding an entire town. She and
Nikki had stayed in touch, so she knew things were
progressing…and that all the Armstrong brothers
were still single. She nursed a guilty pang about not
telling Nikki that she'd grown up in Sweetness, but
she didn't want her friend to inadvertently divulge
information about her to the Armstrongs.

She hadn't counted on Nikki falling in love with

Porter Armstrong. Amy shook her head as memories of the youngest brother came back to her—cute and reckless. It was hard to imagine Porter all grown up and ready to settle down. She wondered if Nikki had ever mentioned her friend Amy back in Broadway. And if she did, would Porter connect the dots? So far, Amy's friend hadn't confronted her. Regardless, Amy was relieved she hadn't shared all the details of her life with the woman she'd met in yoga class scant weeks before Nikki had left to move to Sweetness.

For the time being, anyway, it seemed as if her secrets were still safe.

The shrill ring of the phone on her desk broke into her thoughts. Amy crossed her fingers that the call was an offer for the reservoir job, then picked up the receiver.

"Amy Bradshaw."

"Amy, hi," a deep male voice sounded over the line. "This is Marcus Armstrong."

Amy blinked in surprise, then found her voice. "Hello, Marcus. This is…unexpected. How are you?"

"I'm fine, thanks. And you?"

"Fine," she said automatically.

"Good. I assume you know my brothers and I are rebuilding Sweetness."

She hesitated, her gaze falling on the ad in front of her. "Er, yes, I'm aware of your…project. A friend of mine moved there, and we stay in touch."

"Dr. Salinger, yes, I know. She mentioned your name to Porter and he put two and two together as to why Kendall chose that particular town to run the ad."

She wasn't sure how to respond, so she remained silent.

Marcus cleared his voice. "Look, I'll get right to the point. I'm calling with a proposition."

Wary, Amy sat forward in her chair. "I'm listening."

"We need a bridge designed to replace the old covered bridge over Timber Creek."

A picture of the splendid Evermore Bridge came to her clearly. Lovingly constructed from original stand timber—wood from old-growth forests—and painted a rustic red, the old landmark had been a faithful steward of the safety of all those who had crossed it. How many times had she and Kendall walked there, hand in hand, to stare up at the intricate ceiling trusses and dissect its construction?

"It didn't survive the tornado?" she asked.

"I'm afraid not. It was blown away, like everything else. Only sections of the foundation remain, but I doubt if they're salvageable."

Amy pressed her lips together. "What does this have to do with me?"

"We need a structural engineer to design and oversee the construction. And I understand that's your specialty."

Her heart skipped a beat. She chose her words carefully. "How much do you know about my life, Marcus?"

"More than Kendall," he said evenly.

Feeling light-headed, she sat there, waiting for the floor to open up and swallow her.

"What I propose," he continued in her silence, "is that you return to Sweetness…for the time it would take to rebuild our bridge."

"A new covered bridge?"

"As close to the first Evermore Bridge as possible, considering the original blueprints no longer exist. We have a grant from a preservation society to offset some of the costs and they provided blueprints from a similar bridge in Ohio." He gave her an overview of the project budget and the amount they could offer for her services. "Not a king's ransom, I know," he said.

"No, it sounds very fair," she said, tightening her grip on the phone. Had Kendall told Marcus how much that bridge had meant to her? Rebuilding it would be a great personal achievement. "So…you're offering me a temporary job?"

"That's right. The way I see it, I need a bridge, and it would give you a chance to see if things have changed around here."

If things had changed… He was alluding to Kendall and their old feelings for each other.

"Whose idea was this?" she asked.

"Mine. Kendall doesn't know I'm making this call. As far as I know, he doesn't even know you're an engineer."

Because he didn't care enough to find out? But

even as hurt squeezed her heart, she was grateful Kendall hadn't delved deeper into her life. She wondered again how much Marcus knew.

"And if I say no, what then?" she asked.

There was a hesitation on the other end of the line. "Then nothing. No matter what I think, Amy, you have a right to your privacy."

She exhaled. "Thank you, Marcus. You don't know how much I appreciate that."

"Then you'll think about it?"

Amy's mind swirled with the possible outcomes of returning to Sweetness. It had taken years for the sharp pain in her heart over Kendall to subside to a dull ache. If she returned now, there would be more at stake. Much more. And it was more than she was willing to gamble.

"I'm sorry," she said with as much conviction as she could muster, "but I'm going to have to pass. I have commitments here that I can't turn my back on."

A regretful noise sounded on the line. "I'm disappointed, but I understand. It's been nice talking with you. Call if you ever need anything."

She smiled into the phone. "Thank you. Goodbye, Marcus."

Amy set down the receiver and sank into her chair. That was close. She sat for a few moments, her mind traveling down the road not taken, wondering if her response would've been the same if Kendall had called instead.

She closed her eyes and conjured up his handsome face, his serious deep blue eyes, his intense approach to everything.

Including lovemaking, she remembered with a smile. He'd been her first lover and the only man who'd ever moved her. Every man in her life after Kendall had suffered in comparison to his strong body and keen intellect. If Kendall had been able to commit to her or had loved her enough to come looking for her, her life would've been so different.

Amy gave herself a mental shake. Luckily she had Tony in her life now...a different set of blue eyes to lose herself in. She'd learned long ago that nothing productive came from rehashing the past.

She reached for her computer mouse and returned to the CAD drawing she'd been working on before her chocolate attack, the addition of a wheelchair ramp to an existing structure. A worthwhile project, to be sure...but not very challenging. Even as she double-checked the fine details on the screen in front of her, her mind kept straying to her memories of the Evermore covered bridge over Timber Creek.

Always happy for a reason to get out of the cramped, tension-wrought house where she lived with an elderly aunt, Amy had thought the bridge was the most romantic place in Sweetness—the way it enveloped her and Kendall when they entered one arched portal to slowly walk or ride across the length of it, counting timbers as they went, their footsteps and voices echoing off the plank walls. She would pretend it was their home. They'd certainly shared a lot of intimate moments there, tucked out of sight in the dark corners of the supports, enjoying the vibration of their sandwiched bodies when cars rumbled past.

Unbidden, desire stabbed her midsection. It had been a long time since she'd allowed herself to think about the way Kendall had made her body come alive. In hindsight, the excitement of sexual discovery had clouded her judgment. It had made her believe that Kendall was in love with her, that they shared an unbreakable bond. She had been such a fool.

Still, Marcus had stirred her curiosity about the town's progress. Nikki had mentioned a website, but Amy had purposely avoided it. Now, though, she found herself clicking away from her CAD drawing and on to a search engine. A few keystrokes later, she found the official website of Sweetness, Georgia, *The Greenest Place on Earth.*

Green enough on its own, she remembered, with trees as far as the eye could see. But the slogan was a play on the fact that the Armstrong brothers were rebuilding the town on the industries of recycling and alternative energies. She skimmed the pages of description. The pictures showing the devastation of the tornado still rocked her to the core—those were all places where she'd once walked. The "before" and "after" slide show featured pictures of the overgrown wasteland the town was when the Armstrong brothers had returned to reclaim it, and pictures of the progress that had been made. Nikki was in one of the photos, standing beside the sign for the Sweetness Family Medical Center, next to a short bespectacled man who, from his white lab coat, appeared also to be a doctor. Rachel Hutchins, the busty blonde who used to be the receptionist for the dermatologist Amy used in Broadway, was in several of the photos, flashing her Miss America smile. Nikki said the woman would probably be mayor when the first elections rolled around.

There was a Lost and Found page listing hundreds, maybe thousands of items that had been found after the tornado and warehoused until they could be returned to the rightful owners. Former residents of Sweetness were encouraged to sign up on an email list to be kept apprised of developments. A social network site for the town had also been established.

On the About page, Amy found what she'd been looking for. A picture of the three Armstrong brothers standing outside, dressed in dusty work clothes. Amy instantly recognized each one of them. Porter, always the ham, was grinning at the camera. Marcus, the stoic one, looked highly inconvenienced at having his picture taken. And Kendall…

Her heart stuttered. Kendall had grown from a beautiful boy into a devastatingly handsome man, his shoulders wide and muscled, his skin tanned, his brown hair streaked by the sun. He wasn't quite smiling and he wasn't quite scowling. As always, he

was square in the middle of his brothers' tempera-
ments. He had the same deep blue eyes as Marcus
and Porter, but where Marcus looked stern and
Porter, mischievous, Kendall was the calm one.

The cautious one. The one who couldn't commit.

With a sigh, she closed down the page and re-
opened the CAD drawing, hoping to lose herself in
the details of the diagram. But her mind kept wandering and she kept making mistakes. Then she inadvertently pressed a key that undid an hour's worth
of work.

"Dammit!" she muttered.

The ring of the phone offered a welcome distrac-
tion from her burgeoning frustration. Out of habit
from the past few weeks, she crossed her fingers and
picked up the receiver.

"Amy Bradshaw."

"Ms. Bradshaw, this is Michael Thoms from the
Greater Michigan Water Commission."

Her pulse spiked—the phone call she'd been
waiting for. She strove for a calm tone. "Yes, Mr.
Thoms…I've been expecting your call."

"I have to apologize for the delay. Funding for the
Peninsula Reservoir was held up in legislature, so we
were holding off on filling positions on the project
team."

"I understand," she said, her chest tightening with
anticipation.

"I'm sorry, Ms. Bradshaw. The project manager

position went to another engineer who had slightly more experience."

Her shoulders fell in disappointment, but she rallied her voice. "I understand."

"If it's any consolation, you were in the top three and the decision was close."

She smiled. "That's very kind of you to share, thank you." After a few more minutes of small talk, Amy returned the receiver and tamped down the panic that licked at her. She'd been counting on that contract to stabilize her work hours and finances for the next two years. With the economy in the hard-hit manufacturing state still struggling to its feet, those kinds of public works projects were few and far between. She looked back to her computer screen. It would take a lot of wheelchair ramps to make up the difference.

Or you could go build a bridge, her mind whispered.

She pushed to her feet and walked over to a bin that held tubes of rolled up blueprints. She flipped through them until she located the cardboard tube she had in mind. It was soft and shopworn from so many moves over the years. She opened the tube and withdrew several yellowed pages, then unrolled them on a drawing table and used paperweights to hold down the curled edges.

Building plans for Evermore Bridge, Sweetness, Georgia, 1920. Official copy, do not remove.

She *had* removed them from the courthouse,

though…stolen them, to be more precise, as she was inclined to do in those days when something caught her fancy.

And now it seemed that things had come full circle. Amy released a bittersweet laugh. It seemed as if the universe was telling her she should go home to Sweetness.

Before she could change her mind, she picked up the phone and scrolled back to the number Marcus had called from, then pushed a button to connect the call. As the phone rang, she wondered nervously if Kendall would answer and if he did, what she might say.

But to her relief, Marcus's voice came on the line. "Marcus Armstrong."

"Marcus, this is Amy," she began, but her voice petered out. She cleared her throat, then rushed ahead before she lost her nerve. "Is that offer of designing your new bridge still open?"

"Yes, it is."

"Then…I'll take it."

"Great. I'm glad you changed your mind. How soon can you get here?"

Tony would not be happy about her leaving. "Um, I need a week to tie up some loose ends. Will that work?"

"Sure. I guess I don't have to tell you that you'll be working with Kendall."

She swallowed. "I assumed so."

"Would you like to talk to him? He's not here, but I can give you his cell phone number."

"No, thanks," she said. She needed to get her story straight before she faced Kendall Armstrong again. "I'll see him soon enough."

3

The more familiar the surroundings became, the tighter Amy's hands gripped the steering wheel. The passenger seat of her SUV was littered with candy bar wrappers and an empty box of chocolate donuts. In hindsight, sugar and cocoa hadn't been the wisest stimulant for the long drive. She was wired, and every sense seemed to be firing on all cylinders.

Despite the winter month, the north Georgia mountains were plenty colorful, with soaring evergreens thriving in red clay, and banks of snow high on rock ledges. Cottony clouds hung in a sky of the clearest, deepest blue…the color of Kendall Armstrong's eyes.

She was, she conceded, a nervous wreck about seeing him again. For a week she'd been giving herself pep talks to steel herself against the onslaught of emotions she knew would hit her, but she wasn't sure the mental gymnastics had done any good. Tony, as she'd expected, wasn't happy about her leaving. Of course, he wasn't happy about many things these days, so it was hard to pinpoint if she was the cause of his discontent or just a target.

When she turned off the state road onto the more narrow one that would take her to Sweetness, a hot flush climbed her neck. When she'd left this place, she hadn't planned on ever coming back. Now, it felt as if the years away were collapsing. The landscape had changed somewhat, had suffered from the decade of neglect after the tornado. Kudzu vine encompassed entire copses of trees and hillsides. She knew from industry journals just how concerned civil engineers in the South were over the encroaching plant. It was referred to as the "mile-a-minute vine" that could consume bridges and overpasses in a matter of weeks.

But the surroundings became more cultivated as she entered the outskirts of the small town. The road was newly paved, she noticed, and wider than before. The fluorescent center and shoulder paint lines looked freshly applied. A low guardrail might seem unnecessary to newcomers, but she knew the railing would keep weeds at bay, and serve as a hindrance for wild animals to wander onto the road.

Her first sign of civilization was a car coming in the opposite direction. Once upon a time, she would've recognized not just the car, but the person driving it. The fact that she didn't know either one made her feel like an outsider.

When she rounded the last curve before the straightaway into town, she glanced to the left for a

glimpse of the Evermore Bridge that had always welcomed people into town. Marcus had told her it had
blown away, but she wasn't prepared for the sinking
sensation in her stomach over the yawning gape in
the landscape where the bridge had once stood. In
fact, if a person didn't know better, they might not
know the fine landmark had ever existed. From an
engineer's point of view, she should be glad the de-
molition of the existing structure would be minimal,
but it was alarming that something that had been so
solid, so...*steadfast* could be there one minute, and
gone the next.

Like Kendall...

The site where the mercantile had once stood was
equally haunting. Once a hubbub of activity where
farmers bought feed and lumber and women bought
fabric and books, it was now an overgrown plateau
covered with scrub brush and spindly saplings.

Just when she'd started to think she would recognize nothing about this place, Amy looked up to see
the water tower perched high on a ridge and her heart
unfurled. The inverted white capsule-shaped tank
was topped by a pointed roof that resembled a hat.
It looked like a stalwart soldier, standing watch and
heralding, "Welcome to Sweetness." When Nikki
Salinger had relocated to the town, she'd called Amy
from the water tower because it was the only place
her phone could get cell service. As Amy drove
closer, she could make out graffiti on the side of the
tank—giant red letters that spelled out "I ♥ Nikki."

Amy smiled. It looked as if Porter Armstrong had resumed the age-old tradition of proclaiming love publicly with a can of spray paint.

And apparently, it had worked. The last time she'd spoken with Nikki, her friend had sounded deliriously happy and in love. Amy felt guilty about not letting Nikki know she was coming, but honestly, she was afraid she might change her mind at the last moment. She'd sworn Marcus to secrecy.

The fact that the historically disagreeable man was being so accommodating only reinforced her belief that Marcus knew more about her life than he was letting on.

The approach into Sweetness was long and flat, giving her a few more moments to collect herself and figure out what to do when she arrived. She slowed as buildings came into view in the distance. To the right was a broken paved road that led up to Clover Ridge where the Armstrongs had lived. She'd spent many hours there with Kendall and, after he'd left to join the Air Force, visiting his mother, Emily. Her heart squeezed. Emily Armstrong was the mother she'd always wanted, kind and cheerful and loving. Amy had been loath to leave her company and go home to her aunt who was perennially bitter that Amy's parents had died in a car accident when she was a toddler and left Amy for her to raise. Aunt Heddy always said that Kendall Armstrong only wanted one thing from a girl like her. In hindsight, she had been right.

After Amy left Sweetness, she'd wondered if Emily Armstrong had persuaded her son that Amy wasn't the right girl for him, that she wasn't good enough to be part of their family. Now, though, she conceded it had been a defense mechanism. If Kendall had rejected her because of her coarse upbringing, he had done it on his own.

She tapped the brake again as she approached what she presumed was the new downtown. The rise where their high school had once stood was now a windmill farm, the enormous white blades turning like a flower garden in motion. Amy kept driving, then squinted. The exterior of most of the buildings looked as if they'd been built with a patchwork of materials—a school, a General Store, a large structure with a wraparound porch that she surmised was the boardinghouse Nikki had mentioned, and other unidentifiable establishments that seemed to be bustling with activity. She stopped to allow a group of children to cross the road in front of her vehicle. From the armloads of books and sagging backpacks, it appeared that school had just let out. Amy smiled when they gawked—the town was obviously still small enough for everyone to recognize a stranger.

She'd dressed carefully in slacks and low-heeled leather boots, a tailored blouse and jacket. She'd had her unruly red curls tamed with a relaxer and wore it pulled back at the nape of her neck. When she'd left Sweetness, she'd been a ragamuffin tomboy. She was determined to return as a successful professional. A glance down at her collar elicited a moan—a smear of chocolate marred the look she'd so carefully orchestrated. So much for sophistication. Amy tucked the collar underneath the lapel of her jacket and gave a self-deprecating laugh.

You can take the girl out of the country, but you can't take the country out of the girl.

Her fingers drummed nervously on the steering wheel as she pondered her next move. She was considering calling Marcus or Nikki when, up ahead, she spotted a familiar sign from the website—Sweetness Family Medical Center. Nikki would probably be there. She'd stop first to say hello to her friend...and buy more time before she had to face Kendall.

Kendall pushed back from his laptop, then walked over to a color laser printer in the corner of the new media room in the boardinghouse to pick up the aerial view printouts. The presentation for the Department of Energy representative had been tweaked and retweaked until it was damn near perfect.

But they were still waiting for the guy to arrive.

"Kendall?"

He turned to see Rachel Hutchins, the informal spokesperson for the original group of women who had arrived from Broadway, standing there in all her blondeness. She was a little flashy for his tastes, but a treat for the eyes, for sure, with her long legs and tight sweaters. It had been months since he'd place that ad—Amy obviously wasn't coming home. Maybe he owed it to himself to start…looking.

He smiled. "Do you need something, Rachel?"

She dimpled. "A picture hung in my bedroom."

He almost balked, then told himself he was over-reacting. "No problem. Let me shut down here." He slid the color printouts into a folder, then stashed everything in his laptop bag. Carrying the bag, he followed her through the hallway of the boarding-house they'd built for the women they'd attracted with the promise of room and board for two years.

The atmosphere was slightly different now, though, since some of the women's children had arrived. He stepped aside as two school-aged boys ran by, roughhousing and shouting. When school let out, the media room was usually packed with children playing video games and accessing social network-ing sites. It was a far cry from the way he and his brothers had spent their extra time.

He often wondered if he ever had children, would he even be able to relate to them. Even if they were raised here in his resurrected hometown, it was ob-vious their experience would be different from his own.

"Hello, Cupid," Rachel cooed as she stopped to scratch the ears of the doe the woman had nursed back to health and domesticated, allowing it to roam free in the house. The animal was even housebroken. Scampering at its feet was Rachel's black-faced pug. For some bizarre reason, the dog seemed enamored with the deer. Rachel crouched and made smooching noises. "Hello, Nigel, baby." She straightened and looked at Kendall. "I think we should expand the pet section at the General Store. Our pet population is almost fifty, you know."

He hadn't known, but he nodded. "That sounds reasonable. Just talk to Molly."

Rachel made a face. "Need I remind you that the Colonel doesn't believe in having animals indoors? I don't think she's the best person to be in charge of ordering supplies anyway."

It wasn't the first time that girly girl Rachel and no-nonsense Colonel Molly had butted heads, but both women had proved their mettle by contributing countless hours and good ideas to the effort of rebuilding the town. The Armstrongs couldn't afford to alienate either one of them.

Kendall offered a congenial smile. "But it makes sense because Molly's ordering supplies for the dining hall anyway."

Rachel sniffed and resumed walking. "We have to do something about that cafeteria, too. It's depressing. When are we going to turn it into a restaurant?"

"It's on the list," he assured her. He indulged in watching her curvy behind sashay in front of him. Amy's build was smaller, more athletic. And she'd had the most beautiful head of red hair.

"Here we are," Rachel sang as she reached for the knob of a door and pushed it open.

Kendall hesitated, then guiltily glanced both ways

down the hall to see if anyone was watching before stepping inside.

When she closed the door behind him, he felt trapped, which made him realize how long it had been since he'd been alone with a woman. The room was built and furnished similarly to others in the house—one window, a bed and dresser, love seat, chair, coffee table, writing desk, closet, and a bathroom.

But the otherwise tidy room was strewn with various pieces of clothing—a silky white nightgown, a tiny pink T-shirt that read "Maybe, Baby," a denim skirt, a pair of tall black boots. Through the bathroom door, two pairs of panty hose were hanging over a towel rack. Kendall's face warmed at the implied intimacy. He glanced at the door and considered bolting, but realized how idiotic that would look. Then he forced himself to relax. Who said Rachel was interested in anything more than a little decorating?

But she was looking at his crotch. "I see you brought your hammer."

He blanched. "Pardon me?"

She pointed to the tool belt he wore so often, he forgot he had it on. "A hammer…for pounding in a nail?" She held up a picture-hanging hook, then pointed to a picture leaning against the wall.

He felt like an idiot. "Oh, right. Where do you want it?"

"Can you hold it up for me?"

"Sure." He reached for the picture, then stopped when he realized it was a photograph of the old covered bridge that had once spanned Timber Creek. "Evermore Bridge," he murmured. "If you don't mind my asking, where did you get this?"

She stepped close to look over his shoulder. Her floral perfume filled his nostrils. "I was going through some photographs in the Lost and Found warehouse, and thought this one was really great."

"It is great," he agreed.

"So you remember the bridge?"

He nodded slowly, assailed with memories. "It was a fantastic piece of workmanship." And it was his and Amy's place.

"Don't worry. This isn't the original photo," Rachel said. "I scanned it in—this is a color copy." Then she bit into her cherry-pink lip. "I hope that's okay."

"Of course," he said, irritated with himself that everything these days reminded him of Amy. "Do you want it hung here, over the dresser?"

"Yes, please."

Kendall held the picture against the wall. He glanced down to see a lacy red bra of considerable cup size lying on the top of the dresser. He averted his gaze to Rachel to take direction from her, but all he could visualize was her wearing that red bra...or worse—*not* wearing it.

She lifted her arms, emphasizing her generous breasts. "Higher."

He stifled a groan and lifted the picture higher.

"To the right."

Good God, if he got an erection while his arms were up in the air, there would be no hiding it.

"No...too much. Back to the left."

He moved the frame again, trying to think of something other than the sexy woman. But when he looked at the picture of Evermore Bridge, he was reminded of all the intimate things he and Amy had done in their special place. His groin tightened.

"How's that?" he blurted.

She angled her blonde head. "Maybe."

"Let's try it," he said, then handed her the picture with his right hand while marking the spot on the wall with his left. He was glad to turn his back because he was definitely sporting wood now, like a damn teenager.

"Can you hand me the hanger?" he asked over his shoulder.

Rachel came up behind him and reached around with a long, tapered arm. "How's this?" she asked, her mouth close to his ear.

"F-fine," he said, but almost dropped the hanger. He held it against the wall, then pulled a hammer from his tool belt. Her perfume was messing with his mind. "Um...you might want to step back a little. We wouldn't want anyone to get hurt."

"Oh. Okay," she said, stepping away.

But the red bra was so close to his face he could

take a bite out of it. He had to get out of here. He
lifted the hammer and brought it down hard…

On his thumb.

Kendall howled, Rachel screamed, blood spurted.

"Oh, my God!" she shouted. "Are you okay?"

"Yes," he managed to say through gritted teeth,
but the jolt of pain shot up his arm and brought tears
to his eyes. He dropped the hammer, which landed
squarely on his foot.

He grunted, then lifted his injured foot to ease the
pressure. Of all days not to wear steel-toed boots.

"You're bleeding. Here." Rachel wrapped something soft around his thumb, which instantly turned
red from his blood. "Let's get you down to the clinic.
Can you walk?"

He nodded, feeling like a damn fool, then limped
out of her room. He tried, but there was no talking
her out of going with him. She trotted beside him,
holding his wrapped hand as if it had been severed.
Her lavish breasts rubbed up against him throughout. They attracted a lot of attention as they walked
through the boardinghouse. He was sure the gossip
had already started before the door closed behind
them. God, he hoped his brothers didn't see him. His
hand and his foot both throbbed, but that was nothing compared to the beating his pride had taken.

The only thought that cheered Kendall as he and
Rachel stumbled in the direction of the clinic was
that surely this day would get better.

4

"I still can't believe you're here," Nikki said, smiling wide over her mug.

"I should've told you that Sweetness is my hometown," Amy said. They were sitting in the clinic lounge drinking strong coffee from the pot on the counter.

"So why didn't you?" Nikki asked, her expression a mixture of curiosity and suspicion.

"It's a long story," Amy hedged, embarrassed to hear emotion thickening her voice.

"Well," Nikki said, reaching out to squeeze her hand. "It sounds like you're going to be here long enough for us to catch up."

Amy nodded and seized on another subject. "This place certainly seems to agree with you. You look fantastic." Nikki's hair was highlighted and cut in a new style that set off her beautiful green eyes. Her cheeks glowed with vitality, although Nikki suspected her high color could be attributed more to Porter Armstrong than to the fresh mountain air.

"Thank you," Nikki gushed. "I'm so happy. Sweetness feels like the home I've never had."

Amy's chest pinged with mixed emotions to hear someone else talk about her own hometown with such obvious affection. She hadn't felt a kinship with the place when she lived here before. In fact, she'd felt constrained and isolated. And she was already fighting that familiar closed-in feeling.

"So are the two of you going to get married?"

Nikki blushed. "The town doesn't even have a church yet. But Porter said he was working on it, so I hope that's a sign. After living with Darren in Broadway and that relationship going south, I don't want to move in with Porter until we're married."

Amy smiled at her friend, remembering the feeling of living in this town and being hopelessly in love with an Armstrong. She hoped it worked out better for Nikki than it had for her.

The door opened and a young bespectacled man Amy recognized from the photo on the website stuck his head in. A pair of safety goggles sat high on his head. His hair stuck out at all angles. He wore fluorescent orange rubber gloves.

"Excuse the interruption, Dr. Salinger," he said in a precise British accent. "We have a walk-in, and I'm stuck…er, I'm *still* giving flu shots to the elementary students."

"I should let you go," Amy said, pushing to her feet. "I need to see Marcus anyway."

Nikki stood, as well. "I'll handle the walk-in, Dr.

Cross. May I introduce my friend Amy Bradshaw? She's in town to build us a bridge."

"Brilliant," he said. "We British are very fond of bridges." He gave Amy a flustered smile. "Very pleased to meet you. If you'll excuse me, I have to get back to some miniature terrorists." He lowered the safety glasses and backed out of the room.

Amy laughed. "How did he wind up here?"

"We worked together in Broadway. He's a great doctor, even if he's a fish out of water here."

Amy felt a rush of sympathy for the man—she knew how he felt. "I'll let you get to your patients."

"I assume you'll be staying at the boarding-house?"

"I honestly don't know. Marcus just said that accommodations would be provided."

"It just dawned on me," Nikki said as she opened the door and held it for Amy to walk through. "You must know the Armstrongs."

"Yes," Amy said carefully as she exited the lounge into a large waiting area. "We grew up together."

Nikki grinned. "You went to school with Porter?"

"That's right, although I knew his brother better."

"Which brother?" Nikki asked.

"Nikki!" came a screeching woman's voice. "Help!"

Amy looked up to see the owner of the voice, Rachel Hutchins, standing there in all her vivacious glory.

"You remember Rachel," Nikki murmured in an amused voice.

"Yes," Amy said, but her gaze was riveted on the man next to her, the man Rachel was holding on to in a very proprietary way.

Kendall Armstrong.

Her heart stood still. He was broader and taller than she remembered. His hair was still dark and wavy, and he was sporting a light mustache and beard, probably in deference to the cooler season. It suited him, she acknowledged, and emphasized his strong jaw. It was jarring to see the boy she remembered matured into a man she didn't know. His deep blue eyes were still as intense, but framed with character lines that, if possible, only made him more handsome. Tony's face flashed in her mind for a split-second comparison. She opened her mouth to gulp air and her heart resumed beating.

Kendall appeared to recognize her at the same time and froze. Time seemed suspended, the air between them thick and gluey. Her blood rushed in her ears. How many times had she rehearsed this moment in her mind? She wanted to say something smart and cool, but her tongue was paralyzed. Kendall's mouth opened, but Nikki interrupted whatever greeting he'd been forming.

"What happened here?" she asked, gesturing to his wrapped hand.

"Kendall was hanging a picture for me and

smashed his thumb with a hammer," Rachel said, unwinding the cloth. "He hurt it really bad."

"I just need a Band-Aid," Kendall argued, still staring at Amy.

Hearing his voice again was a shock to her system. Years of travel and experience hadn't changed his deep tone or his rolling accent. She averted her gaze to his pulpy thumb, fighting the urge to reach out to him. It frightened her how easily she could fall back into old patterns around him, but knowledge was power. She would endeavor to spend as little time alone with Kendall as possible.

Nikki was looking back and forth between Amy and Kendall. "Let's get your hand cleaned so I can have a better look," she said, leading Kendall away.

"I'm coming with him," Rachel announced, confirming Amy's suspicions that she and Kendall were an item.

"Why don't you stay here and wash up?" Nikki suggested in a kind but firm voice, indicating Rachel's own bloodstained hands. Nikki looked back at Amy. "Let's have dinner tonight?"

"Sounds good," Amy called.

Kendall looked back at her, too, as if she were an apparition, then disappeared with Nikki.

Amy exhaled. So much for a dramatic reunion. Apparently Marcus had kept his word to stay mum about her arrival. Was it because he knew that Kendall didn't want her here?

"I hope he's okay," Rachel murmured. "His thumb was bleeding like a stick pig."

"I think you mean 'stuck' pig," Amy volunteered, still stung by the sight of Kendall and Rachel together. Although what had she expected? Of course Kendall had gotten on with his life. Probably many, many times.

Rachel squinted at her. "I know you…Amy, right? You were a patient at the dermatologist where I used to work in Broadway."

"Right. Amy Bradshaw."

"Rachel Hutchins," the woman offered. "Are you just now answering the newspaper ad?"

"No. I'm a structural engineer. I was hired by Marcus Armstrong to rebuild the covered bridge over Timber Creek."

Rachel's face lit up. "You're kidding? I love that bridge. In fact, the man Nikki took away was Marcus's brother, Kendall. He was helping me hang a picture of the covered bridge in my bedroom when he smashed his thumb."

"Really?" Amy was surprised at how normal her voice sounded. Evermore Bridge had been her and Kendall's place. It hurt to know he was sharing the memory of it with someone else.

Rachel nodded. "If you need a picture of the way it looked before, I can get you one."

Amy bit down on her tongue. Rachel couldn't know she'd committed every detail of the bridge to memory. She glanced down at the bloody cloth

Rachel held that had been wrapped around Kendall's thumb—it was a cropped pink T-shirt that read "Maybe, Baby." She'd also memorized every detail of the body of the man Rachel was apparently now cozy with.

"Thank you," Amy managed to say.

"Hello, Rachel."

The women turned to see Dr. Cross standing there, gazing up at Rachel as if she were a movie star.

"Hello, Dr. Cross," Rachel offered as if she were addressing a pesky child.

"Do you need attention?" he asked, then stabbed at his glasses. "Medical attention, I mean."

Rachel glanced down at her hands. "No...this isn't my blood."

His face fell. "Pity."

"Excuse me?"

"I didn't mean it's a pity you weren't hurt...I meant...that is..." He cleared his throat, then tapped the clipboard he held. "I was going through my list of patients who've had a flu shot and couldn't help but notice that your name is missing."

Amy wryly watched the man's bumbling attempt to flirt with the blonde who towered over him by a good eight inches. He was obviously besotted. Like Kendall.

Rachel made a face. "No offense, Doc, but I don't like needles."

"Ah, but you've never had a prick from me."

Amy bit back a smile.

"When I want a prick," Rachel said drily, "I'll let you know."

"You do that," he said cheerfully, then wheeled away.

Rachel looked at Amy, then rolled her eyes. "I think I'll find a ladies' room and wash my hands. Will I be seeing you around?"

"Probably," Amy said. Considering she'd be working with Kendall, and Rachel was attached to Kendall at the hip, it seemed likely. When jealousy toward the blonde beauty threatened to surface, Amy squashed it. She had no claim on Kendall. "Could you tell me where I might find Marcus Armstrong?"

"Marcus usually sticks pretty close to the construction office. It's a trailer down the gravel road that runs alongside the dining hall."

"Is it walking distance?"

Rachel looked down. "Not if you're fond of those gorgeous boots."

"Thanks." Amy lifted her hand in a wave to Kendall's girlfriend and walked out of the clinic tingling head to toe. "Kendall's girlfriend," she murmured. The words felt surreal on her tongue. That person had always been her.

Amy looked up and down the main street of the new town of Sweetness—also surreal…and different.

Both good things, she told herself as she opened the rear hatch of her SUV to remove a pair of sturdy work boots. Because without attachments, it would be easier to leave this place once Evermore Bridge was rebuilt.

5

Kendall squirmed as Nikki wrapped a bandage around his thumb.

"Does that hurt?" she asked.

"No." It did, and his big toe hurt, too, but he just wanted to get out of there.

"You look a little flushed."

He wasn't about to tell her it was humiliation. For years he'd imagined seeing Amy again, yet when the moment had presented itself, he'd been as tongue-tied as a teenager.

Nikki felt for his pulse on his uninjured hand. "Your heart rate is up."

From seeing Amy. "I appreciate your help, Dr. Salinger, but I'm kind of in a hurry."

She nodded. "Rachel is waiting for you."

He grunted. "I need to get back to work." He turned his head for a glimpse out the window through slitted blinds, yearning for another look at Amy, wondering why she was here and terrified she'd leave before he could talk to her. "That woman you were speaking to in the lobby…"

"Amy Bradshaw?" Nikki asked. "She's a friend of mine from Broadway. I thought you might know her—she grew up in Sweetness."

"I used to know her," he said absently. "Did she say why she's here?"

"She said Marcus had hired her to build a bridge."

Kendall blinked. "A bridge?"

Nikki nodded. "Amy's a structural engineer."

He blinked again. "Really?"

"Really. I guess the two of you haven't stayed in touch?"

"No…we haven't."

Nikki smiled. "Looks like you'll have some time to get reacquainted."

Kendall pressed his lips together and looked away, his mind churning.

Nikki patted his arm. "All done. Leave it wrapped for a few days. You'll probably lose the nail, and it'll be tender for a couple of weeks. Use the antibiotic ointment to stave off infection."

"Thanks," he murmured, then stood and walked to the door, trying not to limp.

"Kendall."

He turned back.

"Why don't you and Porter join me and Amy for dinner tonight at the boardinghouse?"

He hesitated. "I don't know…"

"It's the hospitable thing to do, don't you think? To welcome her home?"

He nodded. "Okay. See you later. Thanks again."

Kendall left the exam room and walked out into the waiting area, looking right and left. To his relief, Rachel was nowhere in sight. But neither was Amy. He practically ran to the door and out into the cool air. He spotted an unfamiliar burgundy SUV with a Michigan license plate and wondered if it belonged to Amy. The color reminded him of her deep auburn hair. It was empty. He glanced all around, but didn't see her.

Kendall pulled out his phone and dialed Marcus, determined to get to the bottom of Amy's appearance. When he didn't answer, Kendall lit out walking toward the construction office. By the time he reached the steps leading up to the trailer, his foot throbbed and his temper had ballooned into something he'd never experienced. He burst through the door. Marcus was sitting behind his desk, just disconnecting a call on his cell phone.

"What did you do to your hand?"

Kendall fisted his injured hand. "Cut the crap, Marcus. Amy Bradshaw? You hired Amy Bradshaw to rebuild Evermore Bridge?"

Marcus sat back in his chair and crossed his arms. "Actually, she's only going to design the bridge. You're going to build it."

"And you didn't think it was worth mentioning to me?"

Marcus pursed his mouth. "You were busy getting the presentation together. I told you I'd find a structural engineer, and I did. I guess you ran into her?"

Kendall put both hands on Marcus's desk, his blood pressure rising. "Blindsided is more like it."

"Funny, she didn't mention it."

Kendall straightened. "She was here?"

"Of course. She wanted to discuss the project. I told her she should get settled in first, then we could all meet tomorrow afternoon for a conference call with our contact on the Preservation Society."

"So she's at the boardinghouse?"

"No. She wanted to get right to work. She borrowed a four-wheeler to ride out to the site—"

Kendall didn't hear the end of the sentence— he was already out the door. He bounded down the steps, jogged to where several ATVs were parked and climbed on one. Working the hand grips hurt his thumb, but he welcomed the pain—it cut through the mush in his head. He steered the four-wheeler toward a side trail that ran parallel to the main road and led to the site where the covered bridge had once stood. As the cool air rushed by him, he tried to think of what he was going to say to Amy, but everything sounded lame and inadequate. *Long time no see. How's life been treating you? I've missed you every day we've been apart.*

As he approached the area and spotted the ATV she'd parked, his stomach churned. The fact that

she'd known she was coming here and hadn't contacted him spoke volumes, didn't it?

Maybe there was nothing to say.

He pulled the four-wheeler next to the one parked
and cut the engine. He couldn't see her through the
trees, but he walked toward the area where the old
bridge used to stand. When she came into view, his
feet slowed and his heart sped up. Amy had set up a
tripod and was bent over, looking through the camera
lens. Her trim, athletic figure was silhouetted against
the blue sky. She was all business in her slacks, tailored jacket and field boots, but the wind ruffled her
luxurious hair that had escaped from a clasp at her
neck.

She was, in a word, breathtaking.

He was sure she'd heard the four-wheeler, probably knew she was being observed. But if he wanted
proof he couldn't rattle her, he had it, because as he
walked closer, she didn't move, just kept snapping
away. He stopped a couple of yards away.

"Hello, Amy."

She stopped and glanced up. "Hello, Kendall."
Then she picked up a folded screen and extended it.
"Would you mind holding this in front of the sun so
I can get a few more shots?"

Her voice was the same, but her accent had
changed—her pronunciation was more precise and
more…Northern. He stepped forward and took the
screen, feeling thoroughly dismissed. He fumbled
with it, but finally opened it and held it up.

"A little to the left, please."

He obeyed, flashing back to earlier when Rachel had been giving him similar directions.

"More to the left…and higher."

Kendall poked his tongue into his cheek. "Is this how it's going to be?"

She lifted her head, but was looking at the future bridge site, not at him. "What do you mean?"

He sighed. "I mean, it's been ten years. Don't you think we should talk?"

"Twelve." She snapped a few more photos, then straightened and looked at him. "It's been over twelve years."

He swallowed under the full force of her stare. If possible, she was more beautiful now than the last time he'd seen her. Gone was the gangly freckle-faced teenage lover who'd followed him around. Here stood a woman who'd grown into her skin and her looks and who had an aloof air about her that…well, frankly, impressed him.

And worried him.

Amy's eyebrow arched. "So, what was it you wanted to talk about?"

He gave a little shrug. "How have you been?"

"I'm fine," she said in a tone that indicated she was surprised he'd think otherwise.

"I hear you're a structural engineer."

"That's right," she said. "My resume isn't as exciting as yours, but I've stayed busy."

"Who said my resume is exciting?" Kendall

asked, wondering if Amy had kept tabs on him over the years.

It was her turn to shrug. "I just assumed that if you've been in the Air Force all this time, you've been involved in some interesting things. Actually, I'm surprised you didn't make the Air Force a career."

I missed you too much. "I missed...my brothers."

She offered a flat smile. "Of course. Well, it seems as if you've found a way to be together again. And always."

Kendall detected censure in her voice. "You don't approve of our efforts to rebuild Sweetness?"

"I don't disapprove. I just don't understand why you'd *want* to rebuild the town." She leaned over her camera and snapped more photos. "I suppose you have better memories of this place than I do."

"I do have good memories," he admitted, thinking they were mostly of her and feeling disappointed she didn't share his opinion. "And I think this town deserves a second chance."

"Good for you." She straightened and picked up the tripod, then walked to another location.

Nonplussed, Kendall followed. "I understand you're going to rebuild the covered bridge."

She set down the tripod. "That's right. Marcus called me last week and offered me the job. I take it you didn't know?"

Kendall bristled. "I've been working on something else."

"Does it bother you that I'm here?"

Only every cell in his body. "Of course not. I was just...*surprised* to see you, that's all."

"As surprised as I was to see an advertisement for single women to come to Sweetness in my local newspaper?"

His face warmed and his mind raced for an explanation.

Amy gave a dismissive wave. "Don't worry. I figure that was Marcus's idea, too. He seems to think you and I have some unfinished business."

His tongue was like lead in his mouth.

Her berry-colored lips turned up in a little smile. "I assured him we said our goodbyes long ago."

He nodded, like a puppet.

"And that it wouldn't be a problem for us to work together on rebuilding this bridge."

Kendall finally found his tongue. "Right, no problem. We're...professionals."

"And it'll only be for a few weeks," she added. "I'm thinking three months, tops."

He swallowed hard. He already didn't want to think about the day she'd leave. "Meanwhile, I can't think of anyone better to redesign Evermore Bridge."

When she looked up, her hazel-colored eyes held reproach. "Why?"

He could tell she was ready to deny any emotional attachment to the bridge...or maybe he'd projected his own association with the bridge onto her. "Because you knew every stick of that bridge."

She nodded without acknowledging that she'd memorized the construction of the bridge during the hours they'd spent there together. "Were you planning to give the new bridge the same name— Evermore?"

"I honestly don't know."

She let out a little laugh that left him weak in the knees. "Do you and Marcus ever talk?"

"There's a lot to be done around here. We're usually working on different things."

She lifted an eyebrow. "And you're Head of Picture Hanging?"

At the reference to the injury he'd gotten hanging a picture for Rachel, a hot flush climbed his neck. "I was just doing a favor for a friend and lost my concentration." Too late, he realized he'd made it sound as if Rachel had distracted him, when Amy herself was as least partly to blame.

She pursed her mouth, then leaned down to take another photograph. "Could you hold up that screen again, please?"

Kiss me again, please? Make love to me, please? He'd always teased her for saying please—as if he'd needed any encouragement to touch her or to do things that would make her happy.

He held up the screen while she took more pictures, taking the opportunity to drink in every inch of her that was so familiar, yet so changed. She'd matured into a beautiful woman with elegant taste. Her clothes were sensible, but beautifully tailored to fit her streamlined figure. He had to smile, though, at the smudge on the collar of her blouse—Amy was still a chocoholic.

His hands itched to brush her thick red hair away from her face and pull her lean body against his. It was jarring to realize that he no longer had the right to touch her, and he wondered what lucky man claimed that role these days. The fact that she wasn't wearing a ring on her left hand didn't necessarily mean anything. Lots of people whose jobs required them to be on construction sites didn't risk wearing jewelry.

"Did you marry?" he asked, then held his breath while she took her time answering.

"No."

He exhaled and waited for her to ask the same of him. When she didn't, he volunteered, "Neither did I...nor did my brothers."

She pulled a notebook from her pocket and jotted a few notes with a mechanical pencil. "According to the water tower, Porter's pretty far gone over my friend Nikki."

Kendall smiled. "She's changed him, all right."

The pencil point broke with a snap. Amy clicked down a new length of lead, then continued writing. "I hope she knows what she's getting into."

"With Porter? It's been six months. I think she knows him pretty well by now."

"I meant living here."

Kendall bristled. "I know the town doesn't look like much now, but we have plans."

"I know. I saw the slide show on the website. Meanwhile, it's more primitive even than when you and I grew up here."

He tamped down a spike of anger. "Maybe Nikki is happy in Sweetness because the man she cares about is here."

Amy's mouth twitched down. "I hope that's enough for her."

Kendall felt as if he'd been kicked in the stomach. If he'd wondered about the possibility of Amy coming home to Sweetness to stay, he had his answer. And they hadn't even broken ground on the new bridge.

Unless her mind could be changed. After all, his negotiating skills had been honed by some pretty serious head-butting between his brothers since they'd all taken on this project. Seizing on a classic mediation opener, he asked, "What can I do to make your job easier?"

She looked up from the notebook, her expression wary. "I think I have everything I need for now." She tucked away her notes, then picked up the tripod and moved in the direction of the all-terrain vehicle she'd driven over. Kendall followed her, carrying the folding screen.

He was mesmerized by watching her move. He still couldn't believe she was here…within arm's reach. There were a million questions he wanted to ask her, find out everything about her life since he'd last seen her. But from the closed expression on her face and her tight body language, she wasn't in a sharing mood. And she didn't seem to care what he'd been doing for the past twelve years.

She stopped at the four-wheeler and lifted the seat to stow her camera equipment, then reached for the folding screen he held. "Thanks."

Then she climbed on, started the engine and took off before he could even reach the ATV he'd driven over. He goosed the gas to keep up with her, flashing back to when they were teenagers, riding horses all over this countryside. He had always lagged behind on purpose, so he could see Amy's wild hair fly behind her and watch her tight little behind snug against the saddle. He'd loved chasing her...and apparently things hadn't changed—except for the catching part. He followed her back to the construction office, saddened when the ride ended, already loath to be away from her.

She was off the ATV and striding toward town before he could regroup.

"Can I buy you a cup of coffee?" he called. "Maybe we can catch up."

She turned, still moving, her hands full of equipment. "No, thanks. If you don't mind, I'd like to keep things between us strictly business. I'll see you on the jobsite." Then she turned and kept going.

Kendall watched her walk away and had to keep himself from running after her. He hadn't been successful in convincing Amy to stay in Sweetness last time. But he had three months to do it this time.

Starting with dinner tonight with Porter and Nikki.

6

Amy looked at her reflection in the mirror in her bedroom and worked her mouth back and forth. Was a skirt too dressy for dinner with Nikki downstairs in the rear great room? It seemed like a pretty casual atmosphere, but since Amy was usually in sturdy, sensible clothes on jobsites during the day, she tried to dress up after hours. The memory of standing in the shadow of Kendall's splashy "friend" Rachel cinched her decision not only to go with the outfit as planned, but to add hoop earrings, high heels and the Topaz ring that Tony had given her for Christmas. It was always better to be overdressed than underdressed.

She glanced at her watch—she was still twenty minutes early. Enough time to call Tony, she realized, although it wasn't something she was looking forward to under the circumstances. Guilt stabbed at her, impelling her to pick up her cell phone and punch in his number. When the phone rolled over to his voice mail, she wondered if he was really busy,

or if he was avoiding her calls. He hadn't been over-
joyed about her leaving Broadway without him and
had asked a lot of questions. Had he picked up on
the fact that she hadn't been completely forthcoming about her connection to the town for which she
was building a bridge?

"Hi, sweetie, it's me." She wet her lips. "I just
wanted to let you know that I made it to Sweetness,
Georgia, and I have cell phone service, so call me
whenever you want to." She hesitated, knowing how
much he disliked her being too effusive, but it had
been an emotional day. "I love you," she murmured,
then disconnected the call, her heart squeezing over
all the conflict they'd endured the past year, for
which she felt largely responsible. She was looking
forward to better times once she returned to Broadway…once she got some closure on the situation with
Kendall Armstrong.

She walked across the second-floor bedroom
she'd been assigned—a pretty room decorated in
chocolate-brown and sage-green—and glanced out
the window, down at the new town of Sweetness.
Dusk was settling quickly. A tall light illuminated
the area in front of the boardinghouse. Across the
street, the dining hall was lit up, and the headlights
of two cars rolling down the main street cast beams
on what appeared to be freshly painted pedestrian
crosswalks.

The town would need sidewalks soon. In her
mind, she visualized the wooden forms that would

have to be built to contain the leveled concrete snaking down both sides of the asphalt road. She could pour them in her sleep, even in this cold weather, and she could incorporate recycled materials like tumbled glass to give them a custom look. Maybe she'd suggest to Marcus—

Amy caught herself. This wasn't her town, and she wasn't about to start making suggestions that would add projects to her to-do list. She was here to design a covered bridge—in and out.

She stepped back from the window and walked into the bathroom to frown at her auburn hair that was showing increasing signs of frizz. All those rainy, snowy days in Broadway, and she was able to keep it under control. A few hours in this place in the dead of winter, and it was already kinking up like a pig's tail.

She sighed and ran a boar bristle brush through her thick tresses, knowing it would buy her only a few minutes of smoothness, at best. Then she left her room and descended the stairs to the first floor in search of Nikki. Along the way, she passed several women, all smiling and laughing and apparently happy to be there, lots of children who seemed to travel in friendly packs, and a few men who were apparently only visiting because, as she'd read in the boardinghouse rules, males were not allowed in the boardinghouse overnight.

A quaint regulation…very Southern…but comforting, Amy acknowledged. And clever, because it would spur the town to grow faster since couples who wanted to live together had no choice but to build their own home. She wondered if Nikki and Porter were on the fast track to marriage. She also wondered if Nikki realized what a feat she'd accomplished to corral one of the Armstrong brothers. They had always been the most confirmed bachelors in town. She knew that firsthand.

But what had Kendall said? That Nikki had *changed* Porter. Just thinking about it made her cheeks sting. It left her feeling inadequate that she hadn't been able to *change* Kendall.

She found Nikki in the crowded common kitchen, sliding a pan into one of the large ovens. The atmosphere was festive and aromas tantalizing as women crowded around pots of pasta and shared thick chunks of warm bread. A couple of children ran through, snagging brownies from a plate. Amy looked after the laughing children with a tug of longing that she squashed as quickly as it rose. The family environment took her by surprise, and she could see why it would appeal to some people. But the trade-off was living in a fishbowl where opportunities were limited. She hadn't left to educate herself only to come back and settle for something less than she could become.

"I hope Chicken Kiev is okay," Nikki said, her cheeks pink from the heat. "I don't have much of a cooking repertoire."

Amy gave a little laugh. "That sounds pretty impressive to me. I usually eat frozen dinners. What can I do to help?"

"Pick up those wineglasses and follow me," Nikki said, nodding to the countertop. She picked up a bottle of wine and a corkscrew and turned toward the opposite doorway.

Amy frowned at the number of wineglasses—four—but gathered them in her hands and followed Nikki down a hallway into the rear great room that apparently served as the main gathering place for residents to dine and watch TV. The computers that lined one wall were another surprise. The new Sweetness was wired and perhaps not as isolated as she'd imagined.

Nikki stopped at a square wooden table situated away from other tables and chairs that were largely occupied. From all the couples dining together, Amy surmised the ploy to bring women to Sweetness as companions for the Armstrongs' workers had succeeded. Noticing the four salads on their own table, Amy balked. "Is someone joining us?"

Nikki cut the foil on a bottle of wine. "I hope you don't mind if Porter eats with us. We typically have dinner together."

"No, that's fine." Although she was a little disappointed that she and Nikki wouldn't be able to catch up, she understood that she was the interloper here. Before she could ask about the fourth place setting, Nikki beamed at someone behind Amy.

"Here's Porter now."

Amy turned and smiled at Porter, who'd been a fresh-faced sophomore when she'd last seen him. He'd filled out and matured, but his wide grin and cleft chin were still prominent and recognizable, along with those infamous blue Armstrong eyes.

"Amy Bradshaw," he said, extending both his hands to her and lowering a kiss on her cheek. "You grew up good."

She blushed. "Still the sweet talker, Porter. The years have been kind to you, you devil."

"I never thought I'd see you in Sweetness again."

"That makes two of us," she quipped. "Marcus can be persuasive."

He grinned. "That isn't the word I'd use, but Marcus seems to know how to get things done. And what good luck that you and my Nikki are friends."

It was so like a Southern man to refer to his girlfriend in a possessive way. Amy expected Nikki to take offense at the "my" part, but instead she seemed inordinately pleased as Porter pulled her to his side for a squeeze.

Amy smiled. "Yes, it's…fortuitous."

"Anyway, it's great to see you again." He looked down at Nikki. "Who's our fourth for tonight?"

"That would be me."

Amy tensed at the sound of Kendall's voice behind her. She slowly turned to see him, dressed in chino pants and filling out a deep blue collared shirt that reflected his eyes perfectly. He looked so handsome, her throat closed.

"If that's okay with Amy," he added, pinning her with his steady gaze.

"I invited Kendall," Nikki said cheerfully. "To help welcome you home."

Amy's cheeks flamed. Nikki was the only one in their foursome who didn't know she and Kendall had a history and had parted on less-than-friendly terms...unless Porter had filled her in.

"That was kind of you," Amy managed to say. "Of course it's fine." She wasn't going to be able to avoid Kendall, so she might as well get used to acting as if he didn't affect her.

As if he didn't make her heart race and her body warm with unbidden desire, just like old times.

Kendall gave her a little smile, as if he knew how much being nice was costing her. Then he stepped forward and handed Nikki a white bakery box.

"What's this?" she asked.

"Something for dessert."

"How nice," Nikki said. "Let me put this in the refrigerator and check on our dinner. Porter, will you pour the wine, please?"

"Sure thing, baby," he drawled, but watched her until she left the room before turning back to them and the wine. As he uncorked the bottle, he whistled happily under his breath.

Baby. Kendall used to call her baby, Amy recalled. She darted a look at him, but when she saw he was looking at her, she glanced all around, settling on the ceiling. "Nice trusses," she offered. "Is this a modular building?"

Kendall nodded. "The clinic, too. And the General Store. We used reclaimed materials for siding on all the buildings except the clinic."

"I could tell," Amy said. "Are you planning to incorporate any reclaimed materials in the covered bridge?"

"We've been putting aside any boards we find that might've been used in the original bridge in the Lost and Found warehouse."

She nodded. "I read on the website about the place where you're storing things you find so former residents can claim them."

"You're welcome to walk through the warehouse," Kendall said, "or look over the lists to see if you recognize anything that might've belonged to your family."

She shook her head. "Thanks, but there's nothing from here that I want." When she realized how brusque she sounded, she conjured up a little smile. "But I'd like to see the materials you have set aside for the bridge."

"I seem to remember the two of you hanging out at the bridge a lot," Porter offered.

Amy swung her head to stare at him and felt Kendall's gaze follow hers. Porter looked back and forth between them, his expression innocent as he handed each of them a glass of red wine. "Oh, so we're not supposed to talk about the elephant in the room?"

"What elephant in the room?" Nikki asked, returning.

"Amy and Kendall used to be a hot item," Porter said nonchalantly, then handed her a glass of wine.

Nikki's mouth rounded and she shot Amy an apologetic glance.

"It was a long time ago," Amy said quickly.

"To old times," Kendall said, lifting his glass, "and to building bridges."

She couldn't very well decline the toast, Amy thought wryly, lifting her glass to clink with the others. The bandage on Kendall's thumb reminded her of his "favor" for Rachel Hutchins, and she took a deeper drink than she'd meant to.

Kendall looked at her over the rim of his glass, his expression soft and blurred. Was he thinking of graduation night, when they'd snuck a bottle of cheap zinfandel to the bridge and sat on the edge with legs dangling, drinking it from paper cups? It had made them tipsy and giggly and Kendall had made promises about all the adventures they'd have together. Afterward, they'd made such sweet love… It was the last really good memory she had of them together.

Days later, he'd left to join the Air Force while she'd been tethered to Sweetness to take care of the sickly aunt who'd taken her in. Amy's loneliness had been exacerbated by her aunt's bitterness and the nagging sense that she was missing out on the life she was meant to have. But when her aunt had passed away a scant few weeks later, Amy had been besieged with guilt, yet eager to leave. When Kendall had come home for the funeral, he'd backpedaled on the promises he'd made. He'd told Amy they shouldn't be in such a rush to get married, that she should take some correspondence courses and that he'd be back for her. Heartbroken, she'd packed a bag and left Sweetness to strike out on her own.

And here she was, Amy mused, back in Sweetness and sharing another bottle of wine with the man who'd driven her away.

"Let's sit," Nikki offered, now noticeably nervous about the situation she'd created.

Amy felt compelled to put her friend at ease. After all, it was her fault for not mentioning sooner her true connection to the Armstrong family. Kendall held out her chair and she thanked him politely, then took a seat, not entirely pleased when he sat in the chair adjacent to hers. But in deference to her friend, Amy tried to relax and keep the conversation on neutral topics as the meal progressed.

Since the future seemed a safer subject than the past, she asked questions about the progress of the town, mostly directed at Porter and Nikki. If Kendall chose to respond, she took a bite of food or a drink from her glass to avoid eye contact. Twice under the table his knee brushed hers. She couldn't tell if it was accidental or purposeful, but she was unnerved all the same by the sensations that bolted through her. Instead of growing more calm in his presence, every minute seemed to heighten the feelings she'd spent years trying to suppress.

The affection between Nikki and Porter was obvious. They often touched and shared private smiles that made Amy's heart squeeze with admiration and envy. As the night wore on, she found herself stealing glances at Kendall and trying to figure out what he was thinking. But Kendall, ever the placid Armstrong, remained inscrutable.

When Nikki unveiled the "dessert" Kendall had brought, Amy's pulse jumped.

"Double-fudge brownie cake," Nikki announced, setting the decadent concoction on the table. She smiled at Kendall. "I didn't know you had such a sweet tooth."

Amy squirmed. Had he remembered her penchant for chocolate? The round cake was three layers high, dripping with dark fudge icing and topped with dark chocolate shavings. The sweet, rich aroma alone made her mouth water, but she steeled herself against the cravings that surged in her body. To her, the chocolate cake represented a meager effort to appease her. And after all these years, after all she'd been through, it was too little, too late.

"None for me, thanks," she said when Nikki started to serve her a slice.

"Are you sure?" Nikki asked. "It looks so yummy, and you're so trim, you can spare the calories."

"Thanks, but I'm stuffed," she said, then took another small sip of wine. She'd nursed the one glass all evening because she didn't want to become too sentimental.

"Hello, all."

Amy looked up to see Rachel Hutchins standing there wearing a pink sweater dress that looked as if it had been knitted onto her curvy body. Kendall shifted in his chair and his knee brushed Amy's. She pulled away.

"Hi, Rachel," Nikki said. "Have you met Amy Bradshaw?"

"We met earlier," Rachel said, smiling in Amy's direction. "Are you getting settled in?"

"Yes, thank you. And Nikki was kind enough to cook dinner."

Rachel glanced at the table. "Ooh, chocolate."

"Would you like a slice to take—" Nikki began.

"I'd love one," Rachel said, then pulled a chair over to sit between Kendall and Amy.

Amy moved her chair to the side to make room. "Here, you can have mine," she said, sliding the untouched slice of cake toward the woman.

"You don't like chocolate?" Rachel asked, picking up a fork.

"Not tonight," Amy murmured.

Rachel's gaze dropped to Amy's hand. "What a gorgeous ring."

Amy fingered the chunky topaz solitaire. "Thank you…my guy gave it to me."

Kendall made a small choking noise, then pounded his chest and stretched his neck.

"You okay, bro?" Porter asked.

"Sorry," Kendall squeaked. "Wine went down the wrong way."

Rachel reached over to pat his shoulder and coo as if he were a pet—*her* pet—until he recovered. Then she cut into the cake, ate a big bite, and moaned.

"Oh, this is *so* good," she said thickly. She continued to make noises that bordered on orgasmic as everyone around the table squirmed. Kendall in particular seemed on edge, his eyes still watering. Amy, on the other hand, was enjoying his discomfort.

"Another piece?" she asked sweetly when Rachel polished off the last bite and licked the fork clean.

"No, thanks," Rachel said. "I actually just came over to remind Kendall that he left his laptop in my room." She turned to him and batted her impossibly long lashes. "Do you want to come up and get it?"

A pregnant pause enveloped the table. Amy realized it was up to her to ease the awkward moment and pushed to her feet. "Why don't we call it a night? I'll clear the table."

"I'll help," Nikki said, jumping to her feet.

"Me, too," Porter said, then shot Kendall a look that told him he was on his own.

Amy didn't glance at Kendall as she grabbed plates and stacked them on her arm, a talent honed from years of waitressing to put herself through night school. She felt rather than saw him stand.

"Amy," he said. "It was nice to…reminisce."

She looked up and gave him a breezy smile. "Good night."

"Will I see you tomorrow?" he asked.

"I'll be at the bridge site," she said simply, then turned and walked toward the kitchen.

At the last second, she gave in to the urge to see them together, as a couple. She turned and watched as they walked away, Rachel stuck on him like a big piece of pink lint. Kendall glanced back over his shoulder and caught her gaze. Amy just smiled, then kept walking.

7

The smile was still frozen on Amy's face when she walked into the kitchen and joined Nikki at the sink to scrape their dinner plates.

"I can't apologize enough," Nikki said, her expression and voice anguished. "I had no idea that you and Kendall were once… I mean, I can't believe Porter didn't tell me."

"It's okay," Amy said quickly. "I should've told you. But it was a long time ago, and I didn't want to stir up anything. Besides, it looks as if Kendall has definitely moved on."

"I wouldn't be so sure," Nikki murmured.

"It doesn't matter anyway. One of the reasons we split in the first place is because he wanted me to stay here in Sweetness, and I wanted to get away from this place. And on that matter, nothing has changed."

Nikki's jaw suddenly dropped. "Your connection to Sweetness—is that why the ad for single women was run in the Broadway newspaper?"

Amy chose her words carefully. "According to

the website, Broadway was chosen because of its high unemployment rate and distance from Sweetness. The Armstrongs theorized that women who traveled a long distance and with friends would be more committed to stay." She didn't want to raise suspicion on why Marcus might have been keeping tabs on her and wanted to lure her home.

"They were right," Nikki said, glancing around the bustling kitchen. "The women have become very close, even more so after their children arrived."

"Did any fathers come?"

"A few of the women's exes came and signed on to work on a crew. I know one couple that even got back together after the ex-husband relocated here to be close to his daughter."

"That's nice," Amy murmured.

"There've been a few squabbles, but for the most part, everyone tries to get along."

Porter walked up carrying more dishes. "We've got this," Nikki said, shooing Amy away. "You must be exhausted—you should rest."

"I am tired," Amy admitted. Plus she felt like a third wheel and wanted to give the lovebirds some time alone. Besides, the emergency chocolate store in her suitcase was calling. "I think I will call it a night."

Nikki gave her a hug. "I'm glad you're here."

Amy was far from glad, but she didn't want to upset her friend. So she just smiled and said goodnight. On the way to the stairs she bypassed the great room to avoid the scene of a happy community, voices raised in laughter. She was a visitor here, no more.

As she entered her darkened bedroom, her thoughts flickered to Kendall and Rachel, and what they must be doing at this moment in the blonde's room. She wasn't jealous, really. She was glad that Kendall was occupied with someone else, that he had no delusions about them picking up where they'd left off.

She opened the closet door, leaned over to reach into a side pocket of her suitcase and pulled out a dark chocolate candy bar. Amy tore off the wrapper, then crammed the entire bar into her mouth.

No delusions at all.

Kendall stood at the door of Rachel's room, reluctant to step inside.

"Come on in," she invited with a smile. "I have a bottle of wine open."

Kendall took in the bottle of wine and the single glass sitting on the low table in front of the television. He imagined Rachel sitting on the couch watching romantic-comedy movies and drinking wine alone, and he felt contrite. He hadn't considered that the woman was probably lonely. Rachel was the talk among the workers, but as much as they enjoyed looking at the striking blonde, they were all intimidated by her.

"No, thank you," he said with true remorse because he didn't want to hurt her feelings. "I've had enough to drink for tonight."

"We could watch television," she suggested.

"Maybe another time."

Rachel sauntered up to him, then walked her fingers up the buttons of his shirt. "You don't have to be in such a hurry to leave."

He shifted and the door slipped out of his hand, closing with a thud and sealing them inside…alone. Kendall's pulse jumped, more out of nervousness than desire. "Actually, I have a long day tomorrow."

"Oh, come on, you have a few minutes," she cajoled, stepping closer. "After all, I can't keep you too late. Men have to be out of here in forty-five minutes. But that's enough time to do something fun."

She smelled so good. Kendall's mind raced for a graceful way to extricate himself. "I…I really need to get going." He closed his hand around hers to pull it away from his collar.

She pouted. "Do you have time to at least hang my picture? You left your hammer here." Then she bit into her lip. "That is, if your thumb doesn't hurt too much."

She turned his hand over in hers and traced her long, manicured fingers over his big bandaged thumb. Kendall couldn't help but compare her pretty, feminine hands to Amy's natural, neat nails, hands that were suited to the demands of a jobsite.

"It's kind of late to be pounding nails," he protested.

"Okay," she said with a flirtatious smile, now leaning into him. "You can come back tomorrow."

And go through this again? "I guess driving in one little nail wouldn't make that much noise," he said.

He sidestepped her and moved toward the dresser where he'd left his hammer earlier today. He understood forgetting about his laptop, but wow, he must've really been distracted to leave behind a favorite tool.

He lifted the framed photograph of Evermore Bridge and set his jaw against the memories that assailed him. With Amy's face so fresh in his mind, it was impossible not to be affected when he looked at the place they'd once rendezvoused and had made their own.

At least in his mind. It was apparent by Amy's detachment to the project that she didn't share his fond recollections. He supposed the man who'd given her the pretty ring she'd worn at dinner had replaced all those memories with new ones.

Kendall steered his mind back to the matter at hand lest he smash another finger. They went through the harangue again about making sure the picture was in the right spot before he passed the picture to Rachel and held the nail up to the spot in the drywall he'd marked with his finger. Her perfume had enveloped him, and her seductive voice had set his nerves on edge. He quickly tapped in the slim nail of the picture hanger, then reached for the framed photo. He pulled out the slender wire and hung it carefully on the hook, then adjusted it until it was level, and stepped back to look at it.

"How's that?"

"It looks great," she gushed. "Thank you, Kendall." Then before he knew what was happening, she raised on her tiptoes and kissed him on the mouth. And lingered.

Her lips were smooth and tasty—like plump cherries. And Lord, when had he last had a woman's mouth on his? He gave in to the sheer pleasure of it. It was only a thank-you kiss, after all.

A loud crash interrupted the amiable exchange. Rachel gasped and gripped his arm in alarm. Kendall jerked his head around. The picture hanger had come out of the drywall, leaving an ugly gash and sending the framed photo crashing to the dresser with enough force to crack the glass. An ugly web of lines obscured the photo underneath.

"Oh, no!" Rachel cried, hurrying over to pick up the picture.

Kendall winced. "Sorry. Guess I should've looked for a stud to nail into. I'll have it reframed, and I'll fix your wall."

She made a rueful noise. "You don't have to do that."

Guilt stabbed him. She could sense he didn't want to be here. "I insist," he said, taking the picture from her. "I'll come back soon to patch your wall, and I'll bring the photo when it's ready to rehang."

She dimpled. "Okay. If you insist."

Kendall cleared his throat and gestured to his laptop bag sitting next to her bed, as if it wanted to be there. "I should be going."

"Okay," she said, her tone reluctant.

He was relieved to fill his hands with the bag, hammer and the framed picture. She opened the door and ushered him out with a fragrant breeze and a sexy smile. "See you soon?" she asked, looking at him through a fringe of lashes.

"Right," he said, then nodded curtly and turned on his heel. He was in a flop sweat—the woman packed a powerful punch. At the top of the stairs landing, he stopped to put the belabored hammer in his computer bag, then looked down the opposite hallway. He'd pulled up the online directory Marcus maintained for the boardinghouse and knew Amy's room was just a few steps away. She was probably still downstairs, he told himself as he made his way to her door, so she probably wouldn't answer. He knocked, then waited. And if she did answer, he'd make up something about—

The door swung open and Amy stood there, still dressed in the clothes she'd worn to dinner, save for the strappy shoes, which were next to her bed where she'd kicked them off. His heart jumped to his throat. Her deep red hair had partially succumbed to the kinky waves he was more familiar with, but he knew she hated. She stood in stocking feet, her hazel eyes questioning. "Yes?"

His mind raced for an explanation as to why he was standing there. "I just wanted to…make sure you got settled in."

"Yes," she said simply, "I did."

"And your room is comfortable?"

She looked him over and seemed to stiffen. "Yes, very."

He swallowed. "Marcus told me about the conference call tomorrow afternoon with the Preservation Society. I was wondering if you'd like to get together before the call to get our ducks in a row."

She gave him a flat smile. "I told Marcus I'd be there an hour beforehand. We can talk then."

He shifted. "Do you have plans for the morning?"

"Yes, I'm going to survey the site."

"What time?"

"Early," she said vaguely. "But *you* don't have to be there."

At the slight, anger sparked in his stomach. "We're working on this project together."

"While I'm working on the design, I assumed you'd be getting a crew together. We'll need someone who knows how to pour concrete in this weather, and a good mason if you have one. And I assume you have some talented welders and carpenters at your disposal."

He nodded. "No problem."

"Okay, then. I'll see you tomorrow afternoon." She started to close the door.

Desperation emboldened him. He caught the door

with his hand. "Baby—" He stopped, surprised that he had so easily fallen back into calling her his pet name. And he could tell from the look on her face that she didn't appreciate the slip one little bit. "Sorry…Amy. I know things didn't end well between us, but I'm hoping we can start fresh."

She pursed her mouth and nodded. "I don't see why we can't be friends."

He wanted to be more than just friends with Amy, but he acknowledged he had a long way to go to win back her affection. He was counting on the amazing chemistry they'd once shared to rekindle that affection. He leaned in and gave her a smile that had always softened her. "You have chocolate on your mouth."

She angled her head. "And you have pink lipstick on yours. Good night, Kendall."

He pulled back just in time to protect his nose from the slamming door. He swiped at his mouth, feeling like a fool, then frowned at the smear of bright pink on his hand. Now Amy was probably convinced he and Rachel were an item. He puffed out his cheeks in an exhale, then stared at her door. Did he dare knock again to correct her assumption?

Amy leaned against the closed door and closed her eyes. He'd called her "baby," just like old times. Her heart pounded and her mind swirled with confusion. She'd hoped everything would be clear when she got to Sweetness and saw Kendall again, but it had only clouded things more. And instead of being glad he was involved with someone else, she was— Amy groaned in dismay—jealous.

She pushed away from the door and padded over to her phone to see if Tony had called, bitterly disappointed to see he hadn't. Feeling a little desperate, she dialed his number again. While Tony's phone rang, Amy opened her wallet to his picture and ran her finger over his handsome face for reassurance. After three rings, he picked up.

"Hello?"

"Hi, sweetie, it's me," she said, almost weak with relief to hear his voice. "Did you get my message earlier?"

He sighed. "No, I haven't had time to check."

"Oh. Well, I made it to Sweetness, Georgia, this afternoon, and my cell phone works here."

"Duh. How long are you going to be in Hicksville?"

She tamped down irritation. "Like I told you, about three months. But I'll come back in a couple of weeks so we can see each other."

"They couldn't get someone else to build their stupid bridge?"

She bit down on her tongue. "They could've, but they asked me."

"Whatever," he mumbled.

"I miss you," she offered.

He grunted in return. "I hate this place."

"It's a good place," she said earnestly. "You promised you'd give it a chance."

"I gotta go."

She pressed her lips together, awash in helplessness. "Okay. I love you, Tony."

He sighed. "Love you, too, Mom."

Amy disconnected the call, her heart pounding in her chest. She studied the picture of Tony, her twelve-year-old who had recently morphed from a sweet boy into a sulky adolescent. No matter what she did lately, it was wrong. She had never begrudged raising him alone, but recently she'd begun thinking it would be easier if he had a male father figure around.

Or his father.

And Tony looked so much like his father, she acknowledged with a squeeze of her heart. From his tall frame and square jaw…to his deep, cobalt blue eyes.

Kendall leaned against the door, wishing he'd walked away when he had the chance. Hearing Amy profess her love for someone else was like a kick to his gut. The guy who'd given her the topaz ring, no doubt.

It was his own fault, he acknowledged. He'd let Amy get away over a decade earlier, and had gone against his instincts to go to her. Of course another man had recognized how special she was and had wormed his way into her life.

Kendall turned and strode away, lasering unreasonable, but palpable, dislike toward this Tony, the guy who had replaced him in Amy's heart.

8

The next morning when Amy rode out to the bridge site, she was still churning over the previous night's encounter with Kendall, and her subsequent conversation with Tony. The sun was just breaking over the eastern wall of the bowl of mountains that surrounded the little town. The air that whipped her hair behind her was frosty…as frosty as Tony had grown toward her.

Maybe she'd made a mistake by enrolling him in a military school, but his increasing disobedience and recklessness while attending public school had alarmed her, and when he'd been arrested for vandalizing school property last fall, she'd had few options at her disposal. The school counselor had said he was in need of discipline and a male role model. It was the closest she'd ever come to contacting Kendall and informing him he had a son—who was incorrectly channeling the Armstrong traits of stubbornness and arrogance—and she needed for him to step in. But like all the other times she'd had that conversation in her head, she'd talked herself out of it.

She'd raised Tony by herself through some pretty lean and lonely times, but had savored the chocolate-covered kisses, first words, faltering steps, hand-print art, the shedding of training wheels and other happy little-boy milestones. It didn't seem fair to call Kendall when things with Tony had gotten bumpy. Besides, she'd prided herself on being able to keep a lot of balls in the air—working, getting her education and taking care of Tony. It hadn't been easy, but she'd thought she'd managed well enough…until the phone call from the police. A quarter in a military boarding school had seemed like a viable, albeit expensive, alternative for instilling discipline while giving him an outlet for his excess energy. They'd argued about it—Tony had accused her of trying to off-load him—but she'd pointed out that he'd made his own bed and in the end, he'd gone willingly, if reluctantly, a sign to her that he was taking responsibility for his actions.

But she harbored a lot of guilt herself. She'd done some things she wasn't proud of when she was a teenager and had had her share of run-ins with authority. She and Kendall had argued over her penchant for trouble and occasionally taking things that weren't hers. It was, she'd decided, why he hadn't asked her to marry him. Like everyone else in town, he'd considered her tainted. Part of her was afraid that if she called Kendall for help with their son, he would accuse her of being a bad mother...a bad person.

Dropping Tony off at the school after the holidays was the hardest thing she'd ever done. In that instant, he wasn't a tall, troubled adolescent on the verge of manhood—he was her little boy on his first day of preschool begging her with his eyes not to leave him. She'd cried all the way home. Tony had performed and behaved well enough at the school to earn cell phone privileges, but she knew, from his increasingly short and quiet conversations, that all wasn't as fine as it seemed.

Her heart squeezed. She missed him so much it hurt. Their little house in Broadway had seemed big and empty without his clutter and the chatter of his soccer friends and the sound effects of his video games. He was basically a good kid. Bright, too— he was always near the top of the class, had excelled in math and taken home ribbons in science fairs. Schoolwork came to him more easily than it had to her at that age. Even though she had controlled the nurturing part of his development, there was no denying that when it came to nature, he was his father's son.

Except for the getting arrested part...

Amy crested the top of the hill where she'd parked yesterday to find Kendall already there, sitting sideways on an ATV, drinking from a travel mug. Seeing him after being so deeply mired in thought about him and the son he wasn't aware of made her nervous.

She suspected that Marcus knew about Tony, and while he'd respected her privacy thus far, she had a feeling the clock was ticking on that matter.

Amy tried to school her face into a neutral expression as she parked the four-wheeler nearby, but she was still smarting over the fact that he'd knocked on her door after a make-out session with curvy Rachel Hutchins. Years ago, he'd wanted to put Amy on a shelf while he went out into the world, taking for granted that she would always be there, waiting. Or maybe he was hoping she'd just take the hint and move on. That was partly her fault, she acknowledged, for idolizing the man, for being grateful that he'd allowed a poor little girl from the wrong side of the tracks into his life. Of course, he would assume that since she'd come back to Sweetness, she was still hung up on him, and would accept whatever attention he had to spare for the time she was here.

Wrong.

When she cut the engine, he waved. "Good morning."

He looked so good dressed in dark jeans, sturdy boots and a gray sweater. By comparison she felt like a lumberjack in her fleece hoodie and wool pants tucked into knee-waders. "Good morning," she said through gritted teeth. "I distinctly remember saying you didn't have to be here."

He gave her a disarming smile. "I'm here to learn. Besides, this project means a lot to me, too."

Too… There he went assuming again. "I prefer to work alone when I'm in the design stage."

He made a zipping motion across his mouth. "You won't even know I'm here."

"Suit yourself." She climbed off the ATV and opened the storage compartment to remove her heavy-duty laptop built to withstand the elements, and another small bag of equipment.

"Can I carry something?" he asked.

"Nope." Amy shouldered the bags and turned toward the bridge site. Kendall followed her, staying a few steps behind. When she reached the top of the hill overlooking the site, she glanced down at the rushing stream of Timber Creek. The water was crystal clear and at this spot, about waist high. From this vantage point, remains of the three stacked-stone piers that had once supported the bridge were evident. They would have to be replaced, of course, but their presence would help guide the rebuilding efforts. She erected one tripod for her laptop and another for a laser measuring device. Kendall hovered throughout.

"Can I help?" he asked.

"Nope."

"Do you want some coffee? I have a thermos."

Amy pursed her mouth, then gave him a pointed look.

"Right," he said. "I'm not here."

But darn it, his coffee smelled good and a caffeine

headache was working its way up her temples. "Do you have an extra cup?"

He grinned. "Sure do." He removed the top of the thermos that doubled as a cup and filled it, then handed it over.

"Thank you," she murmured. "The creek seems deeper than I remember."

He nodded. "Debris from the tornado created lots of logjams. We've cleared most of the larger ones, but there's still enough filler to raise the water level by at least a foot. The one good thing is that the fallen trees and rubber tires kept the banks from eroding."

She nodded. "I'll inspect the abutments, but they're in much better shape than I expected. We're still looking at the same bridge length, but what about live-weight load? Do you expect heavy-duty trucks to be using the bridge?"

"Yes. The land on the other side is going to be zoned commercial. Porter is working with a scientist who wants to build a lab there, and we thought it was a good site for the recycling plant, too."

She took a sip of the coffee. "That sounds like a lot of traffic for a one-lane bridge."

"An inconvenience, maybe, but worth the sacrifice to restore one of our landmarks. Can you design it to support a commercial load and give it the clearance height it'll need?"

Her back stiffened. "Of course I can. But it complicates the execution. And I can't stay past the three months I committed to." Tony would be out of school then.

"We'll get it done," Kendall said, his voice smooth and confident.

We. It was a word he used to throw around a lot when they were together, making her believe they were a team. Amy took another drink of the coffee, then set to work.

True to his word, Kendall was quiet as she took careful measurements with a laser ruler and entered them into her CAD program. She moved the tripod around at various intervals, then waded into the creek to assess what was left of the support piers and take more measurements from those angles.

She felt his gaze on her as she moved and measured, but standing shin-deep in icy water and dressed like a man, she felt more self-assured than she had last night at dinner. Here, she knew what she was doing. She could fall back on her education and instinct. Satisfaction bloomed in her chest. If she had to come back home to Sweetness, at least she could stand toe-to-toe with Kendall on professional aptitude.

"How many bridges have you designed?" he asked, offering her a hand as she scaled the creek bank with her equipment on her back.

"A few, none of them noteworthy." She ignored his hand, but struggled and slipped. Kendall caught her, and the contact sent a jolt of awareness up her arm. Even after she made it to level ground, his hand remained.

"Are you okay?" he asked, his voice husky.

She looked up at him, into those amazing blue eyes and, to her dismay, she realized how easily she could get used to being around him again.

Except being around him meant living in Sweetness.

"I'm fine," she said in a choked voice, then pulled away. She quickly packed up the rest of her equipment and returned the cup he'd given her.

"What have you designed other than bridges?" he asked, picking up the conversation where they'd left off.

Her chin went up as she headed toward the four-wheeler. "I've done a little of everything—pedestrian skywalks, parking garages, a couple of monuments, even a roller coaster."

"That sounds fun."

Her tongue burned with questions about projects he'd worked on, but she really didn't want to hear about all the adventures he'd had without her while she'd worked in day cares so she could be with their son, then went to night school, and waitressed on weekends.

"Do you have a favorite project?" he asked.

"If I had to choose, I'd say sidewalks for two inner city neighborhoods."

His eyebrows went up. "Sidewalks?"

"There's an art to designing sidewalks that will foster community growth," she said defensively.

"I don't doubt it," he said, but she felt foolish as she repacked the storage compartment of the ATV. All she'd ever wanted to do was impress Kendall, yet she always wound up feeling inept. Maybe not much had changed after all.

"I'll see you before the conference call," she said.

He glanced at his watch. "Actually, I was wondering if you had time to take a look at the materials we recovered from the old bridge."

Amy bit down on the inside of her cheek. If she was going to incorporate the original materials, she'd have to know what they were working with before she completed the design. "Okay."

"Follow me to the dining hall," he said, then climbed on his four-wheeler.

"I'm not hungry," she said, climbing on her ATV.

"But I am," he quipped. "Besides, Molly McIntyre runs the dining hall as well as our Lost and Found warehouse. I know she'll want to see you."

Amy balked, then fired up the engine. Molly McIntyre was a friend of the aunt who had begrudgingly taken Amy in after her parents had died. The women had exchanged letters while Molly was in the Armed Forces—the Army maybe? Amy couldn't recall which branch. But she was sure her aunt had kept the woman informed of all the trouble her unwanted niece had caused her. Worse, when Amy was twelve, the woman had visited her aunt and while they were talking, Amy had taken a ten-dollar bill from Molly's purse to buy a pink blouse at the five and dime, one she had coveted but her aunt had said she didn't need. Molly had caught her red-handed, and after giving Amy a private but thorough tongue-lashing about stealing, had told her to keep the money.

But Amy had felt so guilty about taking it, she'd dropped the bill in the church offering plate instead. She wished she could say it was the last time she'd ever stolen anything, but it wasn't. Still, that lecture had meant something to her. Not so much the words, but the fact that Molly had cared enough to actually talk to Amy about what she'd done, instead of screaming and hitting. It had been a turning point for her, one she would reflect on many times as she grew older, and when dealing with her own son.

Amy pushed aside the poignant memories and rode side by side with Kendall over the trail that ran parallel to the main road. The moisture content in the air was rising, which was never good for construction. Not every engineer had a built-in hygrometer like she did—she thought ruefully of the red hair she could practically hear kinking up—but it did come in handy at times. She'd have to remember to ask Kendall to obtain weather forecasts for the next twelve weeks.

They pulled up to the dining hall, a long ugly building with a scrappy sign. She'd heard they intended to make it more of a diner in the near future, but for now it was little more than a cafeteria. Still, it was an efficient, popular place, crowded with construction workers, women and school children. She felt conspicuous walking in wearing her heavy work clothes and rubber boots, but conceded that she'd looked worse after leaving a jobsite.

Of course, the first person they ran into was Rachel Hutchins, looking like a Playmate in black corduroys and a long-sleeve T-shirt with a picture on the front that was stretched beyond recognition.

"Hi," she said to Kendall with a special smile.

"Hello," he said, smiling back.

Rachel turned to Amy and gave her a once-over. "Looks like you've been…working."

"That's right," Amy said agreeably.

"We came in to get a bite to eat," Kendall said. "Then I'm going to show Amy the Lost and Found warehouse."

"That's nice," Rachel said to Kendall. "When are you planning to stop by to see me again?" *Flap, flap,* went her lashes.

He shifted his feet. "Soon."

"I'll cook dinner for us."

"Okay," he said.

"Do you have any special requests?" Rachel asked. *Flap, flap.*

"I hear you make a mean chicken salad," Amy offered, remembering the story Nikki had relayed about Rachel giving Porter food poisoning on a picnic. Apparently the woman was working her way through the Armstrongs.

"Anything you make will be fine," Kendall interjected. "If you'll excuse me, I need to talk to Molly."

"I'll see you later," Rachel sang after him.

Amy waited until he was out of earshot, then said in a conspiratorial tone, "I heard Kendall say he likes spicy food."

"Really?"

"The spicier, the better."

Rachel smiled. "Thanks for the tip. See you later." Then she walked away, hips sashaying.

Amy nursed a tiny pang of guilt for lying. Then she remembered the lipstick on Kendall's mouth when he'd knocked on her door last night and the casual way he'd called her "baby" with those lips. She smiled to herself.

Paybacks were hell.

9

Kendall picked up a tray and smiled at Colonel Molly McIntyre, a bulldog of a woman who ran the kitchen like a mess mergeant. Retired from the U.S. Army, she'd grown up in Sweetness and answered the call for help when the Armstrongs needed someone to feed the workers who were rebuilding the town. For a long time, Colonel Molly had been the only woman within miles, and remained lukewarm about the infusion of Northern females brought in to get the new town off the ground. Her respect was hard-won.

"What can I get for you, pigeon?" she asked, referring to Kendall's stint in the Air Force.

"Two plates of bacon and eggs over easy, wheat toast."

She began dishing up the food from warming containers. "Hungry this morning?"

"Ordering for two. We have a visitor." He nodded toward Amy, who stood across the room checking her phone—probably seeing if her boyfriend, Tony, had called, he thought miserably. "Do you remember Amy Bradshaw?"

Molly looked thoughtful. "Heddy Bradshaw's niece?"

"That's right. Heddy took her in after her parents were killed in a car accident."

"Weren't you sweet on her?" Molly asked.

Kendall's face warmed. "I guess you could say that."

"Heddy used to write me letters about how sure she was that you were going to ruin her niece."

Kendall gave a little laugh. "Why would she say that?"

"She said there was only one reason a boy like you would be hanging around a girl like her."

Anger sparked in his stomach. "That wasn't a very nice thing to say about her own kin. Amy was a little rough around the edges, but she was a good girl. Besides, Heddy wasn't exactly the motherly type. Amy practically raised herself."

"Heddy was a hard woman," Molly conceded, serving up the plates. "What's Amy doing back here?"

"She's an engineer. She's going to help us rebuild Evermore Bridge."

Molly looked nostalgic. "I used to love riding horses over that bridge when I was growing up." Then she made a face. "That was before your time, pigeon."

"I did the same thing." *With Amy.*

"Well, sounds like the girl did well for herself," Molly said, handing over the plates. "Is she going to stay on after the bridge is built?"

Kendall looked over at Amy, who was putting away her phone and heading their way. "I'm working on that."

When Amy walked up, he noticed her eyes looked troubled—problems with "her guy"? He managed a smile. "Amy, do you remember Molly McIntyre?"

"Of course," Amy said. Her voice was friendly enough, but she looked nervous for some reason. "You were a good friend to my aunt Heddy…and to me. It's nice to see you."

Molly smiled. "You've changed quite a bit since the last time I saw you."

"I hope so," Amy said, holding Molly's gaze.

Kendall had a feeling he was being excluded from the moment, but let it pass. "Molly, I'm going to show Amy the timber we recovered from the original bridge to see if any of it can be salvaged."

"Betsy will probably be there," Molly said, referring to the programmer who maintained the Sweetness Lost and Found webpage. "But if not, you know the key code." Molly smiled. "Welcome home, Amy."

Amy blinked, then inclined her head. "Thank you, Ms. McIntyre."

"Molly," the woman corrected with a wink.

Kendall watched Amy closely as he retrieved fresh coffee from a beverage station then walked to a table and set down the food tray. She followed, but seemed lost in thought—back in time, or hundreds of miles away?

"I got you some breakfast," he said, sliding one of the plates in front of her. "The food in here leaves a little to be desired, but breakfast is usually passable. Eggs over easy, just the way you like them."

She bristled. "Thanks, but I'll just have the toast and coffee."

He pressed his lips together. Eggs over easy was a Southern tradition…and it was becoming increasingly clear that Amy had rejected things that reminded her of her heritage. While she ate, she watched the people around her warily and seemed ill at ease, constantly checking her phone.

"Expecting a call?" he asked.

"As a matter of fact, yes," she said. "I still have a life in Broadway, you know."

He nodded. A *boyfriend*. "How long have you lived there?"

"A few years," she said vaguely.

"Is that where you went when you left Sweetness?" he prodded.

"In that general area."

"And do you like it there?"

"It's been a decent place to live and work."

"Until lately?"

She shrugged. "The state was hit hard when the manufacturing layoffs started to cascade, but I've managed to stay busy."

"I'm surprised you had the time to work on our project."

Her mouth twitched. "Actually, I was in the running to lead a reservoir repair project that would've meant a two-year commitment, but someone else was chosen."

"Ah. Well, their loss was our gain."

Her tight smile telegraphed that she would've rather had the reservoir project.

"You didn't want to come back home, did you?" he asked.

"This isn't my home anymore," she said quickly, almost harshly.

"Fair enough," he murmured.

She took a sip of coffee. "And, no, this project wasn't my first choice," she added, her tone softening. "But I appreciate the opportunity and I'll do a good job."

"I know you will. But you seem…on edge."

"Being here stirs up a lot of bad memories."

That hurt. "A few good ones, too, I hope."

Her hazel eyes were unreadable, then she nodded to his empty plate. "Are you ready to show me this reclaimed timber?"

"Sure," he said, feeling helpless to alleviate her uneasiness, especially since he knew he was partly to blame. She helped him clear the table and stack the trays and plates on the edge of the conveyer belt that would send them through a commercial dishwasher.

"No paper plates?" she asked.

"Right, and no plastic utensils. We're trying to control our waste output, especially since the dump is brimming with tornado debris that couldn't be recycled."

"But doesn't it take hot water and energy to clean the dishes?"

"Our windmill farm supplies more than enough electricity to run the town, and we use water-saving appliances."

"Does that include the hot water heaters in the boardinghouse?" she asked drily. "I had to take a cold shower this morning."

He made a rueful noise. "Sorry. Porter's working on it."

"Nikki says that Porter's also working on building a church?"

Kendall smiled, but then wiped it away with his hand. "Eventually."

Amy gave a little laugh. "You mean never."

"Not never. Just not right away."

"Meaning, he's not ready to get married?"

"Meaning, there are other priorities, like the bridge."

He led her to a rear exit. They walked outside into the brisk air. Amy pushed a springy lock of hair behind her ear, and shivered in her fleece coat. A few yards away from the dining hall sat a tall, long metal building that featured two garage doors and a regular door. They walked to the regular entrance and Kendall knocked.

"Come in," came a woman's voice.

Kendall opened the door and held it while Amy walked through. It was a warehouse, lined with rows of shelves and pallets chock-full of everything from furniture to farm implements to canoes to a golf cart.

"You found all of these things?" Amy asked, astounded.

"Yep. When Marcus and Porter and I arrived last year and started working the land, we realized we had to have a place to store the things we found. Molly and other volunteers clean and repair everything, then they get matched to a list of items residents declared missing after the tornado. If the former resident can be located, the items get shipped to them, or people can come to pick them up. If an item isn't on the list, it gets tagged and shelved."

To the right of the entrance was a work area with a long desk, tables, file cabinets and utility sinks. A teenager with jet-black hair sitting at the desk looked up from her laptop and removed earbuds. "Hiya, Kendall."

"Hi, Betsy. This is Amy Bradshaw. Amy, meet Betsy Hahn."

They exchanged greetings, but he noticed that Amy remained aloof.

"Betsy maintains the Lost and Found webpage," Kendall said. "Thanks to her, former residents can sign up to be notified if their belongings are found.

Or they can browse the unclaimed items and file a form to prove ownership."

"That's nice," Amy said.

"Where are you from?" Betsy asked conversationally.

Amy squirmed. "Here, originally."

"No kidding? Bradshaw, did you say? I'll look you up while Kendall shows you around."

"I wasn't living here when the tornado struck," Amy said.

The young woman shrugged. "Still, there might be something that belonged to a relative."

Kendall watched Amy's face. He knew she was thinking that if something of her aunt's had been unearthed, she didn't want it. The day she'd left, her car had been packed with a photo album holding pictures of her parents, a couple of garbage bags of clothes and as many books as the backseat could hold. When he'd asked her about the things in her aunt's rental house, she'd said, "Let it all rot."

His heart had broken then for the hand that life had dealt her, depriving her of her parents, and it broke for her now.

"The timber?" she prompted, as if she were reading his thoughts.

"This way." He led her to a large wire cage marked "Evermore Bridge." Stacked inside were enormous timbers and various pieces of wood that Amy studied intently. "This is all virgin timber, isn't it?"

He nodded. "Original stands taken right off this mountain."

"Incredible," she breathed.

Kendall's heart swelled with pride. He didn't know very many women who could recognize and appreciate the historical significance of what they were looking at.

"This could be a heel plate," she said, then pointed. "And those are chords, and maybe a lateral member." She ran her hand over the smooth aged surfaces. "The rest are probably floor beams and treads. I'll bet if we look hard enough, we'll find numbers on them to correspond to where they were installed."

He was amazed she could so readily identify these disparate parts. "That's great, but numbers won't do us much good without the original blueprints. Unfortunately, they blew away with everything else stored at the courthouse."

"Marcus mentioned they weren't available," she murmured.

"But the Preservation Society sent us blueprints on a similar bridge in Ohio. Do you think you'll still be able to use these pieces?"

"Maybe, if they're in good shape," she said, giving each log a pat or a rub. "Can you have them moved to the site?"

"Absolutely."

It was the first time since Amy arrived that he'd seen a familiar light in her eyes. Her cheeks were pink and she was animated, her quick mind turning over the details of the project before them. A wide smile lifted her mouth.

"Oh, Kendall, this is…" She looked up to lock gazes with him. Kendall's senses leapt to feel the old sizzle between them.

"Yes?" He took a step toward her.

Then her smile faded, and he knew he'd lost her again.

"I mean…that would be great," she said, visibly reining in her enthusiasm. Then she straightened. "I should be getting back. I'd like to change and get a few things ready for the conference call."

He nodded, disappointed, but closed the door to the cage and backtracked to the front of the warehouse.

When they passed one section of furniture odds and ends, though, Amy stopped. "That looks like your mother's dish cabinet, the one she kept in the dining room."

He smiled. "It is, minus the glass. And that's Mom and Dad's bed. And the coffee table—"

"From the family room," Amy said.

"That's right. Marcus made it for her."

"How is your mother?"

"Right as rain," he said. "After the storm, she moved to Calhoun to live with her sister, but she's determined to come back to Sweetness someday. We're holding all this stuff for her until the town is stable and we can build her a house to move into."

"She was always good to me," Amy murmured.

"She'd love to see you," he said.

Amy gave him a rueful smile. "Except I won't be here when she comes back." She jerked a thumb over her shoulder. "I'll find my own way out."

Kendall watched her go, his arms aching to reach out to her. She always seemed to be walking away from him. And he always seemed powerless to stop her.

10

When Amy arrived at the construction office for the conference call with the Preservation Society, she was surprised to find Marcus alone.

"Come in," he said, standing. "Have a seat. Kendall should be here shortly. Something came up at the last minute and I needed him to take care of it."

Meaning, he wanted to speak to her alone for a few minutes.

Amy leaned her portfolio against his desk, then sat in a chair opposite him with a sense of impending doom.

"How's it going so far?" Marcus asked, settling back into his chair.

"The bridge site seems stable. I have all the measurements and pictures I need. For the first day, I'd say things are good."

He gave her a flat smile. "I meant with Kendall."

She shifted in her seat. "For the first day, I'd say things are good."

"When are you going to tell him he has a son?"

Amy released a pent-up breath. "How long have you known?"

"A few months."

"*How* did you know?"

"When I started researching Broadway, I came across your name in a professional listing. I dug a little. When I found out you had a child, the timing seemed right, and when I found a picture of him on the internet, it was pretty clear that he's an Armstrong."

"His name is Bradshaw," Amy corrected.

"You should've told Kendall you were pregnant, Amy. He would've married you and taken care of you both."

Amy bit her lip. "Probably. Kendall always does the right thing. But I didn't want to be part of a package deal, and it was clear that Kendall didn't want me for myself."

Marcus pulled his hand over his mouth. "Look, I'm sure you had your reasons for not telling him, but if I found out, he can find out, too."

She gave him a tight smile. "And yet, he hasn't, has he?"

Marcus sighed. "Are you going to tell him?"

"I have my son to think of."

"He doesn't know who his father is?"

She shook her head.

"They both need to know."

Amy pressed her lips together. "You're right, but I need time. This isn't going to be easy for anyone."

"Where is the boy now?"

"Tony is in military boarding school this quarter."

Marcus smiled. "Kendall will be happy about that."

Not when he found out why, she mused. "Marcus, I appreciate your discretion, but I need to handle this situation the way I see fit."

He nodded. "I agree that you should be the one to tell Kendall. But know that if you don't tell him, I will."

The door banged shut and Amy turned to see Kendall standing there, his cheeks pink from the cold. "Tell me what?"

Amy's heart stood still.

"Uh, we were just talking about the project," Marcus said, obviously trying to buy time.

"So what don't you want to tell me?" Kendall asked, shrugging out of his coat.

Marcus looked at her expectantly.

Her mind spun. "I didn't want to tell you that… that I have the blueprints for the original covered bridge."

To his credit, Marcus didn't bat an eye.

Kendall smiled. "You do? But that's great! Why didn't you want to tell me?"

A hot flush climbed her neck. "Because I stole them."

He looked confused. "Stole them? From where?"

"From the courthouse, long ago." With her heart clicking, she reached for the portfolio leaning against the desk, then carried it to a table and unzipped it. Kendall and Marcus both crowded around, but Kendall moved more slowly. She was keenly aware of Kendall's hip in proximity to hers. As relieved as she was to have narrowly diverted the conversation, she was still nervous over the close call.

Inside the portfolio were the sheets of yellowed, brittle blueprint paper with the official stamp, dated 1920.

"How did you manage to steal these?" Kendall asked with a frown.

"I smuggled them out one page at a time in a sketch pad," she said in a small voice, feeling dirty. It had taken her months to avoid raising flags with the hawk-eyed archivist who'd maintained the town's historical documents.

The blueprints showed front and side elevations of Evermore Bridge, along with many dissection diagrams, with each piece of wood numbered.

"I guess now we can reuse the timbers we found," Kendall said, but his tone was dry…and critical.

Amy looked up to find censure in his expression. He didn't realize that she'd taken the blueprints so she would always have a piece of their bridge with her. Good. Let him think that she'd stolen them for the thrill of it.

"Kendall, this is good news," Marcus said.

Kendall lifted his hands. "I guess so. How lucky for us that Amy stole these historical documents from a federal building."

Hurt barbed through her chest. *He still thinks I'm trash.*

"Yes," Marcus said pointedly. "How lucky for us, how lucky for this town."

But the damage was done. Amy tingled with shame. "Of course the town can have the originals back. I'll work from a copy I made." She closed the portfolio, zipped it and handed it to Kendall. It was hard to make eye contact, and she wished she hadn't. He looked at her with such distrust, as if he were asking, "What else don't I know about you?"

A lot, she conceded silently.

Marcus cleared his throat. "I suggest we get our notes together for the conference call."

Amy was happy for the diversion. She booted up her laptop and retrieved project notes she'd already made and questions she had for the Preservation Society representative. As they compared notes among themselves, Kendall was perfunctory, and she remained aloof, as well. They both addressed Marcus more than each other, except when they disagreed.

"I think you should invest in a two-lane construction bridge here," Amy said, pointing to a narrow portion of Timber Creek south of the covered bridge site. "That will allow us to work both sides of the creek and provide an alternate route for emergencies. And later, for bringing heavier loads to and from your recycling plant. I'm thinking something fast and strong, like prefab steel."

"That's not in the budget," Kendall argued. "Besides, I thought you said you could design this covered bridge to withstand commercial loads."

"I can," Amy said, her ire rising. "But a construction bridge will cut assembly time of the new bridge in half."

"So you can leave even sooner than you'd planned?" Kendall lobbed back.

Amy's anger sizzled as they glared at each other. The ringing of the telephone broke the moment.

Marcus glanced at the handset. "Can you two call a truce until we wrap up this phone call? Remember, these people are giving us money. It would be nice to present a united front."

Amy and Kendall exchanged brooding glances, then took seats opposite Marcus, their body language stiff. When Marcus answered the call and made introductions all around, Amy pushed down her emotions, and went into presentation mode. She'd worked with preservationists before and spoke to their concerns and motivations. They were delighted to hear the original blueprints for the bridge had been "located," and ran down a list of forms they would need before releasing the grant money.

"Who is the primary construction contact?" the representative asked.

"I am," Amy and Kendall said in unison, then frowned at each other.

"Actually," Marcus said with a deceptively mild tone as he glanced back and forth between them, "*I* am. Please send those forms to the attention of

Marcus Armstrong. Thank you for your time." He pushed the disconnect button, then presented both of them with a flat smile. "I need a covered bridge in twelve weeks. Work it out." He stood and retrieved a coat from a peg, then walked out.

When the office door banged shut, Amy pursed her mouth. "I thought you said we could be professional."

"We can be," he said, his jaw set stubbornly...so much like Tony. "I guess that means we'll have to agree to disagree."

"We're very different people," she added.

"Always were," he confirmed.

His comment stung, but she preferred the truth to fantasy.

"But I'm starting to see the wisdom in building a construction bridge," he said.

Amy met his gaze. So she could leave even sooner than she'd planned.

"Who knows," he said casually, "maybe we could cut assembly time down to ten weeks."

"Or even eight," she offered.

He nodded. "I'll get a crew on it tomorrow."

"Good," she said.

"Good," he said.

11

For the next couple of days, Amy concentrated on updating the Evermore Bridge plans to support the deadweight of the bridge itself, along with the live weight of whatever vehicles and loads would be transported over it. She added expansion joints to allow for the extreme temperature swings here in the mountains, and steel crossbeams that should, if ever tested, withstand the forces of an F4 tornado in the unlikely event a similar disaster ever befell the town again. Reinforced concrete in the center of the stacked-stone piers would keep the bridge rooted more securely, and strategic openings near the roof would allow wind to pass through the bridge rather than buffeting it side to side.

She sat on a boulder overseeing the site where workers were deconstructing the piers as carefully as possible to preserve the stones to be used again. The rock and concrete abutments that supported the bridge where it met land and water were in surpris-ingly good shape, but would be shored up with reinforced concrete. A crew was building walls to divert creek water away from the abutments to allow the area to dry before the pouring could begin.

When Nikki Salinger had first arrived in Sweetness, the workers had balked at being treated by a "female" doctor, so Amy wasn't sure what her own reception would be. But thus far, the workers had been responsive to her instructions and respectful of her authority. She had to admit, it was satisfying to return to a place where she was once a nobody, now a somebody. A somebody in the position to give orders.

Amy shivered deeper into her fleece jacket and studied a diagram of the proposed lattice truss roof system on her laptop, also more fortified than the original.

If only people could be reinforced so easily—a buttress here, a bracket there—to support their deadweight and live weight. The encounter with Marcus had left her shaken and feeling as if time was closing in for her to tell Kendall about his son. But considering how aloof Kendall had been since their conference call, she was starting to think there was never going to be a right time.

And Tony was being uncommunicative, his sporadic phone calls leaving her more concerned than secure. The worrisome flip side of telling Kendall was revealing to Tony his father's identity. He'd asked about his father a few times when he was younger, but Amy had always been vague, never revealing Kendall's name, for which she was now glad. Tony was technologically adept and might've attempted to locate Kendall before she was ready.

Amy squeezed her eyes shut. Who was she kidding? She would never be ready.

But this seemed like a particularly precarious time to dump something so life-changing on Tony. It would be better to wait until he'd finished the quarter at the military school and was back home, in more familiar surroundings. If she told Kendall after the bridge project was complete and he wanted to see Tony, he could visit them in Broadway.

She exhaled slowly, her breath a white cloud in the cool air. Yes…that seemed like the best plan.

The whirring sound of a tractor approaching caught her attention. After years on jobsites, she could recognize just about any kind of machinery. She closed her laptop and shaded her eyes against the bright sun. Kendall's broad shoulders were silhouetted in the driver's seat. Even at this distance, he made her heart pound faster. The tractor moved slowly, pulling a flatbed trailer. Stacked on the back were the thick timbers and wooden parts she recognized from the Lost and Found warehouse.

She stood and watched as he pulled the load off to the side of the road onto a level area, close enough to be handy to the work site, but still out of the way. He expertly parked the bulky trailer, and Amy found herself admiring the fact that even though he'd probably been the boss on most jobsites, it was clear he could hold his own with the workers. He shut off the tractor engine. "Is this spot okay?" he shouted to her.

"Fine," she called back.

He jumped down and walked to the rear to unhitch the trailer.

She enjoyed watching him move his big, athletic body. She idly wondered if making love with him now would be different than before.

Not that it was bad before...

She pushed aside those wayward thoughts as he strode toward her in mud-spattered jeans and boots and a heavy red flannel shirt...with pink sweater fuzz all over it. She bit down on the inside of her cheek—he'd obviously been nuzzling with Rachel again.

He came to a stop before her. "Marcus wanted me to tell you the Preservation Society okayed the blueprints this morning."

"That's good news."

He didn't offer commentary. "Our fabricator is delivering the metal for the construction bridge tomorrow morning."

"That was fast."

"I thought fast was what you wanted."

Amy bit her lip. "That's right."

His mouth tightened. "It's a short span and the parts are standard, so they had what we needed. Anyway, while the fabricator is here, he's going to pick up lumber for the covered bridge, and a materi-

als list to take back with him. So we need to deter-
mine which of these reclaimed pieces we can use."

His brusque manner straightened her back. "Are
you offering to help me?"

He gave a curt nod. "The clock's ticking."

"You won't be missed?" she asked.

He squinted. "By who?"

She reached forward and picked a pink ball of
fuzz from his shirt, then let it fly away in the breeze.

He shifted and his face turned as red as his shirt.

Amy's phone rang. She pulled it out and glanced at
the caller ID: *Tony.* The fact that her son was calling
while she was talking to his father made her blood
pressure spike.

"I need to get this," she said to Kendall. "Excuse
me."

She walked away a few steps and answered. "Hi,
sweetie. This is a nice surprise."

"Hey," came the sulky reply. "How's Hicksville?"

"Fine," she said patiently. "What's new with you?"

"Can you come and get me?"

She gripped the phone tighter. "Is something
wrong?"

"Yeah," he said, "I'm bored."

She relaxed and kept her voice steady. "We talked
about this. I have to be here for a few more weeks,
and you have to be there for a few more weeks. We
can get through this, right?"

A labored sigh sounded over the line. "I guess so."

"Good. I have to get back to work, but call me tonight, okay?"

Another sigh. "Okay."

"I love you."

"Love you, too," he mumbled, then hung up the phone.

Amy disconnected the call with a fond smile, then turned back to Kendall, who was staring at her. She panicked, wondering if he'd overheard any of her conversation. Her mind spun back over the phone call, trying to remember if she'd said anything that would make him suspicious. They stared at each other, and she swallowed hard, waiting for him to demand an explanation.

His mouth tightened as he jerked a thumb toward the load of recovered timbers. "Let's just get this done."

"Okay," she said, exhaling with relief. "If you start looking for numbers, I'll pull up the blueprints." She opened her laptop and retrieved the old and new blueprints in side-by-side windows. "Ready when you are."

He climbed up on the trailer to stand among the pieces, then crouched to inspect a timber on the end. "Fourteen."

She found the corresponding piece on the old blueprints. "It's a crossbeam." Then she checked the updated blueprints to see if that beam would have the same dimensions. "Yes, we can use it if it's in good shape."

He took off his heavy work gloves and ran his hands over the length of the smooth wood, then picked it up with a grunt and turned it over. The amount of effort it took for a strong man like Kendall to lift one of the pieces gave her renewed fear and respect for the ferocity of a storm that had left the sturdy covered bridge little more than a pile of pickup sticks.

"This piece needs to be sanded," he announced, "but it's solid."

"Good. Except that crossbeam is now number... eighteen." She reached into the pocket of her jacket and pulled out a small bottle of spray chalk. "This should do until we can burn or chisel the numbers into the wood."

While Kendall marked the piece, she deleted it from the materials list.

"Next," he said, "is...thirty-five."

They methodically worked through each of the two dozen pieces of wood and over a dozen pieces of wrought iron stacked on the trailer. It was tedious work, but in the end, they were able to salvage more than half of the pieces. And sometime during the rapid-fire back and forth, voices had softened and body language had eased.

Amy caught Kendall's gaze. "I guess we can work together pretty well if we try."

"I guess so." He looked like he wanted to say more, but he didn't.

She was getting used to the beard and mustache—

it suited him. Unbidden, the thought slid into her mind that it would feel good to be kissed by him. All over. Suddenly her fleece jacket was too warm. She casually unzipped the front to let in cool air, but was further unnerved that he seemed riveted to the movement.

"I'll get Marcus the updated materials list," she said unnecessarily, then cast around for an intelligent work-related question. "Do you know what kind of turnaround we're looking at with the fabricator?"

"A little longer than usual because of the metal parts, probably a week."

A week was still very good. Glad to have her mind back on the project, Amy asked, "Are they reliable?"

He nodded. "We've worked with them on every modular building in town. When they deliver, every piece is inspected and checked off the materials list before they leave the site. Then it's just a matter of putting together the puzzle pieces."

She gave a little laugh. "Right…child's play. I have to warn you, building a bridge is a bit more complicated than putting together a prefab building."

He chewed on her comment. "I know that."

Those questions she'd never asked him—the exciting projects he'd worked on…without her. "So you've built a bridge or two?"

"Or three," he said mildly. "Nothing as ambitious as this one, of course."

"Same here," she admitted. "In fact, I'd have to say this is…" She tapered off, afraid to reveal too much about the emotional attachment she felt to this bridge.

"Special?" he prompted.

All of the memories they'd made there together, most likely the place where they'd conceived their son. She simply nodded.

Their gazes locked and the moment stretched on. Finally Kendall cleared his throat and nodded toward the workers standing in the creek bed. "So how's it coming?"

"Fine for now. How about at the other site?"

"I was just going up to check. Hop on and I'll take you with me." He smiled. "Just like old times."

The smile almost did her in—it was Tony's smile, the one he gave her when he was trying to talk her into saying yes. Now she knew why she could never resist it. She remembered riding on a tractor with Kendall around his parents' place, just to keep him company when he plowed or bush-hogged a pasture. Along the way, they would stop and take advantage of any soft pile of hay or shady tree. It was almost embarrassing to think back on. Such a rural thing, courting on a tractor. And she'd loved every minute of it.

But she wasn't that girl anymore.

"I'll pass," she murmured. "I want to get this materials list to Marcus and render the specifications for the fabricator."

If he was disappointed by her response, he didn't let on. "Suit yourself." He turned and walked away, then looked back. "I almost forgot—Colonel Molly asked me to tell you to stop by when you have a chance."

Amy was immediately suspicious. "Did she say why?"

"Nope." Then he grinned. "Good luck."

Amy opened her mouth to call after him and say she'd changed her mind about going with him, but was stopped by the sight of his backside in work jeans that were worn in all the right places. She was feeling too vulnerable right now to be pressed up against him on the tractor, with everything vibrating and throbbing and bouncing around.

Amy closed her eyes and sighed. Colonel Molly was the lesser of the two evils.

12

Amy stopped by the construction office to print the materials list for the covered bridge for Marcus and to launch the rendering program that would provide exact specifications for each piece in the updated blueprints. The fabricators would use the specs to cut each part of the bridge to precision, and number them for assembly.

To her great relief, Marcus was strictly business and didn't bring up anything about Tony or her talking to Kendall. But she knew from his arched eyebrows and tight-lipped answers that the subject was simmering just beneath the surface. Individually, the Armstrong brothers were a force to deal with, but together, they were formidable. Family came first. And she knew Marcus well enough to know he wouldn't let a blood relation—especially a *male* blood relation—escape from the fold.

Deep down, it was what she feared the most, Amy admitted. That once Tony found out about his heritage, he would choose his father—and this place—over her.

This place, she thought as she walked down the main street toward the dining hall, this place that seemed to put barbs in the people who lived there and hold them down, hold them back, *draw* them back. The name of the town was so deceiving. Sweetness. It sounded simple and idyllic, yet in her experience, it had been anything but.

Amy reluctantly returned smiles of people she passed. Some faces were becoming familiar to her, which spooked her a little. She didn't come here to become part of the community, she was strictly a temporary contractor.

She walked into the dining hall and her stomach growled, reminding her she hadn't yet had lunch. Not that the gray mystery meat patties looked very appetizing—Nikki had told her a food revolt was on the horizon—but she needed some type of fortification.

"Amy!"

She looked up to see Nikki walking toward her, carrying an empty tray. "Hi, Nikki."

"Good to see you. How are things going?"

Amy nodded and smiled. "On schedule."

"I wish we could talk, but I have to get back to the clinic. How about dinner tomorrow evening at the boardinghouse?"

Amy hesitated.

"Don't worry, I won't invite Kendall," Nikki said, then added, "unless you want me to."

"No, no," Amy said, holding up her hand. "But don't exclude Porter. I'd like to get to know him better." In case her son would be spending time with him in the future.

"Okay, dinner tomorrow," Nikki said. "But I'll make plenty if you change your mind about inviting Kendall."

Amy gave her a tight smile. "I won't, but thanks."

They said goodbye, then Amy joined the food queue. Molly McIntyre wore a camouflage apron and lorded over the serving line like a drill sergeant, especially where the school kids were concerned, putting the food on their plates that she deemed appropriate before shooing them on their way. Even the adults seemed to cower and accept their fate as gelatinous fare was plopped onto their plates. Amy's nerves jumped as she neared the front, but she had to admit, she was curious as to what the woman wanted. Molly's eyes lit up when she saw her in line.

"Amy! Your hair is more like I remember."

Corkscrews, Amy acknowledged wryly. Her flatiron couldn't conquer the winter humidity. She smiled back weakly, thinking whatever Molly wanted couldn't be too bad if she was being friendly. "Kendall said you needed me to stop by?"

"It can wait until you eat lunch," Molly said, dipping a ladle into a vat of something thick and unidentifiable.

"Actually," Amy said, "I need to get back to the jobsite, so maybe just something portable, like fruit?"

Molly looked disappointed, but handed her ladle to a helper and came around from behind the serving counter carrying an apple and a carton of yogurt. "I guess you got hooked on this sissy food when you moved to the North."

"Er…yes. Thank you." She put the items in her pocket to eat later. "What did you want to see me about?"

"Follow me," Molly said, then turned on her heel and walked off, assuming Amy would follow.

She did, trotting to keep up as the sturdy woman exited the building, then walked toward the Lost and Found warehouse. Amy was starting to get a bad feeling—she didn't want to go back into that sad place full of forgotten belongings. "Molly, if you found something of my aunt's—"

"It's not something that belonged to Heddy," Molly said over her shoulder, and kept walking.

Amy frowned, but followed her into the warehouse. Betsy sat at the desk working on a laptop. She smiled at Amy and removed her earbuds.

"We found something of yours! And it's wicked."

Molly looked at Amy and rolled her eyes. "I think she means it's nice."

Betsy walked over to a file cabinet and unlocked it, then rifled through for a few seconds before removing a plastic bag marked "M. Bradshaw."

Amy's heart skipped a beat. Her mother's name was Marie.

"This belonged to your mother," Molly confirmed, taking the bag from Betsy and opening it to withdraw a gold chain with a pendant.

Amy's mouth went dry when she saw the pendant, a stylized circle of a mother holding a child. The child was represented by a sizable diamond. "I know this necklace," she gasped. "My mother is wearing it in pictures I have."

Molly smiled and handed it to her.

The pendant was heavy, a ball of gold. "But how... Did my aunt have it?"

"Heddy didn't have it," Molly said. "When it was found and turned in, we saw it had the initials MB on the back, but we didn't know who it belonged to."

Amy turned it over and saw the miniscule letters. "How did you know it was my mother's?"

Molly tapped her temple. "Since we met again the other day, something has been nagging at me. I went back and read through Heddy's letters and found this one." She pulled an aged envelope and a pair of reading glasses from her apron pocket, then removed the letter and found her place with her finger.

"'My adorable niece, Amy, is ill, poor child, something to do with her stomach. The doctors say she needs an operation. But Stanley lost his health insurance and Marie is worried sick over how they're going to pay for it. I gave them all I could spare, but when Paul died, he left me with so much debt, I'm afraid I'm going to lose my house. Marie has a nice necklace with a diamond in it that Stanley bought for her with money he won in Vegas. He says it's worth a lot. She doesn't want to sell it, but that woman will do whatever it takes. She loves that little red-headed girl something fierce. We all do.'"

Molly stopped reading, but Amy couldn't see her anymore through the haze of tears. She touched the spot on her abdomen where a faint scar remained from the surgery she had no memory of. "And whoever my mother sold the necklace to…they lost it in the tornado?"

"Looks that way," Molly said, then shoved a handkerchief in Amy's hand. "Could've been someone she knew, or maybe a pawn shop—heck, it could've changed hands a half dozen times since then. But the important thing is it's back where it belongs."

Amy dabbed at her tears, but her throat was still thick with the unfairness of losing loving parents she couldn't remember. In that moment, she softened toward her widowed aunt Heddy, too, who must've been emotionally and financially overwhelmed to have a child thrust on her. Amy knew what that was like…except the child thrust upon Aunt Heddy hadn't been her own. And the child hadn't been particularly appreciative for the safe, if meager, home provided to her.

Shame enveloped her.

She closed her fingers over the pendant. "Thank

you," she said to Molly. "You don't know how much this means to me."

To her surprise, the erect woman gave her a quick, but heartfelt, squeeze. "There, there. Shake it off," Molly said with a hearty sniff. "I need to get back to work."

"So do I," Amy said with a smile.

"I'll walk you out," Molly said, stuffing the glasses and letter back into her apron pocket.

Nursing guilt for rebuffing Betsy on the previous visit, Amy thanked the young woman and said goodbye, then walked out with Molly. "That was a very kind thing to do for someone who once stole from you."

Molly gave a dismissive wave. "Bygones. Besides, you were a child."

"Still, I knew it was wrong. But you made an impression on me."

The woman smiled. "What's the saying? It takes a village to raise a child."

Amy had heard the saying many times, but this was the first time it made sense to her. It was true that so many people in Sweetness had lent a hand in raising her—concerned teachers, nosy neighbors, chiding grocery clerks, meddling ministers. All of them had touched her life somehow.

"Molly, is there an ATV around I can borrow?"

"Take mine," Molly said, pointing to a vehicle painted with mottled camo paint parked under a nearby tree.

"I'll be back in about an hour," Amy promised.

"Take your time and be careful."

Amy jogged to the four-wheeler, stopping long enough to lift the necklace over her head and tuck the pendant inside her blouse. Then she climbed on and turned the ATV toward the main street. She chugged along slowly, conscious of the children leaving the dining hall to return to school for afternoon classes. Her heart squeezed when she looked at their faces. She missed Tony so much. She was counting the days until she saw him again.

After she was clear of pedestrian traffic, she veered left up a broken roadway that led to Clover Ridge, where the Armstrong boys had grown up, and where one of the largest cemeteries was located.

She bit her lip. Had the cemetery survived the tornado? Were the roads clear enough for her even to reach it? She was suddenly overwhelmed with remorse for having been so neglectful of her parents' and aunt's final resting place.

The cracked, weed-choked road gave way to another that was in even more disrepair, then another. Now that she was away from the downtown area, she was starting to get an idea of the amount of work that remained to make Sweetness a habitable place. Kudzu-covered mounds were the only indication that homes had once stood in these places. The opening to the little hollow where she'd lived with her aunt was so overgrown, it was impassable. Her heart lodged in her throat, and she fought back tears. Their little rental house hadn't been much to speak of, but it didn't seem right that it had been wiped from history.

She kept riding across the ridge, slowing when she reached the Armstrong property. She swallowed hard—the house where she'd loved to spend time with Kendall's family was gone, but the land was cleared. At the end of the fragmented driveway the newly painted black mailbox heralding "Armstrong" made her smile—a pronouncement that the Armstrongs were back to stay.

In the field next to the lot, uniform logs were stacked in a crosshatch pattern for drying. Nikki had told her the homestead property now belonged to Porter. It looked as if he were contemplating building a home for them sometime in the near future. Then Amy gave a little laugh—Porter's time might be better spent getting that church built.

She goosed the gas and continued past more abandoned rubble, out to the cemetery where her family was buried. She expected it to be a tangled jungle of weeds, but the place was in decent shape—the Armstrongs had obviously made it a priority to keep the graveyard in check out of respect.

Her heart swelled. That was the kind of men they were—mavericks…heroes…leaders. It was comforting to know there were still people like them in the world.

She pulled up next to the tall gate that had received a new coat of paint recently and cut the engine. After walking inside, she surveyed the sea of gravestones—some of them dating back to the Civil War—and was filled with shame that she wasn't quite sure where her family plot was located. There had been a tree nearby, she remembered, and a small stone bench.

She scanned the area and headed in the direction of the remains of a large tree. The bench was gone, but as she walked, she felt sure she was on the right track. She swung her head back and forth, scanning headstones, recognizing the names of families that had once inhabited the town: Maxwell, Cole, Smithson, Cafferty, Moon. If any headstones had been damaged by the tornado, they had been repaired. No surprise, the Armstrong plot where Kendall's father was buried was perfectly manicured. The brothers took care of their own.

And Tony was one of their own.

The thought was both comforting and worrying.

She proceeded through tall grass to the rear of the cemetery and the lots that were less level and not as scenic. She searched her memory, but it was the cleared area that drew her attention to the Bradshaw plot marked with a simple white cornerstone with an engraved "B." To her amazement, the graves were neat and the marble headstone that marked her parents' grave was clean. *Beloved husband and wife, Stanley and Marie Bradshaw.*

Who had tended their graves? As soon as the

question flitted through her brain, she knew the answer: Kendall.

Amy crouched to touch the stone, her tears flowing freely now for the people she knew only from a handful of hazy photographs. Their lives had been cut short, and here they lay, neglected and forgotten by their only child. When she'd left Sweetness, she'd turned her back on every memory, the good with the bad. She put her hand over the lump of the pendant underneath her shirt and made a silent vow that when she left this time, she would come back to visit regularly.

She glanced over to her aunt's grave, two plots over from her parents' resting place. When she'd left, Aunt Heddy's grave had been a mound of dirt and clay, covered with the drying remains of a few bunches of flowers that friends had sent for the funeral. It had apparently settled and grass had taken hold…but her aunt didn't have a headstone.

Amy took a deep, cleansing breath. That, at least, she could remedy.

The wind picked up, tossing the ends of her springy hair. She surveyed the sprawling cemetery as the breeze kicked up leaves, giving life to the quiet place. The breeze swirled around the headstones, whispering and moaning. It was as if the long-gone residents of Sweetness were speaking to her. *Don't forget us.*

It was what she'd feared most about coming back here, that she would be swept up in the inexplicable pull of this place and these people. She tugged the mother-child pendant from her shirt and looked down at it, all the more meaningful because she had a child of her own.

A child without a village.

13

"What's in the bag?" Porter asked, loping up next to Kendall.

Kendall didn't break stride but continued walking toward the General Store with a package under his arm. "None of your business."

"I thought your mood would improve when Amy got here, but you've gotten downright morose."

Kendall pursed his mouth. "So go find someone else to talk to."

"But I want to talk to you."

"Don't you have a church to build?" Kendall asked pointedly.

Porter frowned. "You don't have to get ugly. I just wanted to see how things are going on the bridge. Dr. Kudzu will be here in a few weeks and I want to make sure we're in a position to start building that lab."

"We'll be ready. She'll be gone before you know it."

Porter squinted. "What?"

He hardened his jaw. "I mean, she'll be *up* before you know it—the bridge, I mean." He stopped and pinched the bridge of his nose. "Go away, Porter."

"Hey, talk to me, bro. Things not going well with Amy?"

"That would be no."

"Then how did you get pink fuzz all over your shirt?"

Kendall swiped at the front of his shirt. "I ran into Rachel at breakfast this morning. She must have brushed up against me. Amy noticed, too. She thinks there's something going on between me and Rachel."

"Well, if that's the only thing standing between you, tell Amy the truth—that you're still carrying a torch for *her*."

"It's not the only thing standing between us. She has a boyfriend in Broadway, some guy named Tony. She can't wait to leave here again and keeps thinking of ways to make the bridge project go faster."

"Well, she's not gone yet. And if she's noticing you and Rachel, that's a good thing."

Kendall frowned. "How's that?"

Porter clapped him on the back. "Because, you idget, it means she's jealous. Just like you're jealous over her boyfriend. And you can't be jealous unless you have feelings for someone."

Kendall brightened. "I guess you're right."

"Of course I'm right," Porter said with a grin. "I'm a genius when it comes to women. I got Nikki, didn't I?"

"You got her *attention* by writing on the water tower while she was on her way out of town," Kendall added. "Whether you manage to keep her is yet to be seen."

Porter frowned. "I'm going now."

"Thought you might." Kendall resumed walking, but he had a lighter step. He turned. "Hey, Porter."

Porter looked up.

"Thanks."

Kendall turned and kept going until he reached the General Store. He jogged up the steps onto the porch. Firewood was stacked in small cabled bundles, and children's four-buckle galoshes were on sale. He opened the door and stepped back as two boys burst out the door, squirting each other with water guns. Caught in the cross fire, Kendall caught a wet shot in the face.

The boys froze. "Sorry, Mr. Armstrong."

"Yeah, sorry. Don't tell my mom, okay?"

He wiped his eyes, then gave them a chagrined smile. "Only if you promise to practice your aim, Justin."

The boys grinned, then ran down the stairs, yelling and soaking each other.

Kendall gave a laugh, then walked into the store, inhaling the good scents of winter—peppermint and evergreen. Despite Rachel's complaint that Molly wasn't the right person to order supplies for the General Store, the place was actually pretty cozy. And while the merchandise fell a little short of Macy's, the basics were covered: dry goods, cleaning supplies, underwear, outerwear, tools, toys, candy and occasional baked goodies if one was lucky enough to be there when the bread truck pulled up on Mondays and Thursdays.

The store was bustling with customers, always good to see. Monica Kinsey, who apparently used to work in a department store in Broadway, was a cheerful, helpful head salesclerk. From behind the long front counter, she smiled. "Hi, Kendall. What can I do for you?"

He set the wrapped package on the counter. "I broke the glass in this frame. Can you replace it?"

"That shouldn't be a problem. Give me a couple of days?"

"Sure, just call me when it's ready."

"Okay." She grinned. "The bread truck will be here tomorrow. Want me to set aside another chocolate cake for you?"

Kendall pursed his mouth. Maybe he could take it to Amy as a peace offering. She hadn't had any the first time, but he knew she'd wanted it. Maybe it would wear down her defenses. Maybe she'd even let him feed it to her. He smiled at the fantasy. "Yes, I'll take one, thank you."

"You got it."

The sound of raised voices caught his attention. To the right, Rachel Hutchins, still wearing that shedding pink angora sweater, and Dr. Jay Cross, dressed in his white lab coat, were having some sort of disagreement.

"All I'm saying is that a flu shot is the surest way of staying in tip-top shape this winter," the doctor said in his precise, polite tone. Then he punched at his horn-rimmed glasses and looked her up and down. "Although admittedly you already look like you're in tip-top shape."

Kendall winced for the man.

Rachel peered down at him. "And all I'm saying is, I don't care. I don't do needles."

"But we can achieve our goal orally."

Rachel leaned down to be eye to eye with the shorter man. "Did you just say something dirty?"

"N-no," he stammered. "I mean, I can give you the vaccine orally." Then his Adam's apple bobbed and he looked hopeful. "Do you want me to say something dirty?"

Rachel reached forward and fisted her hands in his lapels. "Listen, you prissy little—"

"Whoa, whoa, whoa," Kendall said, walking over to intervene. "Everybody just take a deep breath."

Rachel saw him and smiled. "Kendall, hello again." She released the lapels of Dr. Cross's jacket and gave them an ineffective pat. "Dr. Cross and I were just…talking, that's all." She twisted a lock of golden hair. "I should've asked you this morning at breakfast, but I was wondering if you'd like to come over tomorrow evening and take care of that little matter in my bedroom we discussed."

Kendall worked hard to maintain his smile. After all, he was the one who'd put the hole in her wall. "Sure. I'll bring a stud finder."

She dimpled. "A stud finder seems redundant if you're already in the room."

He gave a nervous little laugh. "What time should I be there?"

She stepped closer and her sweater jumped all over his shirt. "Come at seven. I'll make us dinner first."

Dr. Cross and a few other shoppers were listening in. With an audience, he didn't see a graceful way out. "Okay. I'll see you tomorrow evening at seven."

"Maybe you could bring that chocolate cake again?" Rachel suggested.

So much for the peace offering to Amy. "Will do."

He escaped the store and strode away, running his hands over his shirt to remove any pink sweater fuzz. He slung the downy fibers from his fingers in frustration, already dreading tomorrow's dinner with Rachel and feeling guilty about it at the same time. It wasn't her fault that he would rather be with Amy.

Or that Amy would rather be with someone else.

He fisted his hands, feeling at loose ends. The presentation for the impending Department of Energy rep had been tweaked to the nth degree, and the metal parts for the construction bridge wouldn't be delivered until tomorrow, but he felt antsy and needed to do something productive.

The cemetery plots could use a trim, he decided.

And it was always a good place to go to be alone with his thoughts.

He walked to the garage where they kept work vehicles and hooked a four-wheeler to a small trailer that held a push lawn mower. Then he headed for Clover Ridge, happy for the punishing sting of the cool air on his face as he climbed.

He'd tried to live his life with purpose, first by joining the Air Force, then joining forces with his brothers to resurrect their hometown. So why did he suddenly feel as if he'd done everything wrong?

Because he'd underestimated his need for Amy. The day she'd said goodbye, she'd called it right—he *had* put everything before her. He thought they had plenty of time, that if he'd experienced the world, it would be enough for both of them. He'd thought she would wait for him. When she hadn't, he con-vinced himself she didn't really love him. In hind-sight, though, he saw the impossible situation he'd put her in. She'd always hated Sweetness, yet it was where he'd expected her to stay until—

Kendall cursed under his breath. Until what? Until he was ready to commit to her?

No wonder she'd told him to leave her alone. No wonder she'd fled hundreds of miles away. No wonder she hadn't wanted to come back here, and was eager to leave again as soon as she could.

He topped the ridge and rode past his family's homestead, now Porter's land. He and Marcus had happily given it to him and the logs stacked nearby showed his intent to have a home with Nikki, even if he wasn't in a hurry to build that church.

He kept going, dodging potholes and fallen branches, until he reached the cemetery where his father and grandparents were buried, where his mother would be buried next to their father, and where he and his brothers would be laid to rest when their time came. When he pulled up to the gate, he spotted Molly's telltale camouflage-painted ATV and for a selfish moment, he was disappointed he wouldn't be alone with his thoughts after all.

Then the gate opened and he saw Amy emerge, and his heart tripped double-time.

"Hi," she said.

"Hi." He climbed off the four-wheeler and walked toward her. She'd been crying—visiting her parents' graves, no doubt. He wanted to put his arms around her, but forced himself not to reach for her.

"You've been tending my family's graves, haven't you?"

He'd done it out of respect for her, but now realized that she might find it presumptuous, or invasive. "I meant no harm."

And suddenly she was in his arms. After years of drawing on memories of how she'd once felt pressed up against him, of fantasizing how she might feel today, he was staggered by the jolt to his system. She was softer, more womanly. He tightened his arms around her waist and buried his face in her hair. She smelled like the sun and wind, and everything good.

When she raised her face to his, he lingered only a second to look into her hazel eyes before lowering his mouth to hers for a joyous reunion.

He'd meant the kiss to be slow and sweet and poignant, but as soon as her tongue touched his, he lost control and hungrily ground her mouth against his. In the back of his mind, he was afraid he'd never get the chance to kiss her again, and wanted to make up for lost time, and any time in the future that she might deny him. He groaned into her mouth and gathered her closer, desperate to reconnect with her.

Then as suddenly as she was in his arms, she broke free.

"I'm sorry," she said, covering her mouth with her hand as if she wanted to wipe away the kiss. "I can't do this."

He jammed his hand into his hair. "Amy—"

"No, Kendall," she said, chopping her hand in the air. "I can't do this, and I won't do this." She climbed on the ATV and started the engine, then gave him one last look before driving away.

14

Amy sat in her SUV at the future site of the construction bridge and stretched high to yawn loudly. That impulsive kiss had kept her up all night. She'd tossed and turned in her bed, replaying it in her head over and over, had relived every touch, every nuance, trying to convince herself it had meant nothing to her more than the thank-you she'd meant it to be.

Who are you kidding? You came undone.

And falling for Kendall again would mean being tied to this place, not to mention tying her son to this place.

And there was still the matter of *telling* Kendall he had a son.

She closed her eyes and groaned. Things were complicated enough without getting her heart mired in the middle. She had to keep her head about her for everyone's sake until the bridge was complete. Meanwhile, she suspected the kiss had meant nothing to Kendall other than curiosity and proximity.

After all, her pink sweaters weren't as generous as Rachel Hutchins's.

Amy lifted her hand to her cheek. His beard and mustache had been soft and tingly against her skin. She touched her lips. And his mouth…she'd forgotten how passionate he could be, how he could ignite her entire body with a flick of his tongue and a squeeze.

Other men had kissed her since Kendall, but none had ever roused her like he had, and when they'd pressed for more, she'd always shied away. She hadn't wanted to confuse Tony by having strange men around, and it was hard not to feel like she was cheating on Kendall, considering she saw his face every time she looked at Tony. Besides, she'd had too many other things on her plate to be concerned about dating. Tony, school and work had consumed her the way that loving Kendall had once consumed her.

Tony. Her heart pinged. He'd called her last night, as promised, but had grunted his way through the conversation before abruptly saying goodbye and hanging up. She knew moodiness was part of adolescence, but it was difficult to tolerate. She felt as if her sweet boy was slipping through her fingers.

And it gave her renewed appreciation for the handful she'd been for her aunt Heddy.

Amy sat forward when she saw a work truck heading toward her. Kendall was driving. She assumed that, like her, he'd deemed it too cold this morning to ride an ATV to the site. Her heart began to pound, but she tried to act nonchalant when he pulled in beside her so their driver's-side doors were next to each other. He rolled down his window and she buzzed hers down.

"Good morning," he said, his tone friendly enough. He appeared well rested.

"Good morning," she offered, wondering if he could tell by the circles under her eyes that she hadn't slept at all.

"You didn't have to be here for this," he said. "It's a metal bridge in a box—my men and I can handle it."

She shrugged. "I figured since it was my idea, I should be here to help any way I can."

His mouth tightened, obviously still not sold on the merits of erecting a construction bridge. "Coffee?" he offered, holding up his thermos.

"If you have enough." She'd already drained the cup she'd brought with her.

"I do," he said so formally that it made her think of how solemnly he might say those words in a wedding ceremony if he ever found someone he wanted to commit to. Their gazes caught for a moment as if he, too, realized what he'd said. Then he handed a steaming cup across the space between them.

"Thanks," she murmured, shivering in the cold.

"No use in having the windows down. I'll park and join you." He didn't wait for her to respond, just pulled away a distance, then got out to walk back toward her SUV.

She glanced around, scrambling to rid the passenger seat of candy bar wrappers before he opened the door and climbed in.

"Nice ride," he said, looking around. "Four-wheel drive?"

Amy nodded. "It's kind of necessary in Michigan."

"Right."

She took a drink of coffee, then her gaze landed on a sunglasses case in the console monogrammed with "Tony." Kendall noticed it at the same time and a frown furrowed his brow.

To distract him, she lunged forward to look at the gray sky. "Looks like we might have some rain rolling in later."

He sipped his coffee and nodded. "The forecast for tomorrow is sleet and freezing rain."

"I noticed that. But a warm front is coming through afterward so hopefully we'll be able to make up for any lost time."

He nodded to two truckloads of workers pulling in. "I'll push to get as much out of the daylight today as we can." Kendall waved at the men, then checked his watch. "The driver is always punctual. He should be here any minute."

"I can't imagine it would be easy pulling a cumbersome load like bridge parts over these winding roads."

"Nothing in or about this town has ever been easy."

"That's an understatement," she said. "I noticed when I was driving around yesterday how grown up the side roads are. I realize the town limits are part of the federal experiment, but do you and your brothers own the outlying land?"

"No. It belongs to the original deed holders, as long as they maintain property taxes."

"Do you expect all those people to return?"

"We hope so. A few already have. But most are wary about rebuilding before we meet the deadline."

"The federal deadline?"

"Right. There are checkpoints we have to meet along the way, the most important of which is the two-year mark—that's when we'll know if we get more funding to keep going, or if the land in the city limits will be relinquished back to the government."

"What will you do if that happens?"

"It won't," he said with a confidence that would've been laughable coming out of someone else's mouth. "I know we have a lot of work left to do, but it'll all come together. It has to. People are counting on us."

Amy's heart squeezed. Kendall had always been a leader, a rock to so many people—the first person asked to spearhead any effort, and the first to respond in a crisis. He was good at bringing people together. Unfortunately, when the two of them were together, she'd always felt as if she took a backseat to his causes.

"I suggested we have a homecoming weekend event this summer," he said, confirming her reflections. "Invite anyone who ever lived in Sweetness to come home to celebrate...and hopefully stay."

"That sounds nice," she lied. In truth, it sounded claustrophobic.

"Meanwhile, we can use all the engineers around here we can get. The pay is lousy, but the food—" He stopped and scratched his head. "No, wait, the food is lousy, too."

She laughed. "You're going to have to work on your sales pitch."

"I'm practicing for our next checkpoint visit from a Department of Energy rep. He should be here any day now."

"What's the purpose of the meeting?"

"To make sure we're on track, and establish priorities for the next six months. It would help if I could bring him around to talk to you about the covered bridge."

"Okay, sure."

"And if you could play up the fact that you used to live here and what the bridge meant to you, that might score us some points."

"I'll see what I can do," she said drily.

He looked sheepish. "Sorry if I sound pushy, but sometimes these inspections are so subjective, every little bit helps." He frowned suddenly, then reached beneath his hip and pulled out a squashed chocolate bar.

Amy's cheeks went hot. "Sorry."

"No trouble," he said easily, then laid it on the

console next to the sunglass case. He nodded to the case. "Is Tony the same guy who gave you the ring you were wearing the other night?"

He'd remembered her comment that "her guy" had given her the topaz ring. Just hearing him say his son's name made her stomach flip. "That's right," she said carefully, thinking maybe she should just get it over with and tell him. She wet her lips. "Kendall—"

The roaring sound of a big truck engine sounded, and the cab of an eighteen-wheeler suddenly came into view.

"Right on time," Kendall said, opening the door. Then he stopped. "You were saying?"

"It can wait," she said, frustrated and relieved at the same time.

The next couple of hours she didn't have time to think about kisses and near-misses as the metal bridge parts were unloaded and assembly of the construction bridge immediately began. A worker drove a log truck down to park next to the eighteen-wheeler and Kendall used a tractor boom to transfer the enormous yellow poplar logs that would be used for cutting the covered bridge parts to the big rig's trailer. When all was secure, the driver took the materials list and climbed back into his truck for the return trip down the mountain.

Amy's heart pounded with excitement. The next time they saw the poplar, it would be sawed and planed into steadfast wooden bridge parts.

"There goes our bridge," she said to Kendall, and their gazes locked. She'd forgotten how blue his eyes got on cloudy days. Then she caught herself. "I don't mean 'our' bridge, I mean…the town's bridge."

He looked as if he wanted to say something, but was distracted by the appearance of another vehicle, a white extended-cab pickup with a Department of Energy insignia on the side.

"Looks like this is my guy," he murmured, then waved to flag down the driver.

The truck pulled in near Kendall and Amy and the window came down. A tanned man with dark blond hair stuck his head out. "Hello, I'm Dale Richardson, D.O.E. I'm looking for someone named Armstrong."

Amy squinted and stepped forward. "Dale? Dale, it's me—Amy Bradshaw."

Recognition dawned on his face. "Amy Bradshaw. Long time no see."

Dale had been one of those men who had tried unsuccessfully to interest her in more than kissing. "I'd heard you were working in D.C.," she said.

"I was for a while, but I transferred to the Atlanta office last year. What are you doing in this neck of the woods?"

"I'm here to build a covered bridge."

"You don't say? Is Tony with you?"

Amy's heart stuttered—she'd forgotten that Dale had met Tony briefly. "Uh…no." She turned to Kendall, who seemed to be paying close attention to the exchange. "Dale, meet Kendall Armstrong."

Kendall walked forward and Dale stuck out his hand. "I think you're the man I'm looking for. I have a few things on my list to check off."

Kendall shook the man's hand. "My brothers and I have been expecting you. I'm driving that black truck. Follow me up to the construction office and we'll get started."

Kendall turned to Amy. "I'll send Porter down to oversee the men."

"I've got it covered," she said. "I'll call Porter if I need anything."

He looked as if he didn't want to leave, but nodded. "Okay. See you later."

Amy made small talk with Dale until Kendall climbed into the truck, then said, "Dale, this might sound strange, but I'm actually from this town. No one here knows about Tony and I'd like to keep it that way."

He looked anguished. "I'm sorry for bringing up something personal."

"Don't worry about it. But please don't mention it again in front of anyone."

"No problem." He looked at the black truck, then back to her. "I remember what Tony looks like. That man is his father, isn't he?"

She pressed her lips together. "Please don't say anything."

"I would never betray a confidence," he said.

She believed him. "Thank you." Dale was a good guy, just…not Kendall. She realized in that moment how attached she was getting to Kendall. Again. Her heart crimped. It had been a disaster the first time around, and had even more potential of ending worse this time.

Dale grinned. "Hey. I forgot to tell you…I'm engaged."

She grinned back. "Good for you. When's the big day?"

He blanched. "Well, we haven't exactly gotten that far yet."

She laughed. "How long will you be here?"

"Just today. But maybe we can have dinner? I'm not sure what the restaurants are like around here, though."

Amy's mind raced. She was having dinner with Nikki and Porter, but Nikki had said she was making plenty. "Join me and my friend Nikki and her boyfriend, Porter, for dinner at the boardinghouse in the middle of town. Nikki is cooking. Porter is Kendall's brother—you'll probably meet him later."

"Sounds good. See you later." He waved, then pulled away to follow Kendall.

Amy waved, then exhaled loudly. That was close…again. What were the chances that she'd run into someone here who knew her and knew about Tony? Her friend Nikki didn't even know about Tony.

How was it that the world seemed smaller in Sweetness?

15

Kendall realized the Department of Energy representative had said something and was waiting for a response. "I'm sorry. Could you repeat that?" He was definitely off his game today.

Dale Richardson put down his pen. "Maybe we should take a break. We've been going at it for a while, and I realize I pulled you off a job."

It wasn't the job he was missing. He was frustrated at not being able to spend the day with Amy, possibly even revisiting that scorching kiss that had left him tossing and turning last night.

"No, it's fine," Kendall said. "The job is in good hands."

"Oh, yeah, Amy's the best."

Kendall angled his head. "Just curious—how do you know Amy?"

Suddenly, the man's expression shuttered. "Uh… we worked together…on a couple of state projects."

"In Michigan?"

"Er, yeah." Richardson picked up his pen. "We

really should get back to this if we're going to finish today."

"Right," Kendall said, recognizing the blow-off. The man didn't want to talk about Amy. He knew Tony, the man she was involved with, but maybe Dale and Amy had something going, too. Maybe that's why he'd asked if Tony was around, to see if the coast was clear.

Kendall gripped a pencil until it bit into his fingers. He'd assumed that she'd dated and—*gulp*—slept with other men. He just didn't want to meet them. The pencil snapped in two, startling Richardson.

"Sorry," Kendall said. "Maybe we should start the tour. We can talk while we walk."

"Sounds good." The man seemed relieved for a change of venue.

On the way out of the office, they ran into Porter. Kendall made the introductions.

"I'm having dinner tonight with you and your fiancée," Richardson said as they shook hands.

Porter paled. "Nikki and I aren't engaged...yet."

"But soon," Kendall said, clapping Porter's shoulder. "Because Porter is going to build a church next."

Porter shot daggers at him.

"Amy Bradshaw invited me to dinner," Richardson said. "I hope that's okay—Amy and I are old friends."

Kendall set his jaw.

"No, that's great," Porter said, then turned to Kendall. "Why don't you join us, bro? You know Nikki always makes plenty."

He opened his mouth to say yes, then remembered he'd promised Rachel they would have dinner tonight and he'd fix her bedroom wall. He toyed with the idea of both of them joining the foursome, but he was afraid of what Rachel might say in front of Amy to give her the wrong impression…again.

"Thanks, but I already have plans," he mumbled, now truly in a sour mood.

Porter clapped him on the back. "Too bad." Then out of the corner of his mouth, Porter hissed, "Smile, bro."

This time Kendall was the one shooting daggers. But he tried to rally during the foot tour, reminding himself that Richardson held their purse strings.

True to their adopted slogan that Sweetness was "The Greenest Place on Earth," they had incorporated energy savings and recycling into every aspect of living in Sweetness. He tried to make a production of showing off their efforts, but seemed to be foiled at every step.

While they were at the school, a prankster pulled the fire alarm, and bedlam ensued. At the windmill farm, the air was dead—nary a blade moved. The organic garden had gotten perhaps a little too natural—their experiments with compost fertilizers had created such a stench, both men had to stand with their sleeve over their nose and mouth.

At the mulching operation where rubber tires were

being shredded into mulch that wouldn't break down, the conveyor belt had broken so the impressive process couldn't be observed. At the clinic, Nikki and company were dealing with an influenza outbreak, and it was clear Richardson was a germaphobe by the way he recoiled every time someone sneezed. At the General Store, Kendall had to extinguish a small fire from an overly ambitious candle display. And at the Postal Counter, the postmistress's fourteen-year-old (obviously *not* a federal employee) was giving out mail. At the boardinghouse, the first occupant they encountered was the injured doe the women had domesticated and given run of the place.

Given the calamitous nature of the day, Kendall was more than a little reluctant to take the man up the mountain on four-wheelers to climb the big white tower that provided the town's water supply. After all, Porter had fallen off twice and broken bones both times. But Richardson seemed keen on making the climb, so Kendall went up with him, holding his breath the entire way. Thankfully, they made it to the platform that surrounded the tower intact.

"Now this is something you don't see every day," Richardson said, scanning the breathtaking view of the mountains that surrounded Sweetness and the gorge at the bottom.

"We like it," Kendall agreed, breathing in air so clean it burned his lungs. "See that tall evergreen next to the rock that's shaped like a horn? That's our cell tower."

"Clever." His guest gestured to a swath of land where the tree growth was uniformly shorter than the areas around it. "Is that damage from the tornado ten years ago?"

"Right," Kendall said, then pointed. "The funnel cloud formed at that end of the valley."

"And the mountains funneled the twister right into your town?"

Kendall nodded. "Because of this natural bowl, it had gained terrific force by the time it reached Sweetness. I wasn't living here at the time, but my younger brother, Porter, was home on leave from the Army, and the devastation…well—you've seen the pictures."

Richardson nodded. "Stunning. It's a miracle no one was killed."

"We think so, too," Kendall said, then tapped the handrail that surrounded the water tower. "This is where the twister was spotted and the alarm was sounded. Otherwise, who knows how many lives would've been lost."

"I didn't realize tornadoes struck at this altitude."

"They don't usually. We get lots of powerful thunderstorms, but that twister was a freak of nature."

"Let's hope lightning doesn't strike twice. I'd hate to see all your hard work get blown away."

"We're better prepared this time," Kendall said. "Stronger buildings, better communication systems. But yes, I hope we don't ever have to see how well we could withstand another monster like that. Ready to move on?"

"Sure." Richardson patted his stomach. "I'm looking forward to checking out your diner."

Kendall maintained his frozen smile. "Actually, it's more of a cafeteria than a diner," he said in an effort to lower the man's expectations. "There is no cost to residents since it's part of the free-room-and-board program."

"Sounds good," the man said.

But just as Kendall feared, it wasn't.

When they walked into the crowded dining hall, Molly and Rachel were engaged in a shouting match over the salmon croquettes that were being served for lunch. Kendall had to admit the greenish pucks didn't look appetizing. Ditto for the gray mashed potatoes.

"This food is inedible!" Rachel shouted. "And we're tired of eating crap in here!"

Behind the serving counter, Molly's face was a mottled red. "Then go eat crap somewhere else!"

"There isn't anywhere else to eat!"

"Precisely!"

"Ladies," Kendall soothed, moving forward. "We have a visitor."

He prided himself on being able to mediate just about any situation, but they completely ignored him.

Rachel picked up one of the salmon patties and pounded it on a stainless-steel counter for effect. "This isn't food, it's a weapon!"

Molly's face screwed up. "Let's just see about that!" She picked up a patty, wound up and threw it at Rachel, who thankfully had the agility to duck.

Richardson wasn't so lucky. It nailed him in the neck.

"Ow!"

"Jesus!" Kendall yelled. "Everyone, calm down!"

But it was too late. A bona fide food fight had erupted. Salmon croquettes landed like grenades, and mashed potatoes rained down like hail. Kendall braved the melee to snag a couple of protein bars from a side counter, then grabbed Richardson's arm and dragged him out of there, but not before they both were pelted.

Kendall shut the door behind them and gave the man a weak smile. "I guess it goes without saying that all of that food will go into our compost bins."

Richardson returned a flat smile, pulling mashed potatoes out of his hair.

Kendall handed him a handkerchief and a protein bar, then pulled out his phone. "Excuse me just a moment." He stepped away, then dialed Marcus's cell phone number.

"Hello," Marcus said.

"Wherever you are, get to the dining hall. All hell finally broke loose."

Marcus cursed. "Can't you handle it?"

Kendall lowered his voice. "I'm babysitting the D.O.E. guy, who, by the way, just got hammered with a piece of flying fish."

Marcus released a string of curses this time. "I've had it with those women! I—"

Kendall disconnected the call, then offered Dale Richardson a smile. "Have you heard about our Lost and Found warehouse?"

He pocketed his phone, then led the man in the direction of the large building, extolling the virtues of the program that matched former residents with found belongings.

But throughout the tour, he had a sinking feeling their checkpoint review was going to be negative, at best. Why, today of all days, did everyone and everything in town have to go to hell? He needed to leave the day on a high note, so after a leisurely tour of the warehouse, he described the pending arrival of the scientist who wanted to study the medicinal qualities of the prolific kudzu vine.

"Hence the need for a bridge to provide access to that section of land," he said. "Let's go talk to Amy about the covered bridge she's designing based on the original that was destroyed by the twister. She's even using some reclaimed materials."

But he could tell Richardson's attention was waning. The man glanced at this watch. "Amy and I can discuss the bridge at dinner. Which reminds me, I brought a change of clothes. Is there a place where I can shower before dinner?"

"There's a shower in the office," Kendall said, irritated that this man was going to get to spend the evening with her. "Help yourself, the door's unlocked."

"Thanks. Also, I was wondering if there's a place where I might pick up dessert." The man grinned. "I seem to remember that Amy has a thing for chocolate."

Kendall bit down on his cheek. "Sorry...can't help you there."

"Okay, thanks for the tour. I'm going to interview a few residents before I get cleaned up. I'd like to get a sense for how people feel about this place as a community. After all, this experiment is about more than reducing the carbon footprint, isn't it?"

"Right," Kendall said, managing a smile. Considering the black cloud that had settled over the town today, they were sunk.

"I hope to see you again before I take off." Richardson extended his hand. "If not, good luck, Armstrong, with...well, with everything."

Kendall had the oddest feeling the man was talking about something other than the checkpoint report. "Thanks."

As soon as the man climbed into his vehicle, Kendall headed back to the construction bridge site. The cloudy day had ushered in an early dusk. Workers were calling it a day. But he could tell from this vantage point that a lot of progress had been made on the metal bridge—more than he'd expected. He spotted Amy and his pulse picked up. No other woman could look so sexy in a hard hat.

He walked over and she looked up, then smiled and removed her hat. Her amazing red hair tumbled down in all its wildness. Her face was smudged with dirt and her shoulders drooped, but her eyes were bright. She loved her work…and he loved that about her. He loved the strong, capable woman she'd become. More than anything, he'd like to carry her off to a warm bubble bath to wash away the day's grime and climb in with her.

"How was your day?" he asked.

"From the look on your face," she said, "better than yours. How did it go with Dale?"

"Not great," he admitted. "So if you have the chance to say something positive about the town while you're having dinner, it might make a difference in his report."

Amy's hazel eyes darkened. She looked off into the distance, as if trying to conjure up some good memories of this place.

"I'm sorry to put you on the spot like this," he said, feeling like a heel. "I wouldn't ask if it wasn't important."

Amy looked back at him, then gave him a little smile. "I'll think of something." Then she carried her hard hat to her SUV, climbed inside and drove away.

16

Amy laughed into her dinner napkin at Dale's re-telling of the food fight scene. "I almost wish I'd been there."

"Be glad you weren't," Dale said, then pointed to the strawberry-size bruise on his neck. "I'm not sure my fiancée is going to buy the story that I got this from a piece of flying salmon."

They all laughed heartily, then Nikki fanned her face. "I hate to say it, but that food fight has been brewing for a long time."

"Oh?" Dale asked casually. "Is there a lot of dis-sension among the residents?"

A little red flag raised in Amy's mind. She glanced across the great room of the boardinghouse to where Kendall and Rachel were having dinner alone. On the corner of their table sat a white bakery box, probably another chocolate cake, she thought, her mouth watering. Remembering Kendall's ear-lier plea and her promise to help if she could, Amy squashed her feelings of jealousy and turned a smile in Dale's direction. "Sweetness is the most peaceful place on earth. That's what makes the food fight so funny."

"So you have good memories of growing up here?" Dale asked.

Amy managed to maintain the smile. "That's right. There's nothing like growing up in a small town." The sameness, the isolation…the sameness.

"So tell me about this covered bridge you're building. Is that what you were working on today?"

She shook her head. "That's the construction bridge that will give us access to the other side of the creek so we can build the covered bridge more quickly." She conjured up a picture of Evermore Bridge in her head. "The covered bridge will be just north of there, on the most picturesque part of Timber Creek, in my opinion. The old bridge was spectacular, the truss work alone was a work of genius. Did you know it was built from virgin timber in these mountains? Imagine, trees that have been growing for three hundred years, maybe more."

"Kendall mentioned you were able to incorporate some of the original wood in the new design?"

"Only because of the recovery efforts. Kendall recognized pieces of the bridge and stored them in the Lost and Found warehouse in the event they could be used again. He gets all the credit."

They were all staring at her. She realized how dreamy her tone had sounded. "Porter and Marcus, too," she added quickly.

"Not me," Porter said, shaking his head. "I always thought the covered bridge was a neat landmark—Marcus, too—but Kendall was the one completely fixated on it." He looked at Amy. "Not sure why."

She tingled. Porter had to know it was where she and Kendall had rendezvoused. "I'm sure it was the budding engineer in him," she offered. Then she smiled at Nikki and changed the subject. "Dinner was delicious. Thank you."

"You're welcome," Nikki said, all smiles.

"Nikki is from Broadway, too," Amy said to deflect attention from herself. "She seems to have acclimated well to small-town living." She winked at her friend.

"And are you the same Nikki referenced on the water tower?" Dale asked.

Nikki darted a glance at Porter, then grinned. "I am."

"Quite a statement," Dale said, tipping his wineglass to Porter.

Porter put his arm around Nikki and squeezed. "It seemed to work."

Amy watched the couple, so obviously enamored with each other, and gave in to pangs of envy. She sneaked another glance across the room to Kendall and Rachel. The curvy woman was setting plates of food on the table. Their mouths moved in what she assumed was easy banter, not the tense, barbed remarks that she and Kendall traded. No wonder he preferred the blonde's company.

She watched him smile at Rachel, then bring a loaded forkful of food to his mouth. He chewed, then stopped, the expression on his face changing from pleasant to confused to painful. His eyes widened and he swallowed, then reached for his water glass. Amy remembered telling Rachel that he liked his meals spicy and cringed.

Maybe she'd overdone it a little.

The water seemed to make matters worse. Kendall choked and sputtered, gasping for breath. Everyone turned to stare, and Nikki was instantly on alert.

"Is Kendall okay?" she asked Porter, then pushed to her feet and headed in his direction. Porter followed.

Amy took another drink of wine, hoping the moment would pass. But Kendall couldn't stop coughing. It was clear that whatever had caused the reaction was pretty potent. His face was red and he wheezed, clutching his throat. He leaned over at the waist, gripping the edge of the table as he coughed with enough force to cause the dishes to clatter.

Rachel was on her feet, beating him on the back. "I used super-hot peppers," she told Nikki, then sent a glare in Amy's direction.

Amy squirmed and emptied her wineglass.

"Let's get him to a sink," Nikki said. "Rachel, find some bread for him to eat. It'll soak up the capsaicin."

Porter helped Kendall to his feet and they walked him, still gasping for air, out of the room.

"This is an interesting little place," Dale said. "Lots of character."

Amy managed a smile. "Yes, indeed."

"Were you living here when the tornado struck?"

"No, I got out—" She checked her words. "I mean, I left Sweetness before the storm hit."

"I can see why," he said. "It's quaint, but I'd be bored to death here."

Unbidden, her defenses rose. This city boy had no right to judge a lifestyle he couldn't possibly understand. "Not everyone's cut out for this kind of life," she agreed. "It takes a strong, independent person to live off the beaten path."

Dale blinked. "I meant no offense."

"None taken," she said, regretting her response. "I apologize. It's been a long day."

He nodded. "I should be going. It'll be late when I get back to Atlanta." He stood and reached for his jacket on the back of the chair.

"It was great to see you again," Amy said, standing to give him a quick hug. "I appreciate whatever you can do for this—" she caught herself again "—for *my* hometown. The Armstrongs are trying to do something good here."

He nodded. "I can see that. Take care."

She smiled and waved as he left. Then she sighed and cleared their table of dishes, hoping to be gone by the time Kendall and Rachel returned. Just as she made her final trip to the kitchen, Nikki and Porter walked back in.

"He'll be fine," Nikki announced. "Maybe a little hoarse for a while."

"Amy probably remembers what a wimp Kendall has always been when it comes to spicy foods," Porter said.

Amy gave them a tight smile. "Dale had to leave, and I think I'll call it a night, too."

"Okay… Good night," Nikki said, tucking into Porter. The couple were obviously glad to have some time to themselves.

"Good night," Amy said.

On her way out of the room, she cast a covetous glance at the white bakery box still sitting on the table Kendall and Rachel had abandoned. She was completely out of her chocolate reserves, and she could really use some comfort food tonight. As she climbed the stairs, she reflected on what a mess she'd made of things. She seemed doomed to keep making the same mistakes.

How could she be falling for Kendall again?

Her aunt had always said Amy was a glutton for punishment, and she was starting to think Aunt Heddy was right. Because giving her heart to Kendall again would not only expose her to rejection again, but it would expose Tony to rejection, too. And she couldn't bear to see her son hurt like that.

When she got to her room, she picked up the phone and punched in his number, gratified when he answered on the second ring.

"Hi, Mom."

She smiled. "Hi, yourself. You sound like you're in a better mood."

"Whatever. How's the bridge coming along?"

"We're making headway," she said. "How are your classes?"

"Boring. I've already learned all this stuff."

"Then it'll be a good review," she said cheerfully.

He sighed. "There aren't any girls here."

Amy winced. It was too early for him to be thinking about girls...wasn't it? "I should hope there aren't any girls there. It's an all-boys school. Have you made any friends?"

"A couple," he said. "But I want to come home."

"Soon," she promised. "I'll plan a trip back to see you next weekend, okay? We'll do something fun."

"Okay," he said, sounding resigned.

"I love you."

"Love you, too."

She disconnected the call, feeling raw and helpless, the same way her own mother must have felt when she was sick all those years ago. Amy clasped the gold pendant at her neck and tapped into the new connection she felt with her mother. It transcended reason, but she did feel stronger when she touched the necklace her mother had worn next to her heart.

She undressed slowly and slipped into a soft gown and robe. Her body was tired, but her mind was churning, so she curled up on the couch, wondering how she and Tony were going to get through these next few weeks. And the weeks after that.

A knock on her door startled her. Amy pushed to her feet and padded to the door, then unlocked it. In deference to her nightclothes, she opened it only a crack.

Kendall stood on the other side. Her heart skipped a beat.

"Yes?" she said.

He gave her a sardonic look. "I understand I have you to thank for the extra spice in my dinner." His voice sounded raspy.

Her cheeks flamed. "I might have accidentally insinuated to Rachel that you liked spicy foods." She bit her lip. "You have every right to be angry."

"I'm not angry."

"You're not?"

"No. Because Porter reminded me what it means when someone is jealous."

She frowned. "I'm not jealous."

He smiled. "It's okay, I was jealous, too, watching you with Richardson all evening."

Pleasure infused her chest. "You were?"

He nodded. "Can I come in?"

She pressed her lips together, knowing how dangerous that could be.

"I brought a peace offering," he said, then held up the bakery box.

Defeated, Amy grinned, then opened the door. "Okay, but we're only having dessert."

Kendall walked in and she closed the door. He set

the box on her nightstand and reached for her, pulling her into his arms. Her senses leapt.

"Right," he murmured, lifting her chin. "Only dessert," he whispered on her lips before claiming her mouth.

17

Amy knew as soon as Kendall kissed her where this was leading. But she told herself that making love with this man was inevitable, and she was powerless to resist him anymore. So she gave in to the rush of emotions as he kissed her thoroughly and with such tenderness tears pooled in her eyes.

He wrapped his arms around her and slid his hands down her back, pressing her against his hard frame. She moaned into his mouth as her body came alive, fires erupting everywhere at once. His salty flavor, his musky scent, his calloused touch were all familiar. Kendall had been her first lover… She had learned how to make love while experiencing these same sensory details—her brain and body remembered, and responded with elation.

She splayed her hands over his shirt, searching for buttons. She fumbled with them and pulled his shirt from his jeans, eager to touch his bare skin. He helped her, then tossed the shirt.

Amy held him off and drank him in. "Let me look at you."

His wide shoulders were broader, thicker. His once-lean arms were dense with heavily packed muscle. His chest was peppered with dark hair that swirled over the flat planes of his stomach and disappeared into the waistband of his low-slung jeans. The beautiful, sexy boy had morphed into a gorgeous, sexy man.

"All of you," she said.

He held her gaze while he kicked off his boots, then undid his belt and pulled it from the loops, dropping it on top of his boots. Then he unbuttoned and unzipped his dark jeans and pushed them down, peeling off his socks and adding them to the pile. Kendall was still a boxer man. His erection tented the loose white cotton. She wet her lips in anticipation as he pushed them down and stepped out of them, then stood before her nude.

Amy's lips parted. He was so handsome and so sexy, it sent a shudder through her body.

"Now you," he said, his voice husky.

With her heart pounding, she loosened the tie of her robe, then shrugged out of it and draped it over a chair. The pale gown underneath was long but thin, and left little to the imagination. Her dark nipples were budded, straining at the fabric. She lifted the hem of the garment, then pulled it over her head and let it fall on her robe. She stood in tiny pink panties, her chest rising and falling quickly. When she lifted her gaze to his, she found his eyes hooded, his mouth slightly parted. She tried to imagine how her body had changed—more curves from maturity, not to mention giving birth, but more definition, too, from the demands of her job.

"You're beautiful," he breathed, then walked over and stepped behind her.

When she glanced up, she could see them in the mirror over the dresser. He lifted her curly hair and kissed her shoulder, then her neck. Then he wrapped his arms around her and cupped her breasts, his tanned skin against her paleness. He looked up and caught her gaze in the mirror and she knew she would always remember that erotic image of them together.

"What's this?" he asked, fingering the diamond pendant around her neck, squinting at the image. "A mother and child?"

Her pulse skipped higher. "I didn't tell you... Molly gave it to me. It belonged to my mother."

"It's nice. I'm glad you have something special to remind you of family." He smiled against her skin. "For a second there, I thought you might be keeping something from me."

Her throat convulsed. *Tell him...later.*

She closed her eyes so she didn't have to see herself in the mirror. The scrape of his rough-tipped fingers against her nipples sent pleasure reverberating through her body. She moaned and reached behind her to clasp his sex.

He groaned in her ear and she felt the surge of his muscles reacting to her touch. He slid his hands lower, inside her panties, and stroked the curls between her thighs. Her body gushed with pure physical pleasure. She arched her back and touched him lightly, rubbing his erection against her buttocks. He sucked in a breath, then slipped a finger inside her secret folds.

Amy moaned and her knees buckled. He turned her in his arms, then picked her up and walked the few steps to the bed she'd turned down. He kissed her desperately, nuzzling her breasts and laving her nipples until they were stiff and puckered. Then he pressed her into the sheets and rolled down her panties, plying her body with his wonderful hands. She moved against his fingers and an orgasm immediately began to swirl in her womb. She moaned and parted her knees.

He flicked his tongue against her ear. "Come on, baby, that's it, come on…"

The pressure was building. It felt so good she didn't want it to end. He'd always known just how to touch her, how to make her fall apart in his arms. She tensed, willing the climax to slow, but it had taken on a life of its own and flew to the surface before she was ready, exploding like a flood of warm honey.

Her body shook with waves of spasms. She dug her nails into his shoulder and cried his name over and over.

"That's good, baby," he whispered. "So good, isn't it?"

He held her until she stilled, then ran his hands up and down her tingling body.

"God, you're so sexy." He kissed her hard and deep, his body sliding against hers, his erection insistent against her thigh. "I have to have you, baby." Then he stopped and wiped his hand over his mouth. "Sorry, let me get protection."

They'd always been careful...had always used a condom—except that one time. Amy swallowed and closed her eyes. If she was going to stop him from going through with this, now was the time.

But she didn't want to stop. It had been twelve long years since she'd been touched like this. God help her, she wanted to be held and made to feel like a woman. Not a mommy, not an employee, not a boss, but a *woman*.

And Kendall was the only man who'd ever tapped into that secret part of her.

He returned to the bed and handed her the condom, let her roll it on his straining shaft, gritting his teeth throughout. He lowered his big body on top of hers, then he cupped her face. He was so handsome, his eyes so intense, he left her breathless.

"I've missed you, baby," he said, and thrust into her while staring into her eyes.

Their moans comingled. Amy's shoulders rolled with the exquisite sensation of being filled. She slid her hands down his muscled back and pulled his body deeper into hers. She never wanted this to end…

Kendall never wanted this to end…

He stared down into Amy's face, enchanted by her natural beauty, further heightened by her flushed cheeks and slitted eyes. She was so sexy, he almost couldn't bear it and he was going to embarrass himself if he didn't slow down. He wanted their first time back together to be special for Amy. But it was so hard to hold back when this was all he'd ever fantasized about. He was home…

"Come on, baby," she whispered, urging him on by raising her hips to meet his slow, deep thrusts. "I'm going to come with you." Then she gasped in his ear and her body tensed with another climax. "Oh, baby…"

Her voice in his ear sent him over the edge. His body contracted like a spring, then he came with a long groan, thrusting into her deeper…and deeper… and deeper…until he felt lost in her.

As his body recovered, a memory chord strummed. He'd felt like this before. It was why he'd run from her, this desperate feeling of not being able to do without her. And Amy had been too wild to tame…

What about now? Could he convince her to stay in Sweetness this time around? And what about this guy in her life, Tony?

They lay there for a few minutes, bodies pulsing

and cooling. Finally he lifted his head to find her staring at him, her hazel eyes full of questions. Was she thinking some of the same things?

He kissed the tip of her nose. "I'll be right back."

He rolled out of bed and went to the bathroom to clean up, disposing of the condom and washing his hands. When he realized he was whistling under his breath, Kendall acknowledged that for the first time in a long time, he was happy. And it felt good.

Then he heard a movement in the bedroom and was instantly worried, half afraid that when he came out, she would be dressed. Or gone.

When he peeked out, he exhaled. Amy was still lying in bed and had merely crawled under the sheets. But the moment left him shaken. He didn't like the feeling that the day would come when she would be gone again.

Pushing aside those troubling thoughts for now, he walked to the bed and lay down next to her, then pulled her over on his chest, reveling in having her soft curves against him. "That was so good," he murmured against her hair.

"Mmm, yes, it was. How long can you stay?"

He shrugged. "How long do you want me to stay?"

"I thought men had to be out of here by a certain hour."

"I won't tell anyone if you don't."

She leaned up on her elbow. "Are you taking liberties because you're the boss?"

He was distracted by a rosy nipple within kissing

distance. He couldn't believe she was this close… and this naked. "Maybe I am. Do you realize we've never had the luxury of relaxing like this in an actual bed?"

She pursed her mouth and nodded. "You're right. We were always sneaking around, trying not to get caught."

"Making out in some pretty uncomfortable places, as I recall, most of them outdoors. I remember getting stung by a wasp on my backside."

"That was nothing compared to my poison ivy."

He grinned. "I remember that. I got to rub that pink lotion all over your good parts."

She punched him. "That wasn't fun for me."

"So let's enjoy this nice, soft mattress. I'm not leaving until you kick me out. And if you kick me out, I'm taking the chocolate cake with me."

She laughed. "Speaking of the cake, did you happen to bring forks?"

He reached for the box on the nightstand. "Who needs forks?"

They broke off the chocolate cake and ate it with their hands, feeding it to each other, licking icing from their fingers. But when crumbs went astray, Kendall began nibbling on Amy, and before long, the rich cake had been set aside in favor of more decadent fare.

When Amy jarred awake, she was disoriented, unaccustomed to having a big, warm body in the bed with her. When it all came flooding back, she closed her eyes against the onslaught of emotions. Lying here with Kendall's breath in her ear, she could fantasize that things had turned out differently…

That Kendall had proposed after her aunt's funeral, then she'd told him about the baby, and they'd happily planned a life together. In her fantasy, Tony was lying in his bedroom down the hall, and Kendall was the coach of his soccer team. They lived in a midsize house in a midsize town where engineering jobs were plentiful and Kendall wasn't taking on the Herculean effort of resurrecting a town.

A town she hated.

Academically, she knew Sweetness wasn't the same town she'd grown up in. But in some ways, it was worse—smaller and even more confining, isolated and all-consuming. And under the domain of the Armstrong brothers. She hadn't escaped and sacrificed to get an education and raise her son alone only to come back to exist in Kendall's world, on his terms.

Her digital alarm clock read 5:15 a.m. and driving rain sounded on the metal roof of the boardinghouse. The pings against the window told her it was freezing rain. Amy managed to slip out of bed without disturbing Kendall, and shrugged into her robe. She went to the window and looked down on the empty, wet street illuminated by a sole dusk-to-dawn light and smaller lights in front of the General Store, the school and the clinic. It was a bleak picture. She couldn't see what Kendall could see. She didn't share his vision.

His touch on her shoulder startled her. "Hey," he whispered, then wrapped his arms around her from behind. "Everything okay?"

His touch alone sent her body reeling. "I have something to tell you."

His hands slipped inside her robe. "What's on your mind?"

Amy leaned her head back and undulated into his hand. "You should know that I'm still planning to leave after the bridge is complete."

He nibbled on her earlobe. "And you should know that I'm going to try to change your mind."

She moaned, putty in his hands.

"Come back to bed," he murmured. "I say we hide out in your room until it stops raining."

"But that could be for days."

"I'm counting on it," he said, tugging on her hand.

Amy followed him. She couldn't resist pretending for a little while longer...

18

Amy slipped out of her room and checked her cell phone. Tony had left a voice message last night. Guilt stabbed her. What if she'd missed something important? She listened to it, a few words of sullen resignation and preteen angst—he was bored, he wanted to come home—but nothing new. She sighed in relief, then punched in his number, hoping to catch him between classes, but his voice message kicked on.

"This is Tony. At the beep, well, you know what to do."

The beep sounded and she gripped the phone tighter, struggling for words. There seemed to be more that she *couldn't* say. "Hi, sweetheart, it's me. I…"

Woke up with your father this morning. Again.

"I'm just thinking of you and wanted to check in."

The more we talk about what he's been doing all these years, the more I realize how like him you are.

"I hope you're having a good time with your new friends."

I'm going to tell him about you soon. We just need this alone time together to make up for all that we've missed.

"Call me later if you get a chance."

I think I'm falling in love with your father again…

"I love you, sweetie."

She disconnected the call, then walked down the hall and descended the stairs, feeling conspicuous. Did anyone know Kendall was in her room? Had they made too much noise or had people missed her?

Still, she had to come out sooner or later. And since they'd exhausted the chocolate cake, she'd emerged in search of sustenance.

She walked past the great room where a group watched a movie in deference to the blustery, rainy day. Relieved to find the kitchen empty, she quickly made two peanut butter and jelly sandwiches, snagged two bananas from a fruit basket on the counter, and tried to make a hasty exit. But she wasn't quite quick enough.

"Amy!" Nikki said, walking in to put an empty glass in the dishwasher. "Hi. I haven't seen you around for a couple of days."

Amy's cheeks warmed. "I…I've been a little under the weather."

Nikki made a rueful noise. "You should've come to see me. Maybe I could help."

"It wasn't that bad," she backpedaled. "Just a bug. But I've been staying in my room because I didn't want to risk making anyone else sick."

Nikki nodded. "Good idea, because something is definitely going around. Porter said Kendall has been laid up somewhere sick, too."

Amy swallowed nervously. "Really? Gee, with both of us sick, I guess it's a good thing it's raining. We couldn't have gotten any work done anyway."

"That's what I told Porter," Nikki said breezily. "But I hear it's supposed to clear up tomorrow."

"Good. I expect to feel better tomorrow."

"Porter said that Kendall expects to feel better tomorrow, too."

"That's great," Amy said, nodding.

Nikki pointed to Amy's food stash. "Two of everything. Glad to see you're getting your appetite back."

Amy lifted her shoulders in a slow shrug. "Now that I'm recovering, I can't seem to get enough to eat."

"As your personal physician, I hope you'll let me know if there's something you might need but aren't able to get out to buy for yourself."

"Such as?"

Nikki shrugged. "Such as *protection* from this bug that's going around."

Amy pursed her mouth. They *were* down to only one condom. "Now that you mention it, I could use some of that protection."

"How many, um…doses?"

"Say…eight?"

Nikki's eyes widened. "Eight doses? Really?"

"Better make it ten, just to be sure."

"No problem. I'll hang a care package on your room door in a little while."

"Thank you," Amy said, "for being such a good doctor…and a friend."

Nikki smiled. "Don't mention it."

Amy hurried back to her room, feeling flush and naughty. But she had to admit it had been a glorious couple of days. Swathed in their cozy cocoon, they had gorged on chocolate and each other in ways that surpassed her fantasies. He was living up to his promise to try to change her mind about staying in Sweetness…staying with him. In the circle of his arms, listening to his heartbeat, she could almost be lured into thinking that a life together might be possible. It wasn't reality, she knew, but it felt so good, she couldn't stop. Not yet.

She put her hand on the doorknob and closed her eyes, her heart already beating in anticipation of seeing Kendall again, of having his big nude body in her bed and at her disposal.

If only it would keep raining…

Amy turned the knob and slipped inside.

19

Kendall opened the door to Amy's room a crack and looked out. Seeing the coast was clear, he stepped out into the hall and, with one regretful glance back to her sleeping form, he closed the door.

He crept down the hall as quietly as he could in the predawn hour, hoping he didn't run into anyone along the way. His body ached pleasantly from two—or was it three?—days in bed with Amy, but he'd never felt better. For the first time in a long time, he felt as if he had something to look forward it. He'd promised his brothers he would help rebuild Sweetness, yes. But now it meant more to him because he wanted to make it home for Amy again, to give her the kind of loving environment she hadn't had here before.

So that she would stay.

He eased down the stairs and paused at the bottom. From the kitchen came the sound of voices and activity, hushed in deference to the early hour. He gauged the distance to the front door. He'd have to walk past the door to the kitchen and through the front great room, which was mostly used as a sitting room.

He turned in the direction of the back door, but that route would take him through the rear great room that was equipped with TVs and computers and, therefore, more likely to be occupied.

Then he remembered the side door that would spill him onto a footpath leading to the main street. It was a more circuitous route, but he was less likely to run into anyone.

Resolved, he took a step, but at the sound of a growl, he froze. In his path a few feet away stood Rachel's dark-faced pug, Nigel. And he didn't look happy.

"Easy, boy," Kendall soothed.

The dog began barking, a sharp, yapping noise in the same decibel range as a siren.

"Shh!" Kendall hissed, now panicky. "Shh!

"What's all the commotion?"

Kendall looked up to see Rachel Hutchins standing there in pajamas and robe, holding a spatula.

"Kendall? What are you doing here?" She snapped her fingers at the dog, and it quieted.

"I…uh…" He squirmed, wondering when she'd realize he was wearing the same clothes he'd been wearing the night he'd nearly burst into flames after eating her "Special Asian Chicken."

Suddenly Nikki appeared behind Rachel. "Kendall, are you finished already?" She glanced at

Rachel. "Kendall offered to come over this morning and take a look at the leak in the hallway from all the rain we've had." She looked back to Kendall, her expression pointed. "So, is it fixable?"

He nodded. "Yes, it's...fixable. I'll be back later with...tools."

Rachel smiled. "I'll walk you out."

He stifled a groan, but he'd put up with anything to get to the door. He gave Nikki a grateful nod, then strode down the hall.

Rachel trotted to keep up with him, and Nigel trotted to keep up with her. "I hope you're not angry about the other night," she said. "I'm really sorry."

Kendall stopped at the door, then turned. She was a very pretty girl—smart, too. But she wasn't Amy. "I'm not angry at all. It wasn't your fault. You've been nothing but nice to me."

Rachel bit her lip. "But?"

"But...I'm not your type, Rachel."

She angled her head. "You mean *I'm* not *your* type?"

"That, too," he agreed.

"It's that Amy woman, isn't it?"

"Actually, it's always been Amy."

She nodded. "I heard that she's from here originally. You all were sweethearts before?"

"Yes."

"Well, that takes the sting out of it a little."

"I'm sorry. Any guy would be lucky to have you."

She gave him a little smile. "So I've been told."

Then she sighed. "Does this mean you're not going to fix the hole in my wall?"

"No. The hole will be fixed, I promise."

She nodded, but looked as if she didn't believe him.

"Rachel, I am really sorry about everything."

She leaned over to scoop up her dog. "It's okay, I have Nigel." She gave her pooch a smooch, then walked back down the hallway.

He wondered with a pang how many men in her life had let her down, and hated that he was one of them.

He eased the door closed behind him and paused on the front porch to breathe in cool, rain-cleansed air. The sun was coming up and the sky was clear. It was going to be a nice winter day.

But the rain had left pools of ugly red mud in its wake, and he knew the site of the construction bridge would be a mess. Considering how much work Amy and the crew had accomplished the day the metal parts had been delivered, though, they were still on schedule.

In response to his howling stomach, he crossed the road to the dining hall. Remembering the war zone it had been the last time he'd walked in, he gingerly opened the door. But all was calm and Molly seemed happily situated behind the serving line, ladling out lumpy oatmeal, as usual. The hall was crowded with workers, eating early before their shifts began. He walked toward the food line, so famished that for once he was looking forward to rubbery eggs and undercooked bacon.

Suddenly, Dr. Jay Cross stepped into his path. "May I have a word, Mr. Armstrong?"

Kendall came up short to keep from plowing into the small, suited man. "Sure, Doc. What's up?"

"My ire," the man said in his precise, clipped accent.

Kendall squinted. "Come again?"

The doctor stabbed at his dark glasses. "I find myself in the unfortunate position of having to stake a claim on…my woman."

Kendall scratched his temple. "Your woman?"

"As if you don't know of whom I speak—Rachel Hutchins, of course."

He almost laughed at the absurdity of Amazonian, flamboyant Rachel and this petite prim little man, but caught himself when he realized the doctor was serious. "I guess I didn't realize you and Rachel were an item, Doc."

"We're not," he chirped. "But we will be…once I've eliminated you as a competitor."

Kendall lifted his hands. "Whoa, I'm not a competitor."

"Okay," the doctor said, putting his fists in the air and adopting a fighting stance. "Fisticuffs, it is!"

The noise around them quieted, and men scrambled to pull back tables, eager for a show.

Dr. Cross started bouncing from foot to foot, as

if he were in the boxing ring. He was nervous, his face red, his tie askew.

Incredulous, Kendall stared at the man he could easily bench-press. "I'm not going to fight you—"

The man's fist darted out, lightning quick, and jabbed Kendall in the nose.

"Ooh," chorused the crowd.

Kendall frowned. The "punch" felt more like a mosquito bite, but now he was irritated.

Still bouncing, Cross stabbed at his glasses. "Put up your dukes and fight like a man!"

Kendall assessed the situation. He didn't want to hurt the young doctor or break his glasses, both of which he was likely to do if he punched him. But he understood the guy needed to save face. So he "put up his dukes" and let the man dance around him, jabbing and punching at will.

He pretended to fend off the blows as the men around them cheered and provided various sound effects. Then after a few minutes, he raised his hands. "Okay, I give up."

The doctor stopped bouncing and pushed up his glasses. He was sweating profusely. "You do?"

"Yes," Kendall said. "I will step aside so you can pursue Rachel."

The man smiled, then jammed his hands on his hips, pleased with himself. "Very good," he said with a curt nod. "Brilliant decision." Then he extended his hand, and lowered his voice. "No hard feelings, Mr. Armstrong?"

"None at all," Kendall murmured. "Treat her right."

"I will, sir," the little man said, his expression serious—and happy. He ran to the door, no doubt in a hurry to let Rachel know they could now be together. Kendall puffed out his cheeks in an exhale.

He hoped the woman didn't clobber him.

As Dr. Cross was going out, Porter and Marcus were coming in. They looked at Kendall and the pushed-back tables.

"Did we miss something?"

"No," Kendall said with a dismissive wave. "Let's eat."

Porter grinned and clapped him on the back. "Glad to see you've recovered from whatever was ailing you, bro. That must have been some bug. You look like you've been ridden hard and put up wet."

Kendall shrugged, unable to completely stop the smile that crept onto his face.

"Look at that," Porter said. "Is that a smile? Our brother is smiling again, Marcus."

Marcus grunted. "I just hope you're ready to get back to work."

"I am," Kendall said.

"Amy, too?" Marcus asked with an arched eyebrow. "I heard she was down with the same thing that had you on your back."

Kendall wiped his hand across his mouth. "I think she's ready to return to work today, too."

"Good thing," Porter said, "because the fabricator

is delivering the wood this afternoon for the Evermore Bridge."

Kendall blinked. "That's earlier than we thought." Damn—of course the materials for the one project he'd like to delay would arrive ahead of schedule.

"Will you let Amy know?" Marcus asked. "That is, if you think you'll be seeing her."

Kendall smirked. "I'll let her know."

"Need an extra pair of hands today on the construction bridge?" Marcus asked.

"Sure," Kendall said, always happy to work side by side with one of his brothers. They were usually off in different directions. "Have you heard back from the D.O.E. guy yet?"

"Not yet," Marcus said. "I hope his report isn't as bad as you think it's going to be."

"So do I," Kendall said. He now had more reason than ever to want Sweetness to be a success. "So do I."

20

Amy scanned the covered bridge work site where crews were drilling into the muddy creek bed, hoping to hit rock sooner rather than later. All seemed well, so she punched in Tony's cell number, but frowned when it once again rolled over to voice mail.

"Hi, sweetie, it's mom again, just hoping to catch you. Call me when you get this message." She ended the call, telling herself not to be overprotective. Surrounded by other boys his age, he probably didn't want to be seen as the kid who had to check in with his mother all the time.

She discouraged texting as a primary source of communication between them, but decided in this case, she would send one as a secondary measure. Call me soon. Love, Mom. She didn't hear back right away, but reasoned he could be in class. Or he might've done something to have his phone rights restricted.

She admired her son's independence and the fact that he'd always been mature for his age. She'd given him enough leeway to make his own mistakes and that hadn't always turned out, but it was the only way to ensure he would be equipped to deal with the world when he left her nest.

She put away her phone, squashing the niggling worry in the back of her mind. She was probably feeling anxious over Tony simply because she'd spent so much time thinking about how she was going to tell Kendall he had a son.

So many times over the past couple of days while they were lying intertwined she'd started to tell him—until she played through the worst-case scenario in her head: instead of being elated, he'd be angry that she'd kept it from him for so long. And he'd be angrier still that Tony was in military school for being in trouble. He might see it as his duty to try to handle things, perhaps storm the school and demand to see his son. It was the last thing Tony needed right now.

So she'd decided to stick with her original plan—to finish building Evermore Bridge, tell Kendall about Tony before she left Sweetness, and invite him to visit her and Tony in Broadway when Tony got out of school for the quarter and returned home.

Home.

She'd thought about that word a lot lately. Kendall tossed around the word *home* as if it meant the same thing to everyone—going home, staying home, having a homecoming weekend. He had a singular view of "home" because his home always had been and always would be in Sweetness, Georgia. She could feel herself falling in love with him again—her body ached in all the right places from his vigorous attempts to "convince" her to stay. But the fact that he'd dedicated his life to rebuilding a concept that she didn't understand showed just how far apart they still were.

A foreman waved to get her attention. Amy pushed aside the personal thoughts and emotions pinging around in her chest to focus on the task at hand. The parts for the covered bridge would be delivered this afternoon. Although the unpacking and staging of materials alone would probably take days, there was much to do to prep the site before assembly could begin. Everything they could get done before the materials arrived would put them that much further ahead.

And she couldn't afford to get behind—she needed to be back in Broadway by the time Tony got out of school.

For the next several hours, she moved around the site where holes for new piers were being drilled, and the rock abutments were being reinforced. Timber Creek was running angry and red from the recent rains and from the soil displaced by the drilling. Simply getting the heavy equipment down into the creek was a precarious job because the banks were craggy and steep. Safety was a top priority, and Amy was careful to check every detail before giving the go-ahead on any part of the job, no matter how small. Having stringent safety measures in place for seemingly unimportant aspects of the job would help ensure everyone's welfare when the blasting and heavy work began.

Amy was talking to a foreman about the site plan when her cell phone vibrated in her coat pocket. She pulled it out and her pulse rocketed to see the name of Tony's school on the caller ID. She excused herself and stepped away to connect the call.

"Hello?"

"Is this Ms. Amy Bradshaw?" a man asked.

"Yes. Who's speaking?"

He identified himself as the dean of students at the school.

"What can I do for you?" she asked, tamping down concern.

"Is your son, Tony, with you?"

Her heart began to pound. "No. He's supposed to be with *you*. What's this about? Is my son okay?"

"Ms. Bradshaw, I'm sorry to inform you that your son, Tony, is missing."

Kendall crouched to inspect a weld on a stiffening girder, then gave it a pat and stood to move to the next one.

Marcus walked over carrying two cups of steaming coffee and handed one to him. "How does it look?"

"Good," Kendall said. "At this rate, the bridge

should be ready for traffic within a couple of days." He took a sip of the coffee. "Thank you, Marcus."

"It's just a cup of coffee," Marcus said, drinking from his. He winced. "And not very good at that."

"I mean thank you for convincing Amy to come here."

Marcus averted his gaze, always uncomfortable with personal conversations. "No thanks necessary. It seemed like a good fit." He took another drink of coffee. "How are things between you two? Other than the obvious, of course."

Kendall smiled. "Honestly, I don't know. But I still love her."

"God, I certainly hope so after the way you've moped around here waiting for her to show up."

Kendall laughed. "I wanted it to be her idea. Or at least, not mine, I guess. I wanted her to come home on her own volition."

"And is she going to stay after the covered bridge is built?"

"She says she isn't, but I'm hoping to change her mind."

Marcus grimaced and tossed the rest of his coffee on the ground. "Has she said anything else?"

Kendall frowned. "What do you mean?"

The horn of a big truck sounded. Kendall waved to the driver, the same one who'd delivered the metal bridge parts, and walked over to the edge of the road. The driver stuck his head out the window. "Where do you want this load?"

"Just up ahead," Kendall said. "Give me a minute, I'll ride with you."

"Already got a passenger," the driver said, jerking his thumb to someone unseen in the passenger seat. "Picked up a hitchhiker on Route 7 on his way here. Boy says he's looking for his mother. Do you know an Amy Bradshaw?"

Amy's knees buckled at the dean of student's calm pronouncement. "Missing? How can Tony be missing?"

"Apparently, he left campus without permission, and we can't seem to locate him."

She gulped air, trying to stay calm. He'd said he was bored, he was probably with friends, maybe at a movie or an arcade. "When did he leave?"

"Er…yesterday, ma'am."

Her stomach dropped. "Yesterday?" she shouted. "My son has been missing since yesterday and I'm just now hearing about it?"

"We only discovered he was missing a couple of hours ago, ma'am, but the last time anyone saw him was yesterday morning. We do believe he left voluntarily, and that no one else is involved. We've already called the police. I have the name and number of a detective for you to contact."

She felt light-headed. She needed Kendall.

The foreman walked over to her. "Are you okay, ma'am?"

She lowered the phone and grabbed on to the

man's coat sleeve. "No, I'm not okay. Will you get Mr. Armstrong for me, please?"

"Which Mr. Armstrong, ma'am?"

"Kendall," she said, her voice breaking.

He pulled out his own phone then stopped and pointed toward the road. "I think that's Kendall now."

She looked up to see Kendall's black pickup pulling onto the site. He parked the truck and climbed out. She started toward him on wobbly knees.

And then she saw someone get out of the passenger side.

Amy couldn't believe her eyes. *Tony?*

21

Amy's emotions swung from sheer terror to sheer joy to see her twelve-year-old son alive. "Tony!" she shouted, and began running to him.

He started running toward her, too, and they met in the middle. She threw her arms around him and hugged him tight, raining kisses on his temples. "Are you okay?"

"I'm okay," he said, but his voice cracked.

She pulled back and gave him a once-over. He was wearing his school uniform of jacket and khaki pants, both rumpled. Instead of a collared shirt, he wore a gray hoodie underneath the jacket. He was as tall as she, with boxy shoulders and long, lean limbs, ending in big hands and feet. His features were handsome and all boy. His light brown hair had been cropped per the school's rules, but was uncombed. His eyebrows were a few shades darker, to go with the black lashes that set off his blue, blue eyes.

Armstrong eyes.

Now that she was satisfied he wasn't harmed, the

full force of the moment hit her—the moment she'd dreamed about and dreaded all of Tony's life. She lifted her gaze to Kendall, who stood leaning against his truck, giving them privacy. But his face was a stony mask. Even a stranger could see the boy was a carbon copy of Kendall. Of course he'd known he was Tony's father the moment he'd set eyes on him.

She turned her attention back to Tony. "Do you know how much trouble you're in, mister?"

"A fair amount, I figure."

He had a flair for understatement. "What happened?"

He shrugged.

"I asked you a question."

His mouth twitched down. "I missed you."

She gave a little laugh. "Oh, no. You don't get to use that as an excuse to run away from school and scare the life out of me."

He reconsidered. "I got bored. *And* I missed you."

"How did you get here?"

He looked panicked.

"Tony?"

He swallowed, then lifted his chin. "I…hitchhiked."

Amy closed her eyes and counted to ten…twice. A thousand bloody headline scenarios raced through her head.

"I was really careful," he said, his voice belligerent.

She opened her eyes. "You're grounded for the rest of your life."

He looked miserable. "Aren't you glad to see me?"

She exhaled loudly, then pulled him close for another hug. "I'm glad you're safe." She pulled back. "And yes, I'm glad to see you. But we're not finished talking about this yet. I need to call your school, and you, my dear boy, need a bath." She crinkled her nose.

"Mom, I take showers now."

"Pardon me," she said. "You need a shower. Maybe two."

"Who's that man?" Tony asked, nodding to Kendall.

She chose her words carefully. She'd learned long ago to answer only the question her child asked and not to elaborate. "His name is Kendall Armstrong."

"Am I related to him?"

Her breath caught in her chest. "Why do you ask?"

"Because I look like him some, don't you think?"

Amy nodded, trying to keep her emotions in check. Her son needed facts, not feelings. She tried to keep her voice level. "You look like him some because he's your father."

A light flickered in his eyes before his mouth hardened. "Does he know he's my father?"

"Not until a few minutes ago. He never knew I was pregnant."

"How could he not know he got you pregnant?" he asked with a sneer.

She gave him a reproving look. "Watch your tone. I know you must have a lot of questions, and I will answer all of them as honestly as I can—after we get you settled in."

"Okay," he mumbled.

She looked back to Kendall, who was still planted like a tree. "Are you ready for me to introduce you to your father, or do you want to wait?"

He shrugged. "Now is good, I guess."

"All right, then, let's go. Mind your manners."

"I *know,* Mom."

It was his way of telling her not to hover, so she fought her instinct to touch or hug him as they walked toward Kendall.

Kendall straightened, his hands by his sides, as if he didn't know what to expect. Her legs were quaking, so she knew her son must be nervous. But he held himself tall and his eye contact didn't waver as they approached. Kendall was staring at Tony, his expression as close to fear as she'd ever seen. The impact of the moment wasn't lost on her. When they stopped in front of him, Kendall didn't look at her, thank goodness, but she still had to make an effort to keep her voice from shaking.

"Kendall Armstrong, this is Anthony Alton Bradshaw...your son."

"Tony," her son said, extending his hand.

Her heart swelled with pride.

Kendall shook the boy's hand slowly. "Tony. It's

nice to meet you." Her ears heard the unspoken word *finally* hanging in the air.

Tony took back his hand. "So what am I supposed to call you?" His tone was challenging, his jaw set.

Amy bit her lip to stay out of the first father-son exchange.

Kendall's expression was cautious. "What do you want to call me?"

Tony's mouth worked back and forth. "I'll think about it."

Kendall nodded. "Fair enough. Your middle name—Alton. My dad's name was Alton."

"Is he dead?"

"Unfortunately, yes. But my mother is alive and I know she'd love to meet you. And I have two brothers—Marcus, you met at the other jobsite, and Porter, you'll meet him, too."

She could tell by the expression on her son's face that he was starting to feel overwhelmed. He'd never been around family before.

"All in good time," she said. "I'm going to take Tony to get washed up." She looked at Kendall. "I assume it's okay to put him in a room at the boardinghouse?"

"He could stay at the bunkhouse with the men," Kendall offered.

She bit down on her cheek.

"Could I?" Tony asked her. "That sounds fun."

"We'll see," she said. "Remember, you're grounded.

For now, you're staying where I can keep an eye on you."

He made a sour face.

"We'll see you later," she said to Kendall.

"Amy," he said, "can I speak to you a moment? In private?"

It was her time of reckoning. "Sure." She pulled her keys out of her coat pocket and handed them to Tony. "Wait for me in my SUV, please."

He picked up the backpack he'd dropped on the ground and walked to the SUV in the uncoordinated gait of a preteen. He kept looking back, as if to make sure she was okay. She gave him a reassuring smile and waited until he'd closed the door before turning back to Kendall.

She was unprepared for the look of unveiled hostility in his eyes.

"How could you?" he asked, his voice shaking. "How could you not tell me that I have a *son?*"

She'd had more than twelve years to think of a response to that question, but she still didn't have it down pat. "You didn't want *me,* Kendall. I assumed that would extend to a baby, as well."

A muscle ticked in his jaw. "You assumed wrong. I would've taken care of you…both of you."

She noticed the resounding absence of the word *love.* "No way was I going to saddle both of us with a marriage for the sake of a child who would only get torn in half in the process."

"I deserved to know," he said, his voice vibrating with anger.

"It was easier for me if you didn't know," she volleyed back. Then she darted a look to the SUV—Tony was watching them. She exhaled. "See, you've known him for ten minutes and we're already arguing in front of him."

Kendall pulled his hand down his face, then crossed his arms. "I want to spend time with him."

"I don't know if he can stay," she admitted. "He was in trouble already—military school was part of his sentence."

Kendall's eyes widened. "Sentence? What did he do?"

She pressed her lips together. "He's not a bank robber. He vandalized a school."

"That sounds pretty serious to me. Maybe he wouldn't be a delinquent if he'd been allowed to know his father."

Her eyes filled with angry tears. "Are you saying I was a bad influence on him?"

"I'm saying a child needs a mother *and* a father! You of all people should know that."

"Because I'm such a piece of trash? Is that what you're trying to say?"

"You're putting words in my mouth—"

The sound of a car horn split the air. Amy turned her head to see Tony's head stuck out the window. "Come on, Mom! I'm starving."

"I'm coming," she called with a smile. Then she

looked back to Kendall. "I'll talk to the attorney and let you know."

"We'll *both* talk to the attorney."

So this was how it was going to be. She pressed her lips together, then nodded. "Okay, we'll both talk to the attorney. Tomorrow." She turned to walk away, her heart hammering.

"Amy."

She stopped, then turned back. "What?"

"I want his name changed to Armstrong."

She closed her eyes briefly. "That will be Tony's choice to make—not mine…and certainly not yours."

Kendall's jaw hardened.

She turned and walked to the SUV, telling herself to keep putting one foot in front of the other. Her heart ached. Was it only this morning that Kendall had slipped from her bed after making sweet love to her all night?

It seemed like a lifetime ago.

22

"Wow," Nikki said. "You have a son…and Kendall is the father. Now it makes sense why you were warning me about Southern men when I first came to Sweetness."

Amy lifted her glass for a sip. It was after one in the morning and they were sitting alone in the corner of the front great room under quilts, drinking wine and watching a dying fire. "Don't worry, Nikki. Porter's a good guy."

"Kendall's a good guy, too."

"For a woman who wants to live in Sweetness. I didn't, and I don't." She took another sip. "No offense to you."

"I won't pretend to know what it was like growing up here. I'm sure you have your reasons for not wanting to live in Sweetness." Nikki sat forward in her chair. "But how did you keep the baby a secret?"

"I left town before I was showing. I didn't have family here, and I didn't stay in touch with anyone."

"But even I didn't know you had a son."

"I didn't keep Tony a secret from people in Broadway," Amy said with a laugh. "But when you and I met in yoga class, he was starting to get into trouble, and I didn't want to dwell on it."

"So Kendall had no idea you had a child?"

"None. And this wasn't how I wanted them to meet."

"So how did Kendall take it?"

"Not well. He's livid that I didn't tell him about Tony. And he pretty much blamed me for everything that's wrong in Tony's life."

"He's in shock, give him some time to digest things. He cares about you, Amy. The man just spent three days in bed with you, for heaven's sake."

Amy gave a dry laugh. "Sex was never our problem—Tony is living proof of that."

"How's Tony taking the news?"

"Hard to tell. He's in trouble for leaving school and coming here in the first place, and then this was sprung on him."

"He's in shock, too."

"Maybe. He was asleep before I turned out the light in his room. I'll know more tomorrow."

"Did you get a sense of how Kendall and Tony might get along?"

"They were feeling each other out. It's surreal watching them because they're so much alike. I guess it can go either way—they could love each other or hate each other."

"And good or bad, you'll be in the middle," Nikki

said, reaching for the bottle. "I think you deserve a refill." As she topped off Amy's glass, Nikki asked, "Have you thought about things long-term?"

Amy gave a little laugh. "Only that Tony and I won't be living in Sweetness."

"Wow," Porter said. "A son...and Amy is the mother."

"And you had no idea she was pregnant when she left?" Marcus asked.

Kendall lifted his beer bottle for a drink. It was after one in the morning and they were sitting alone around a fire pit drinking beer. "Not a clue."

"Now it makes sense why she told you not to contact her," Porter offered.

"Nothing about it makes sense," Kendall snapped. "All this time I've had a son walking around and I didn't even know." He looked at Marcus. "But you knew, didn't you, big brother?"

"Only for a little while," Marcus said quietly.

"So that's why you asked Amy to come back and build the bridge," Porter said.

Marcus nodded, then tipped up his bottle.

"Did you blackmail her into coming back?" Kendall asked.

"No. She could've said no. Actually, she did at first, said she had another commitment."

Kendall nodded. "I remember her saying something about a project that had fallen through."

"I think she came back to tell you, Kendall. She was just waiting for the right time."

"The right time was twelve years ago."

"Obviously, she felt differently," Porter said mildly. "Amy's a good person, Kendall."

"She's a thief, remember? She stole my son from me. And now he's a delinquent."

"Sounds like a gutsy kid to me," Marcus said. "To hitchhike all the way from Michigan. Cut Amy some slack, Kendall. She didn't want you two to meet like this."

"She obviously cares about you," Porter said. "The woman just spent three days in bed with you, for chrissake."

Kendall gave a dry laugh. "Sex was never our problem—Tony is living proof of that."

"How's the kid taking the news?"

"Hard to tell. He's in trouble for leaving school and coming here in the first place, and now this."

"He'll be fine," Porter offered. "He's an Armstrong."

"I told Amy I want his name changed, but she said it was up to Tony."

"It's cool that she named him after Dad, though," Porter said.

"Did you get a sense of how Amy and Tony get along?" Marcus asked.

"From what I can see, she's way too lenient, and he's way too spoiled."

"So you'll be in the middle," Porter said, reaching

into a cooler. "Brother, I think you deserve another beer." He pulled out a bottle, twisted off the top, and handed it to Kendall. "Have you thought about how things might play out long-term?"

Kendall lifted the bottle to his mouth. "Only that I want my son to live here in Sweetness."

23

Sitting in the construction office waiting for the phone to ring, Amy couldn't stop looking back and forth between father and son. Not only did they look alike, but they had the same mannerisms, she realized. They quirked their eyebrows the same and liked to steeple their hands.

And at the moment, they were easy to observe— they were both ignoring her.

"Thank you for the use of the office," she offered to Kendall. "Hopefully we won't have to wait much longer for Bertram to get back to us."

He nodded. "No problem. I just want to get this wrapped up so we can get back to work."

"I want that, as well," she said mildly.

"What do you think they'll do to me?" Tony asked, chewing on his fingernails.

"That's not a very nice habit," Kendall commented.

Tony's face turned red and he put his hand down.

Amy shot Kendall a pointed look. "Your father

knows," she said to Tony, "because he used to bite his nails, too." Then she reached over to squeeze his hand. "What do you think should happen to you, sweetie?"

He shrugged. "I don't know. I already said I was sorry."

"Sometimes sorry isn't good enough," Kendall said. "You heard the attorney—you caused a lot of damage. The school had to be closed for repairs."

"It wasn't just me," he mumbled.

"We've already been over this," Amy reminded him. "It doesn't matter who else was involved. I asked you what you think should happen to you. What would be fair?"

"They should've made *you* do the repairs," Kendall offered.

"I asked Tony," Amy said, keeping her tone light.

"I don't want to go to jail," Tony said. He lifted his hand to bite his nails again, then darted a look at Kendall and put it back down.

"Let's just wait to see what the attorney is able to work out," Amy said. "No matter what happens, you can deal with it."

He gave her a grateful look and she winked at him.

Kendall cleared his throat, clearly disapproving of the way she was handling things.

The phone rang and when she saw it was the attorney's office, she put the call on speaker. "Hello, Mr. Bertram, this is Amy Bradshaw. Tony is with me." She glanced up and remembered they weren't alone. "Oh, and…Tony's father Kendall Armstrong, is joining us, too."

She supposed she was going to have to get used to saying that.

"Hello, all," Bertram said, his voice brusque and efficient. "Okay, here's the situation. The school is being cooperative because they understand the precarious position they're in with leaving young Tony unsupervised. I've spoken with the dean of students and he agreed to speak to the District Attorney's office on Tony's behalf because he was a model student for the, um…" Papers rattled. "For the two weeks he attended. If Tony agrees to turn in the names of the other boys who were with him, he might be able to get off with time served at the school."

"And if he doesn't give up the names?" Kendall asked.

"Well, I was at least able to get the fine down to five thousand dollars. And he wouldn't have to go back to the school."

"He'll pay the fine," Kendall announced.

Amy looked up. "Mr. Bertram, can I put you hold for a moment?"

"Of course."

She hit the button to exclude the man from overhearing their conversation. "Kendall, I do okay in my job, but I don't have that kind of cash lying around.

The attorney's fees and the tuition at the school already set me back some."

"I'll pay it," he said.

Tony looked at her, his expression hopeful. She knew what her son was thinking—that this having a dad thing wasn't so bad, if he was going to be generous.

"And you'll work it off," Kendall said to Tony.

Tony frowned. "How?"

"However I want you to. Until the covered bridge is built, you'll go to school here and work for me after school and on weekends."

Tony looked suspicious. "But if I give them the names of the other boys, we don't have to pay anything, and I don't have to work for you."

"Trust me, son. If you take the easy way out, you'll be paying for it the rest of your life."

Tony's eyes narrowed. "Don't call me 'son.'"

Amy bit down on her tongue.

Kendall looked at her. "Some help here?"

"It's Tony's future, Tony's decision."

"Like the decision he made to vandalize a school? We're his parents, this is our decision."

Amy tried to telegraph to Kendall that if left to his own devices, Tony usually did the right thing. She'd raised him that way. But when challenged, he did what most of the Armstrong men did—push back. Amy chewed on her lip, playing out the scenario Kendall described. Maybe it would be the best way for father and son to get to know each other, to hash things through.

"Okay," she said, looking at Kendall. "We'll do it your way."

Tony's head come up. "You're siding with him?"

"We both want what's best for you," she said carefully. "And this way, you won't have to go back to that school. Besides, I still haven't forgotten the whole hitchhiking thing."

He scowled. She could feel his frustration. Up came the hand so he could chew on his nails. "Whatever," he mumbled.

Kendall looked at her and gave a curt nod, his body language easing.

Amy hit the button on the phone to resume the call. "Mr. Bertram, we've decided—all of us—that Tony will be paying the fine."

"Okay, I'll draw up the papers and fax them to you there to sign."

"Thank you," she said, then disconnected the call.

Anger and distrust vibrated in the room between father and son.

"Now what?" Tony asked Kendall. "I'm your slave?"

"Watch the attitude," Kendall said. "A thank-you would be nice."

Tony gave him a look saying that was never going to happen.

"Thank you, Kendall," Amy said, then looked at Tony. "Now what happens is we get you enrolled in school here for this quarter. I'll finish the covered bridge and you'll finish school about the same time."

"Then we'll go home?" Tony asked.

She glanced up at Kendall. His expression was expectant. She looked back to Tony. "Yes…then we'll go home."

24

"This is going to make a wicked elapsed time video for the website," Betsy said of the covered bridge work site.

Amy nodded, understanding only about half of what the girl said. She had shown up every day after school to document the erection of the stacked-stone piers, the unloading of the materials and the staging of the timber pieces as they'd be needed for assembly. Four days into the job, progress was slow, but steady.

Amy observed the young girl, so mature and creative. Her clothes were funky and unlike anything Amy would've worn in high school. "How old are you, Betsy?"

"Fifteen. Why?"

"You seem…older."

The girl smiled. "Good."

"Do you know my son, Tony? He enrolled in the school here earlier in the week."

"Yeah, he's a lot younger than me, though."

"Yes, he's twelve," Amy said, smothering a smile.

Betsy rolled her eyes. "All the girls are gaga over him, they think he has dreamy eyes."

Amy laughed. "Thank you, I think."

The girl took a few pictures, then lowered the digital camera and looked at Amy warily. "There's a rumor going around that Kendall Armstrong is his father."

"Yes, Kendall is Tony's father," Amy said. It was getting easier to say, but still not so easy to grapple with. She and Kendall were being civil, but just barely. When he looked at her, his eyes were so accusatory, it chilled her to the bone.

"That's cool," the girl said simply, then went back to taking pictures.

The younger generation were very matter-of-fact about dealing with pieces and parts of broken and melded families, Amy mused. The casualness was a bit unsettling, but reflected reality. She still couldn't tell how Tony was feeling about the turn of events—he breezed over concerns she voiced and gave her monosyllabic answers to questions. Mostly he kept to himself or played video games in the great room. Today Kendall was picking him up from school and bringing him here for his first "job" to work off the fine. They had agreed that Kendall would choose and supervise the chores.

She hoped she didn't regret that decision.

"Hey, are you wearing your mother's necklace?" Betsy asked.

Amy's hand went to her bare neck. "Not at the moment. I don't want to lose it." True, but disingenuous, she admitted to herself. She hadn't worn it in days. In fact, she'd acquired an aversion to it because it had started to represent a connection to this town.

At the moment her emotions were so confusing, she was grateful for the covered-bridge project. The steadfastness of building materials, the certainty of structural load and force, gave her something to focus on. There were a thousand details to handle with the foremen, and two crews of men to manage. It kept her mind occupied for the most part, but her thoughts still strayed to the two men in her life throughout the workday, and how they both managed to push her buttons.

Kendall's black pickup pulled onto the site. Tony sat in the passenger side. As inconspicuously as possible, Amy watched to see how they interacted. They both climbed out and scanned for her. Knowing she looked like any other worker in her hard hat, she lifted her hand. They moved in her direction.

She noticed Tony was wearing sturdy work clothes—Kendall must have bought them for him at the General Store. Her son looked awkward and unsure of himself. Kendall, on the other hand, looked like a tower of power in work-worn jeans and a long-sleeve black thermal shirt that hugged his wide shoulders.

It would be hard, she realized suddenly, to find out your father was a mountain of man with more strength in his hands than most men had in their entire arm. She had no doubt that Tony's physique would be the same someday, but for now, his pre-adolescent body looked scrawny standing next to his father.

His father. As they approached, Amy marveled over the sheer biology, the fact that she and Kendall had made this whole other person. And her midsection tightened with memories of how they'd done it.

"Hello," she called when they were close enough. She resisted hugging Tony, part of her new effort to allow him to look grown up around his father.

"Hey," he said simply, his eyes darting around the site…and stopping on Betsy, who was still taking pictures.

Amy smiled. "Tony, this is Betsy Hahn. She goes to your school."

"Duh, everyone here goes to the same school," he said.

Amy opened her mouth to reprimand him for being rude but Kendall beat her to it.

"Be nice," he said.

"Hi," Betsy said with a tight smile. "I'm from Broadway, too."

"Then you know how boring it is here," Tony said with a laugh, his voice condemning.

"I don't think it's boring," she said, giving him a look as if he didn't know anything.

"There's nothing to *do* here," he said.

Kendall put a hand on his shoulder. "That's about

to change. See that pile of construction debris? I want you to sort through it. Put anything that will burn in one pile, and throw everything else in that green Dumpster."

Tony took in the sprawling pile that was taller than him. "Tonight?"

"Before you leave."

Tony looked at her and pleaded with his eyes for her to intervene. Instead, she gave him a wink. "Think of all the muscles you'll build."

Kendall extended a pair of suede work gloves. "You'll need these."

Tony frowned. "No, I don't." He trudged toward the pile, his body language sullen.

"Suit yourself," Kendall called after him.

Amy looked at Kendall. "You could have one of the men move that pile with a back-hoe in fifteen minutes."

"Yes, I could," he agreed.

"I'm not sure I like the idea of you working my son just for the hell of it."

He arched an eyebrow. "Then think of it as me working *my* son just for the hell of it. The boy needs to get out from behind the computer and those video games."

"He's not a couch potato. He played soccer at his regular school."

"Not baseball?"

Kendall had played baseball in high school. Between them, the Armstrong boys had dominated football, basketball, baseball and wrestling. Soccer hadn't yet made it to the North Georgia mountains in large numbers.

"I think he has a *fantasy* baseball team," she offered.

He frowned. "I'm supposed to know what that is?"

"No, but you can ask him," she said mildly.

"He doesn't seem to use any words. All he does is grunt."

She gave a little laugh. "It takes a while to learn to interpret his grunts."

He gave her a pointed look. "Except I don't have much time, do I?"

Amy couldn't think of anything to make him feel better, so she remained silent.

Kendall sighed noisily, then his shoulders softened, obviously trying a new tack. "I was thinking about a family dinner tonight."

Family. "The three of us?"

"Actually, I'd like for Tony to get to know Porter and Marcus, you know, just us men. I thought we'd do steaks at the bunkhouse…if that's okay."

Ah, *Kendall's* family. Amy tried to hide her disappointment at the slight, as well as her reservations about Tony being pulled more deeply into the Armstrong fold. They were good people, but she didn't want to lose her son to them. "What time do you want to pick him up?"

"I'll just take him from here when he finishes,"

Kendall said, "and I'll bring him back to the board-inghouse after dinner."

"Just remember it's a school night," Amy said. "I like for him to be in bed by ten."

"When he's not hitchhiking?" Kendall asked drily.

That stung.

"Have fun," she managed to say before turning back to her work, blinking back hot tears.

25

Kendall stood in front of his truck in the head-lights that shone over the dwindling pile of debris where Tony still labored. The sun had set an hour ago. Kendall didn't particularly enjoy working the boy so hard, but he knew it was good for him.

Tony stood and wiped his forehead. "I think that's all of it."

"Good," Kendall called, proud that he'd finished. "I'll bet you're hungry."

Tony walked toward the truck, glaring. "I'm too tired to eat."

"You'll sleep good tonight." Kendall opened the driver's-side door and climbed in. "I told your mother you and I would have dinner at the bunkhouse to-night with my brothers. You can shower there."

Tony climbed in the passenger side, moving slowly. "I don't have my soap and stuff."

"It's provided. Are you shaving yet?"

Tony wiped a dirty hand over his jaw. "No."

Kendall bit back a smile. "It won't be long."

On the way to the bunkhouse, Tony inspected his hands in the dark. Kendall could tell they were blistered. The boy would learn. He remembered a similar lesson when he was about Tony's age...over a similar junk pile.

Emotion tugged at his heart. His father would be so pleased to see Tony, to have a namesake, to know the Armstrong lineage would continue. As soon as he changed the boy's name, he thought wryly. Kendall hadn't yet called his mother. He knew Emily Armstrong would pelt him with questions he couldn't yet answer about the boy, and about Amy.

Another tug. Amy Bradshaw would be the death of him. At times he was so angry with her over denying him knowledge of his son that he felt dangerously close to losing control. Her betrayal had cut deeper than anything he'd ever experienced. Even now, when he looked at Tony, he was bereft over all the moments in the boy's life he'd missed out on, all the moments Tony had wondered about a father who wasn't around.

"What's the bunkhouse?" Tony asked.

"It's where the men stay."

"Why do the men and women live separately here?"

Kendall laughed. "Good question. Logistics, I suppose. When my brothers and I started rebuilding the town, we signed on two hundred and fifty men to work for us. But we realized sooner or later we'd have to have some women, or the men weren't going to stay."

Tony grinned for the first time and it lifted Kendall's heart.

"So we advertised for single women, and we built the boardinghouse for them to stay in."

"And their kids," Tony added.

"Their kids came later because we didn't have a school yet, but yes. Sooner or later as couples decide to marry and live together, people will start building their own homes outside of the downtown area. That's how a community grows."

"So you grew up here?"

"Right. Then I went into the Air Force and traveled around the world."

"Were you a pilot?"

Kendall laughed. "No. I'm an engineer."

"Like my mom."

"Yep."

"She's good at her job," Tony offered.

"She's a smart lady when it comes to her job," Kendall agreed.

"She's a good mom, too," Tony blurted, his voice defiant.

"I'm sure she is," Kendall said carefully. Something stirred deep within him to hear his son defend his mother. It was just the kind of thing he would've taught Tony to do, even though he had problems with some of Amy's decisions.

He pulled the truck up to the bunkhouse. "I'll grab

a change of clothes. You can put on the same clothes you wore to school today. Over there's the shower house. I'll meet you inside."

Tony picked up his backpack and headed toward the long block building that housed the showers. Kendall stopped in the bunkhouse to get what he needed from a foot locker, then stopped outside at the grill area to tell Porter and Marcus they'd be out in a few minutes.

At the shower house, Tony waited for him, his dirty face stoic. "There's men in there already."

It dawned on Kendall that Tony had never taken a locker-room shower. He thought back to when he was Tony's age and tried to remember if he'd been modest. He hadn't, but then, he'd grown up with two brothers. "You can shower in your underwear if you want."

Tony thought about it. "Do you?"

"Nope." Kendall walked into the locker area, grabbed a towel and opened a locker, depositing his change of clothes inside. Then he began to undress, noticing that Tony was copying his movements. He whistled under his breath throughout, then wrapped a towel around his waist and slipped his feet into shower shoes. He pulled out an extra pair and dropped them at Tony's feet. "Wear these."

Tony pushed his feet into the flip flops, then followed Kendall to the showers. A dozen men were showering, tossing laughter back and forth.

"Hey, guys," Kendall said, throwing up his hand.

"Kendall, who's the little man?" one of the workers yelled.

"This is my son, Tony." He realized it was the first time he'd said those words.

"Hiya, Tony!" the guys chorused.

Tony waved self-consciously.

Kendall casually removed his towel and hung it on a hook, then turned on one of the many shower heads coming out of the wall. Tony did the same, albeit more slowly. Kendall squirted soap out of the dispenser and lathered up, knowing his son was probably studying his body. It was an age-old lesson that he was happy to pass down. He gave Tony his privacy, joked a couple of times with the men to let his son know he didn't need to be embarrassed.

Then he turned off the shower and retrieved the towel, dried off and wrapped it around his waist again.

"That was fast," Tony said, trying to keep up.

"We try to conserve water here," Kendall said. "Sweetness is a green community."

"That's why there are recycling signs everywhere at school?"

"Right."

"Someone said there are big bins of worms by the cafeteria."

Kendall smiled. "Those are compost bins…and yes, we use mealworms. I'll show you sometime."

He walked to a sink, pulled out shaving cream and lathered up his beard, then pulled out a razor.

"You're going to shave your beard?" Tony asked.

"I always shave for spring, might as well do it now." He passed the shaving cream to Tony. "Do you want to try?"

Tony shrugged. "Okay." He lathered up, too.

Kendall passed him a razor. "Do you know how?"

"Not really."

"It's tricky the first couple of times," Kendall said, using slow, exaggerated strokes. "Don't press too hard."

"Ow!" Tony said, then grimaced at a thin line of blood that comingled with the shaving cream.

"I still cut myself, too," Kendall said. "Keep going."

They shaved in companionable silence. Again, Kendall was taken back to the bathroom lesson his dad had given him. How many special moments like that had been lost in his memory forever because he hadn't been around his own son to trigger them? His anger toward Amy resurged to the surface.

"You have a lot of muscles," Tony said absently.

Kendall smiled. "So will you."

"Is that why my mom liked you, because you had muscles?"

Kendall's smile faded a bit. "You'll have to ask her."

"She won't talk about you."

His hand slipped and he cut himself. "See, I told you I still cut myself," Kendall said with a rueful laugh. "Let's wrap this up—Porter and Marcus are waiting."

They dressed in the locker room, then Kendall said, "Let me see those hands."

Tony worked his mouth, then stuck them out. Bright red blisters and broken skin covered his palms and the undersides of his fingers.

"Yeah, I've been there," Kendall said, turning over his own calloused hands. He handed Tony a tube of antibiotic ointment. "This will make them feel better and heal faster."

Tony opened the tube and squeezed some on his fingers, then handed it back.

"Keep it," Kendall said. "You're going to need it." He closed the locker door. "Got your dirty clothes?"

Tony patted his backpack.

"Towels go over there," Kendall said, pointing, then he smiled. "And now, dinner. Are you hungry?"

Tony nodded. "Thirsty, too."

"Then let's go."

They walked in the darkness, the ground illuminated only by a three-quarter moon. Kendall looked over at Tony, marveling that he and Amy had created this person. He was overwhelmed by the urge to protect him and was scared anew at the thought of Tony hitchhiking on the interstate between Michigan and Georgia. He had a new appreciation for the sleepless nights he and his brothers must have caused his parents.

"What's it like having brothers?" Tony asked.

Another thing that Amy had deprived Tony of, Kendall thought glumly—the chance to have siblings. "Having brothers is the best," Kendall said. "Just don't tell them I said that."

Tony grinned.

"There they are," Porter said, waving from behind one of the many grills set up for the men to use if they were so inclined. Marcus stood next to him, both of them wearing heavy flannel shirts and drinking cans of soda.

"Tony, the ugly guy on the left is your uncle Porter," Kendall said. "And the uglier guy on the right is your uncle Marcus—you met him the other day. Guys, this is Anthony Alton Bradshaw. He goes by Tony."

"Hey, Tony."

"Hello, Tony."

"Hi," he said, then stepped forward to offer his hand to each of them.

Kendall's chest swelled, conceding that Amy had taught the boy manners.

"Sorry, I got ointment on my hands," Tony mumbled.

"That's okay," Porter said. "We can always use some, too."

"Good to see you again, Tony," Marcus said.

Over the boy's head, Kendall met his brothers' eyes and they gave him imperceptible nods of approval—and envy—that left Kendall shaken…and flushed with pride.

"I understand you put in a full day at school, then worked all evening," Porter said. "You must be starved. Steak and baked potato okay?"

"Yeah," Tony said, his eyes alight.

His brothers, especially Porter, had an ease with Tony that Kendall didn't, probably because the relationship was simpler, with no expectations. Kendall observed as Tony interacted and opened up with his brothers about sports and movies, enjoying the banter.

At one point he glanced at his watch and realized with dismay it was already ten o'clock.

Then Tony laughed at something Porter said, and Kendall dropped his arm. He had missed out on too much of his son's life. No way was he going to be deprived of this evening.

It was close to eleven-thirty when he drove Tony back to the boardinghouse. Tony was dead on his feet. Kendall walked him to his room that was just a couple of doors down from Amy's. He shepherded him inside with a good-night, then tapped on Amy's door.

She answered, dressed in the gown and robe he remembered so well from a few days ago. Her curly red hair was coiled up and held with a clip, her face devoid of makeup and naturally pretty. All the anger he'd fostered toward her over the evening disintegrated. He felt the pull of her body on his and had the overwhelming urge to kiss her.

"You're still up," he said unnecessarily.

"I was hoping to say good-night to Tony."

"I just dropped him off in his room. I'm sure he's sound asleep already."

"Okay, thanks." She squinted. "You shaved your beard and mustache."

He stroked his clean chin. "Like it?"

"It's late, Kendall." She started to close the door.

"I'm sorry I brought him home late. We lost track of time."

"I understand."

"It won't happen again," he promised.

She nodded. "It's okay, really. I'm going to have to learn to share him for a while."

"For a while?" he asked, his anger reigniting. "How about for the rest of his life?"

She touched her forehead. "I'm tired, I misspoke."

Through the open door, the bed they had occupied for the better part of three days mocked him. All of those private moments when Amy could've told him about his son, could've prepared him, could've explained why she'd kept their child a secret. But what made him most angry was, despite her cruel deceit, he still wanted to press her down in those sheets and make love to her until dawn.

"Kendall, was there something else you wanted?"

He snapped out of his reverie. "No. Good night."

Kendall turned and strode away, his entire body vibrating with frustration. He needed to persuade

Amy to stay in Sweetness so he could be with his son. But he wasn't sure he wanted her to stay if they couldn't be together.

26

For the next few weeks they settled into a tolerable, if not comfortable, routine of Kendall picking up Tony from school for a couple of hours of work, then delivering him back to the boardinghouse where Amy helped him with homework. On Saturdays, Tony spent the day with Kendall and slept in the bunkhouse. On Sundays, he was with Amy all day.

But the exchanges were contentious because Amy felt as if Tony was always too tired to complete his homework, while Kendall argued that she'd agreed that Tony working to pay off the fine was the right life lesson. And no matter how much Amy prepared herself to see Kendall, no matter how often she promised herself she wouldn't let him goad her into saying something cutting or unpleasant, the mere sight of him undid all those assurances that had seemed so ironclad when she'd made them. Unintended words flew out of her mouth like arrows, and each encounter seemed to escalate. She would always walk away feeling miserable that Tony had witnessed yet another altercation between his parents.

She was afraid the strain was wearing on him.

It was certainly wearing on her.

Kendall had made it clear that he would never forgive her for not telling him about Tony, and that he thought she'd done a substandard job of raising his son. The fact that she knew how he felt about her, yet she still lay awake at nights thinking about his big body arching into hers, left her feeling ashamed.

But hadn't he always been her weakness?

Amy sipped a cup of coffee as she scanned the nearly completed covered bridge. It promised to be a spectacle. By her estimation, they would be finished within another two weeks, which would coincide with the end of the school quarter. If she could hold on and hold out for another two weeks, she'd be home free.

Home. Back in Broadway.

The sight of Kendall's black truck made her pulse jump, as if she'd conjured him up with her thoughts. She frowned when she saw that Tony was in the passenger seat. She glanced at her watch—it was too early for school to be out. When Tony climbed out and looked up, her stomach dropped. He had a black eye.

She strode toward them, trying not to panic. "Tony, what happened?"

"It's no big deal," Kendall said.

She glared at him, angry that he would dismiss

her concern. "I asked Tony." She put her hand under Tony's chin and angled his injured eye toward her. "Tell me."

Tony grimaced. "I got in a fight."

"What about?"

He shrugged.

"I asked you a question, young man."

"It was with an older boy," Kendall said.

She looked up. It was obvious that Tony had called Kendall when he'd gotten in trouble. Not her. "If you don't mind, Kendall, I'm addressing my son." She looked back to Tony. "Who had better speak if he knows what's good for him."

"Leave me alone." Tony swatted away her hand, then turned and jumped back in the truck and locked the doors.

"Tony!" she shouted. "What are you doing?"

"Leave him be," Kendall said, his hand on her arm. "He got into a fight over a girl. He was too embarrassed to call you."

Amy blinked. "A girl? What girl?"

"The girl who comes here every day to take pictures."

"Betsy?"

"Yeah. Apparently an older boy was bothering her, and Tony said something to him and they got into a fight. The other boy definitely got the worse end of it."

She was incredulous. "You're gloating? I can't

believe this—I've taught my son not to fight and you're encouraging it?"

Kendall grunted. "He's a *boy,* Amy! He has testosterone, and a lot of it. He's going to be aggressive at times. I'd much rather see him get in trouble for defending someone than for vandalizing a school!"

"You only think that's worse because it happened on my watch," she said. "But when he does something and he's been under your influence, you find a way to justify it."

"That's not true!" he shouted. "There's a big difference in doing something wrong for the right reason and doing something wrong just for kicks. I've been trying to teach him how to be a responsible man, to stick up for people who can't fend for themselves."

"So he gets hurt himself?" Amy shouted back. "This is exactly the kind of Southern macho bull crap I didn't want him to learn, Kendall! It's just posturing, like the whole surname thing!"

"A son should have his father's name—he's an Armstrong!"

"He has a name already—it's Bradshaw!"

"Stop fighting!" Tony yelled through the windshield.

When Amy turned her head to look at her son inside the truck, he had his hands over his ears. Of course he'd heard everything they'd said—they'd been shouting at the top of their lungs. Amy looked around and realized the machinery on the jobsite had quieted and the workers were staring in their direction, too. Everyone had heard them.

She looked at Kendall and he realized it, too.

"Was he expelled?" she asked, her voice calm now.

"No." His voice was quieter, too. "He has to sit in detention when he goes back Monday."

"What about his eye?"

"I stopped at the clinic on the way here and Nikki took a look at it. She gave him an ice pack and some over-the-counter painkiller. He'll be fine."

"Thank you."

"I thought I'd take him to Clover Ridge on four-wheelers to visit the homestead and do some chores around the cemetery. We can roast hot dogs for dinner. I believe he can handle one of the smaller ATV's...if that's okay with you."

She nodded. "He'd like that. But let me talk to him first. Can you unlock the doors?"

Kendall pulled out his keyless entry remote control and unlocked the truck doors. Amy walked around to the driver's side and opened it to climb in. She closed the door behind her, then sat back in the seat.

After a few minutes' silence, she said, "I'm sorry."

"For what?" Tony asked.

"For yelling at your father in front of you. We both care about you, but we have different ideas about how to raise you. It's not fair to you."

"Mom, when can we go home?"

"Soon. The bridge is nearly finished, and the winter quarter ends in what—two weeks?" She smiled. "I can bear it for two more weeks if you can."

He nodded. "I'm sorry, too, for fighting."

"I know. Listen, your dad wants to take you out on four-wheelers to see where he grew up. Would you like that?"

He grinned. "Yeah!"

"Wear a helmet," she said, wagging a finger. "And don't drive fast."

"Mom."

She smiled. "And have fun."

"I love you, Mom."

How long had it been since he'd offered it first? "I love you, too."

"Don't kiss me."

"Can I at least make the smooching noise?"

"Mom."

"Okay. Be careful." She opened the door and dropped to the ground. Kendall stood there, expectant.

Would he ever stop making her heart thrash in her chest? "We're good. Will you let me know when he's in tonight?"

"Sure." He looked as if he wanted to say something else, but she didn't dare risk another argument, so she turned and headed back toward the jobsite and immersed herself in the details of getting the final touches put on the covered bridge. The full skeleton was up, including the ceiling trusses. The pedestrian sidewalk was also complete. All temporary steel support had been removed and the bridge was now a self-supporting timber structure. Many details remained to be completed, including siding, roof and shingles. But she was very pleased with the progress.

A few minutes later, Betsy arrived, camera in tow. She took a few pictures, then looked all around.

"Ms. Bradshaw, is Tony going to be here today?"

"No. He's out with his father."

Her shoulders fell. "Can you give him a message for me?"

"Sure. What is it?"

"The message is…I think he's kind of cool." She lifted the camera and resumed taking pictures.

Amy shook her head. That Southern macho bull crap had worked on her when she was a teenager. Apparently, it was still working.

27

Kendall stood at the door to his son's room. "Good night, Tony."

"Good night, Dad."

Kendall stopped, surprised.

Tony looked worried. "Is it okay if I call you 'Dad'?"

Damn, his heart was going to burst. "Yeah…it sounds good."

Tony grinned. "Good."

Kendall backed out of the room and closed the door, then exhaled.

It had been a near-perfect evening with his son— riding four-wheelers up to Clover Ridge to show Tony where he and his brothers had grown up, and explaining how the tornado had blown everything away. Tony had been fascinated by the story of his grandmother Emily and uncle Porter taking cover in the root cellar.

They had visited the cemetery and he'd shown Tony the grave of the grandfather he was named for, and the graves of Amy's parents. They had trimmed weeds and cleared branches and picked up litter. Then they'd built a small fire pit next to the stacked logs drying for Porter's house and roasted hot dogs and marshmallows. Tony had told him all about fantasy baseball, and taught him a few soccer terms.

The only way it would've been a nicer evening, Kendall thought as he walked toward Amy's room, was if Amy had been with them.

He knocked on her door and his pulse ratcheted higher in anticipation of seeing her in her gown and robe.

She answered the door, but opened it only a few inches. "Hi."

"Hi. He's in bed."

"Did you have a good time?"

He nodded. "Tony asked if he could call me 'Dad.'"

Her lips parted, and the door opened a little wider, giving him a better peek at the gown and robe. "That's…great."

"So I guess now we're Mom and Dad."

"I guess so." She bit her lip, then gestured into the room. "I have something to show you if you have a few minutes."

As if he would turn down an invitation into her room. "Sure."

He walked in, then closed the door behind him.

Amy had stepped to the closet and appeared to be rummaging through the side pockets of a suitcase. He enjoyed the view of her backside while she stooped and stretched. His jeans suddenly felt a little tighter.

"I remembered something," came her muffled voice. "Ah, here it is." She straightened, then turned, holding a small book. Her face was radiant with a happy smile. "When I used to travel more, I always carried a photo album with pictures of Tony. I thought you might want to see some pictures of him when he was younger."

He smiled. "Show me."

She walked over to sit on the edge of the made bed, seemingly oblivious to what it did to him to have her and a mattress in proximity to each other. He swallowed hard and lowered himself to sit next to her.

She opened the book. "Here is Tony at five days old."

His son already looked like him, the eyebrows, the stubborn chin. Kendall studied the background of the picture, then frowned. "He was still in the hospital?"

"He was born with a respiratory problem, so they wanted to keep him a little longer."

"Was it serious?"

"It was more scary than serious, and he didn't have any permanent damage. He's perfectly healthy now."

His heart gave a squeeze. She'd been young and alone. She must have been terrified.

"Here he is at six months, look how much he'd grown. At that point, he would literally outgrow an outfit before he could wear it twice."

She'd never contacted him for money, or any other kind of support. How had she worked and put herself through engineering school and taken care of a baby? His mind reeled.

"The rest of these were taken on his birthday, every year up until ten."

Kendall could've been looking at his own baby pictures, Tony looked so much like him at every age. But the props were different—the soccer ball cake, the guitar video game he played. Kendall studied the pictures and saw the loving touches in the photos— friends his age, party favors and always a special cake. Amy had been a devoted mother to his son. To accuse her of anything less was only retaliation on his part.

"Thank you," he murmured.

She smiled. "You're welcome. I have more pictures at home, and I'll have copies of everything made for you."

"I meant thank you for raising my son and taking such good care of him."

Her smile wavered. "You're welcome." Then she bit her lip. "I'm sorry, Kendall, for not telling you about Tony sooner. It was selfish of me."

He shook his head. "I'm sorry you didn't feel like you could tell me. I can't imagine what you sacrificed to get by." He lifted a hand to her face. "I admire you so much."

Slowly, he leaned forward to kiss her, prepared to stop if she put up the slightest resistance.

But she didn't. When his lips touched hers, she sighed into this mouth. His senses leapt as he curled his fingers around her neck and pulled her closer for a deeper kiss. He pressed her back into the covers and opened her robe, then skimmed the gown up to her thighs. She pulled his shirt over his head and helped loosen his belt. While he discarded his boots and jeans, she shed the gown. When Kendall came back to her, she reached for him and brought him to near ecstasy with her hands and mouth.

He rolled down the minuscule underwear she wore and tasted her damp folds until she cried out with her first orgasm. Then with the taste of her still on his lips, he sheathed himself, settled between her thighs and drove himself home.

Being buried inside Amy was heaven and torture at the same time. Every movement felt rapturous, but brought him closer to completion, which he wanted to postpone. He pushed his fingers into her hair and whispered encouragement to her and soon, their bodies were rising and falling together in another climax that made his mind spin.

Before his body had quieted, he wanted her again, and began a new, slower rhythm. He clasped her hands over her head and looked into her eyes while he moved inside her. She came apart in his arms, but

still he claimed her, pumping into her until she succumbed a second time...then a third. Finally he took
his own shattering release, clenching his muscles
hard before falling exhausted on her breasts.

Kendall dressed as quietly as he could so as not to
disturb Amy. He moved quickly because the sun was
rising and he needed to get out of the boardinghouse
before anyone saw him. It was Saturday morning,
so everyone would be sleeping in a little later than
usual, but he didn't want to push his luck.

He opened the door a few inches. When he
thought the coast was clear, he opened the door and
stepped out into the hall.

Directly in front of Tony, who was dressed and
headed toward Amy's room.

Kendall froze and watched helplessly as Tony
looked back and forth between his mother's door
and Kendall. Suddenly his expression morphed from
confusion to clarity.

"You slept with my mom?" Tony cried.

Kendall lifted his hands. "Tony, let me explain."
But words failed him.

Amy's door swung open and she stood there in
her robe, her hair disheveled. She took one look at
Tony and her eyes closed. "Oh, no."

"You slept with my mom!" Tony yelled, going
after Kendall with his fists like a windmill. "You
disrespected her!"

Kendall let the boy pummel him, then he caught

his fists. "Okay, settle down. Let's talk about this without disturbing the entire house."

"I don't want to talk to you!" Tony said, pushing away. He was crying now. "All your dumb talk about responsibility and being a man. You weren't being responsible when you got my mother pregnant, and you're not being responsible now! You're a hypocrite!"

Doors were opening and people were coming out into the hall.

"Kendall, you need to leave," Amy said. Tears streamed down her cheeks. "Now."

"Let's talk about this, like a family," he said.

Amy looked at him, shaking her head. "That's the point, Kendall. We're not your family."

He clasped her arm. "Amy, I don't want to leave."

"Leave my mother alone!" Tony shouted, and started punching Kendall for all he was worth. "Get your hands off her!"

Kendall put his hands up and backed away. "Okay, I'm leaving." He spoke to people he passed in the hallway. "Sorry for the disturbance, folks."

He exited the boardinghouse feeling like the world's biggest ass...and the world's worst father. He would never forget the look on his son's face when he realized what Kendall had done, what Kendall had taken. Tony was right—he was a hypocrite.

It was admirable that the boy was so protective of his mother.

And it was shameful that of the two guys in Amy's life, Tony was the bigger man.

28

Amy felt the condemning stares of the women standing in the hallway of the boardinghouse. A choking sense of déjà vu washed over her. She was back in Sweetness, and being judged. Everyone knew everyone else's business, things hadn't changed at all.

"What are you looking at?" Tony shouted at them, putting out his arms to shield her.

They hid their children's eyes and pulled them back into their rooms. Amy lifted a hand to her wild rat's nest of red hair and pulled her robe closer around her. Mortified, she clasped Tony by the shirt-sleeve and tugged him into her room.

She closed the door, then panicked all over again by the disarray—her gown, her underwear, condom wrappers. She turned Tony toward the bathroom and marched him inside. "Stay in there until I tell you to come out. I'm going to get dressed."

When the door closed she took a deep, cleansing breath and held it until her eyes watered, then exhaled, shaking.

This was bad. Her behavior went against everything she'd tried to teach him about intimate relationships between men and women. Heaped on top of his raw emotional state, it could be traumatizing. What had she been thinking to allow Kendall to stay the night?

She hadn't been thinking, of course, only feeling…

To hide the disheveled, tangled sheets, she hurriedly made the bed and fluffed the pillows that clearly held the imprints of two occupants. She collected her undies and gown and tossed them in the hamper in the closet, then pulled on jeans, a shirt and sneakers in case Tony ran and she had to go after him. She wound up her unruly hair and secured it with a clip. The condom wrappers went to the bottom of the trash can, where her mind raced for the best way to handle this debacle.

She decided she'd have to fall back on what she'd always resorted to when it came to parenting Tony—instinct.

She'd have to wing it.

When the room was back in some semblance of order, she knocked on the bathroom door. "Tony? Can I come in?"

"Whatever."

She opened the door and found him sitting in the bathtub, his head on his knees. She climbed in to sit opposite him. Her heart broke for him—he deserved so much better than two parents who couldn't get it right.

After a few minutes of silence, she sighed. "I can't imagine how confused you must be. Adults do stupid things sometimes, things even we don't understand. Kids can't be expected to figure it out."

"I hate him," he mumbled.

Her heart gushed. "Don't hate him, Tony. I'm as much at fault as he is...actually, more, because it's my job to protect you."

He lifted his head. "I thought that was a father's job, too."

"The way he sees it, he *is* protecting you. He's trying to convince me to stay in Sweetness so he can be near you."

"So why doesn't he just marry you?"

She smiled. "Because he doesn't feel that way about me."

"He wants to have sex with you, but he doesn't want to marry you?"

She took her time answering. "Sometimes that goes both ways between men and women."

"You mean you wouldn't marry him, even if he asked?"

Her chest ached. "That's right. Your father's home is here in Sweetness, where it's always been. The reason I left twelve years ago and didn't tell him I was pregnant with you was because I didn't want to live here. And that hasn't changed."

"So why did you come back?"

"His brother Marcus found out about you. Marcus asked me to come here to build the covered bridge to give me the chance to tell Kendall myself." She gave him a pointed look. "But before I could tell him, you showed up."

He picked at a seam on his jeans. "So...I was an accident?"

She reached forward to comb the hair that had grown long since he'd arrived out of his blue eyes. "The best accident in the whole world." She lifted his chin. "I wouldn't trade you for anything, don't you know that?"

"I'm a lot of trouble."

"Yeah...but you're worth it."

He lifted his hand to chew on his nails. "So now what?"

"We still have a plan. I have to finish the covered bridge and you have to finish school. We'll go back home to Broadway, and we'll work out something with your dad so the two of you can see each other as often as you want to see him."

He scowled. "I don't want to see him anymore— here or when we get home."

He didn't really mean that. "Seeing him while you're here isn't an option. You're still working off your fine, remember?"

He looked down. "I remember."

"And today's Saturday, so he'll be expecting you to spend the day with him."

"I guess." He was picking at the jeans seam again.

"Something else on your mind?" she asked.

"Is it his muscles?"

"What do you mean?"

"Is that why you want to have sex with him?"

She pulled back. "That's an inappropriate question, young man."

He shrugged. "I'm just asking because you've never had any other boyfriend. I thought maybe it was his muscles."

Amy leaned her chin on her hand and sighed. She supposed it was as good an explanation as any as to why her heart couldn't break free of Kendall Armstrong.

After the scene at Amy's room that morning, Kendall was uncertain about coming back to pick up Tony for their usual Saturday of work, dinner on the grill and a sleepover at the bunkhouse. But when he pulled up in his pickup at their regular meet time, Tony was standing out front, with Amy.

Kendall's stomach clenched. He'd hated to leave Amy alone to deal with the aftermath of such an awkward situation. It was his fault—he was the one who couldn't keep his hands off of her.

A couple of women and their children exited the boardinghouse and cast a wary glance at Amy and Tony before veering in another direction. Kendall flashed back to the way some girls in high school had treated Amy because she didn't have the nicest clothes and because she'd spent more than her fair share of time in the principal's office.

His gut pinched. Amy was already leery of living in a small town. And now he'd single-handedly ruined her reputation among the women in the boardinghouse.

He emerged from his truck as Amy made her way toward him. Tony stayed behind, shuffling foot to foot. It made Kendall ill to know he was responsible for the pinched look on her pretty face, that, in fact, he'd been responsible for most of the trouble in her life. All because he hadn't scooped her up twelve years ago when he'd had the chance, when she'd still had a light in her eyes for him.

If he had, everything would've been different. Tony would've had a father and he would've had a son. Amy's life would've been infinitely easier.

And he would've had Amy.

His biggest mistake, he now realized, was giving her the time and space to learn how to live—and thrive—without him. She didn't need him. She'd done just fine without him. Other than the great sex, there was no reason for her to be with him. And he knew she could get that anywhere if she were inclined—although the thought of another man in her bed made him sick to his stomach.

Now he'd bungled things so badly, he wasn't sure where things stood with her, or with Tony. Last night his son had called him "Dad" for the first time, and this morning he'd totally blown it. He was sure he'd blown his chance with Amy, too.

"Hi," she said, offering the tiniest and briefest smile.

"Hi. How bad was it?"

"Not good," she confirmed. "But Tony and I talked and things are marginally better. I have to warn you, though, he didn't want to see you today."

That hurt. "I understand."

"But he knows he has a responsibility to work off the fine. Try to get him to talk, and answer his questions as honestly as you can." She gave him a rueful smile. "I have a feeling he'll have more questions for you than he had for me."

"Okay," he said, suddenly nervous.

"Just remember—you're still his father. Don't let him disrespect you."

His admiration for Amy rose even higher. She handled the boy well…and him, too, he realized. She started to walk away, but he put his hand on her arm. "Amy."

She turned back.

He swallowed hard. "How are *we?*"

She gave him a sad little smile. "We're the same, Kendall."

Remorse washed over him as she walked away. But he had to put on a good face for Tony, who walked over and climbed in the truck without saying anything. The way he slammed the door, though, spoke volumes.

"I guess I deserve that," Kendall offered. "Do you want to talk about what happened this morning?"

"No," Tony said, his voice belligerent.

"Fair enough. If you change your mind, let me know." He put the truck in gear. "I thought we'd give your uncle Porter a hand today. He's on the land out past the covered bridge clearing off a spot where we're going to build a laboratory."

Tony's eyebrows furrowed. "What kind of laboratory?"

Kendall checked the rearview mirror, then pulled away. "A scientist wants to come to Sweetness to study kudzu."

"What's that?"

"It's a vine that grows over things—trees, houses, anything in its path if it's allowed to get out of control." He pointed to a copse of trees on the side of the road that had been consumed. "That's kudzu. Down here we call it the mile-a-minute vine because it seems to grow that quickly."

He could tell Tony was interested even though he didn't want to be. "Does the scientist want to figure out how to kill it?"

"No. He thinks it might have some medicinal uses, maybe even cure diseases. And we have a lot of it, so he's putting his laboratory here."

Tony pursed his mouth. "I *like* Uncle Porter."

Kendall didn't miss the indirect dig at his own likability. "He likes you, too."

He drove slowly, relatively sure that Tony had

more to say if he gave him a chance to say it. After a few minutes of sullen silence, the boy began to chew on his nails.

"What you did with my mom was wrong," Tony said finally. "You're not married."

So Amy had impressed upon him the fact that sex was best reserved for marriage. And he'd destroyed that lesson with his irresponsible behavior. "You're right, what I did was wrong. But don't think I don't have feelings for your mother, because I do."

"But that's not enough," he said, sounding wise beyond his years. "I mean, sex is important, isn't it?"

Kendall took a deep breath—this was even harder than he thought it was going to be. "Yes, sex is very important, and very private. You shouldn't have sex with someone unless you really care about them, and only if they feel the same way. And you should always use protection. Do you know what that is?"

He nodded. "Mom told me about condoms. I guess if you'd used one, I wouldn't be here."

Man, the kid didn't pull any punches. "Maybe you would've just been born later, that's all."

"You mean, you and Mom might've gotten married?"

"Maybe."

"She said she wouldn't marry you even if you asked."

Kendall's stomach pitched. "She told you that, huh?"

"Yup."

The sun seemed to dim a little. "So you and your mom, you talk about everything?"

He nodded. "She calls it an 'open-door' policy."

"That's good." Kendall marveled that Amy had been so wise to parenting considering she'd gotten so little of it herself. "So, you know all about sex?"

Tony shrugged. "I haven't done it, if that's what you want to know."

Kendall exhaled. "That's…good. You should wait until you're much older."

"How old were you?"

Kendall pulled the collar of his shirt away from his suddenly too-warm neck. He didn't remember having this particular talk with his father. Growing up in the country, there were always plenty of animal couplings to observe and glean the fundamentals. In hindsight, Marcus and Porter—who'd always been ahead of his years in that department—had filled in the blanks. It was a benefit, or perhaps a detriment, of having brothers. "I was…much older than you."

"Was it with my mom?"

He hesitated, not sure how much to disclose. He wished Amy was nearby to consult or step in. *Answer his questions as honestly as you can.* "As a matter of fact, it was."

"So, are you going to keep having sex with her?"

Jesus, the kid was blunt. "That's between me and your mother."

Tony averted his gaze and lifted his hand to chew on his nails. Kendall was sure he'd asked because he was trying to figure out his parents' relationship and where he fit in.

Kendall was still trying to figure that out, too.

29

If Amy had forgotten what it was like to be the topic of gossip in a small town, she was getting a primer. She noticed the questioning glances of workers on the jobsite, and the whisper of women in the boardinghouse and imagined what was being said behind her back.

She grew up here, got knocked up and moved away. Came back with boss's secret baby. No wonder she got the job. Sleeping with the boss, too, in front of her son. What kind of mother would do that?

But with only one week to go, she could bear it. The best part about waking up in Sweetness this morning was knowing she didn't have to stay. As the days ticked down, she found herself more and more antsy to leave. Tony was, too, she could tell. He was on edge, cranky and sullen, his nails bitten down to the quick…especially after spending time with his father.

A candy wrapper crackled in her jacket and she sighed. Tony nibbled on his nails while she nibbled on chocolate, both biding their time until they could go home.

Home.

Sometimes she felt as if home was anywhere but here.

A white van pulled onto the jobsite. Nikki climbed out, then made her way over to where Amy stood near the east portal of the covered bridge watching shingles being nailed to the roof. Down below workers were spraying a coat of barn-red paint to the exterior walls. Amy walked away from the noise to meet Nikki halfway.

"Wow, your bridge is absolutely amazing," Nikki said, surveying the large structure that was mere days away from being finished.

Amy laughed. "It's not *my* bridge, but thank you."

"I've seen pictures of the original Evermore Bridge. It looks very similar."

"It is similar, except for the pedestrian walkway," Amy said, gesturing to the structure running along the side.

"And it's stronger, I assume."

"Yes, much stronger," Amy assured her. "What brings you out in the middle of the afternoon?"

"I'm supposed to meet Porter here to greet the scientist who's coming to scout the location for his lab."

"That sounds like the kind of project that could bring a lot of attention to the town. Will you be involved?"

"If and when he needs a medical doctor's input, I'll make myself available. Me, or Dr. Cross."

"Is Dr. Cross from Broadway?"

Nikki nodded. "By way of England, of course. We used to work together at a family practice in Broadway."

"And how is he acclimating?"

"Amazingly well. He's a modern physician, but he's fascinated by old mountain remedies. There's a man here, Riley Bates, who's been teaching him everything he knows." Then she leaned in. "Between you and me, though, I think he's more fascinated by Rachel Hutchins."

Amy laughed. "I noticed that myself. But they seem like an unlikely match." Especially since she suspected Kendall and Rachel would pick up where they left off as soon as she left town.

Nikki nodded. "But stranger things have happened." She pressed her lips together and Amy had a feeling Nikki was beating around the bush about something. "Uh, Amy...I know this isn't the time or place, but I've been hoping to run into you since the, um, incident that happened last weekend at the boardinghouse."

Amy's cheeks warmed. "You mean Tony catching Kendall leaving my bedroom and freaking out?"

"I heard a rumor...or two."

"I'll bet you did. We had quite an audience."

"Look, if people have been unkind, please just ignore it. They don't know you. Porter spent more than one night with me in my room before the children arrived. Since then, everyone's been more strict about the no-sleepover rules."

"As they should be," Amy said. "It was all my fault."

Nikki's eyebrow arched. "You dragged Kendall inside and made him spend the night?"

"No, but I had more to lose than he did, so I should've hit the stop button." She shook her head. "You'd think I would've learned that by now. But when it comes to Kendall, I seem to have a blind spot for trouble."

"It's those blue Armstrong eyes," Nikki said with a rueful smile. "They're hypnotizing." She angled her head. "So, I don't mean to pry, but how are things between the two of you now?"

Amy shrugged. "We're keeping our distance, trying to make things as smooth as possible for Tony until he and I leave."

"And afterward?"

She sighed. "I don't know. I'd assumed that Kendall and Tony would see each other, but they're not getting along at all. Kendall is pushing him on the work thing, trying to teach him a lesson. Tony told me again last night that he doesn't want to see Kendall after we go home. I know it's going to be a fight because Kendall won't accept that."

"Armstrong father versus Armstrong son. I guess it's inevitable that they clash, especially at Tony's age."

"You're so right. I've spent all these years wondering when would be the right time to tell him about his father, and as it turned out, my timing couldn't have been worse."

"I understand *you* didn't pick the time at all, that Marcus made that decision for you."

She nodded. "But I can't blame Marcus for this mess. His allegiance is to Kendall. He was only doing what he thought was best for his brother."

The sound of another vehicle arriving caught their attention.

"There's Porter now," Nikki said.

Porter climbed out of the driver's seat. A rear door opened and Kendall appeared. Amy's heart betrayed her and started thumping against her ribs.

"I didn't know Kendall was going to be here," Nikki said.

"No worries," Amy said breezily.

Another door opened and another man, presumably the scientist, emerged. Amy arched an eyebrow.

The man was over six feet tall, as broad and buff as an underwear model, with chiseled features, a real tan, an Italian suit and a headful of white-blond hair.

The man was…perfection.

"Wow, he doesn't look like any scientist I've ever seen," she said to Nikki, who seemed equally as stunned. The closer the man came to them, the better-looking he got. He smiled at something one of the men said and went from beautiful to gorgeous.

"It's like looking at the sun," Nikki murmured.

Porter sidled up to Nikki and whispered. "Your mouth is open, baby."

"Is it?" she murmured back, unable to take her eyes off their visitor.

Amy smiled—a little jealousy might get Porter moving on that proposal Nikki seemed to think was forthcoming. She met Kendall's gaze and acknowledged him with a nod. He returned the favor.

"Ladies," Porter said, "meet Dr. Barry Devine."

"Devine?" Nikki asked, her voice high. "How… unusual."

Porter frowned. "Dr. Devine, this is my *girlfriend,* Dr. Nikki Salinger."

Dr. Devine smiled at Nikki, his eyes mischievous. "Charmed. So you're not married yet?"

She put out her hand and he lifted it for a kiss. "N-no," Nikki stammered.

Amy swallowed a smile as Porter's jaw hardened. "And this is Amy Bradshaw," he said, his voice vibrating with irritation. "Amy's the engineer who designed this fantastic bridge."

Dr. Devine turned the full force of his affable smile on her. "This town is full of beautiful, talented women," he said, also bussing the hand she offered.

"Thank you," she said, annoyed with herself for not responding more to the man's charm, especially since she felt Kendall's gaze on her throughout. But she couldn't help compare the two men and, despite Dr. Devine's height, he fell short of the rugged man next to him.

"Your lab will be up on that ridge," Porter said, pointing.

Dr. Devine looked up, then back to Amy. "So this lovely bridge will be my view. Wonderful. Red is my favorite color."

He might've been talking about the painted bridge, but he was looking at her hair. She had to laugh at his outrageousness. "Only the bridge will be here, Dr. Devine. I'll be leaving after the ribbon-cutting ceremony next weekend."

"I'll be here through next weekend," he said. "I'm preparing a paper to present to an engineering conference next month about the effects of kudzu on static structures. Perhaps I could pick your brain."

The man was smooth. "I'm sorry, but I'm going to be swamped this week with inspections. Kendall is an engineer—I'm sure he'll be glad to help."

"Oh…of course," the doctor said.

She wasn't sure who looked less enthusiastic about the idea—Dr. Devine or Kendall.

Porter clapped his hands. "Okay, what do you say we go take a look at the property I staked off?" He smiled at Nikki. "*Darling,* if you'd rather stay here and visit with Amy, I understand."

"Don't be silly, *pumpkin,*" she said sweetly, tucking her hand into their guest's arm. "I'm looking forward to hearing more about Dr. Devine's research."

Porter frowned as they walked away.

"Actually, Porter, I think I'll stay," Kendall said,

clapping Porter on the shoulder. "You're on your own. Good luck."

"Thanks a lot," Porter muttered, but hurried after the couple when Nikki laughed at something Dr. Devine said.

Amy laughed into her hand as she watched them leave.

"I think that guy's going to keep Porter on his toes," Kendall said.

"Porter doesn't have anything to worry about," Amy said. "That woman is head over heels in love with him. He just needs to make it official." When she realized what she'd said smacked of the reason their own romance had ended, her smile dissolved. "But that's between Porter and Nikki."

He nodded, then turned to look at the covered bridge. "It's really something, Amy. No one else could've done it justice."

"Thank you," she said, tingling under his praise. "But something tells me you didn't come by to admire the bridge."

He wiped his hand over his mouth. "I want to talk to you about Tony."

She glanced around to make sure they were alone, noticing but ignoring the elbow-pokes and sly smiles that passed among the workers. *Only seven more days*.

"I'm listening," she said.

"I'd hoped things would get better since last weekend, but they seem to be getting worse. He doesn't talk, he defies everything I say. He's impossible."

"He told me you've been working him too hard," she offered.

He threw up his hands. "That's ridiculous! If anything, I've been easy on him this week because I feel so damn guilty about what happened."

She gave him a little smile. "Welcome to parenting."

His mouth tightened. "Are you enjoying this? Watching me struggle with my son?"

Her earlier fears that Tony would prefer Kendall and the Armstrongs to her flitted through her mind.

He looked incredulous. "You *are* enjoying this, aren't you?"

"No, Kendall. How could I enjoy a situation that isn't good for Tony?"

"Maybe because you think it'll be less trouble in the long run if I'm not involved with my son. Let's face it, if Marcus hadn't found out about Tony and forced your hand, I would've never found out about him, would I?"

Amy crossed her arms. "I honestly don't know. I did plan to contact you if Tony ever asked me to, or if he asked for your name."

His eyes went dark. "So you say."

Her heartbeat stuttered. They were back to square one. She glanced around, knowing they were starting to attract even more attention from the workers.

"Okay, just hear me out," Kendall said, his voice

calmer. "We need sidewalks, and you said it's what you do best. Would you be willing to stay on to manage that project to give me more time with Tony?"

She bit her lip, panicked at the idea of spending more time in this place—more time around Kendall—when she was so close to escaping. On the other hand, she didn't have any big projects to hurry back to. She'd have to start canvassing for freelance work as soon as she returned. Desperation pulled at her.

In her pocket, her phone vibrated. Happy for the diversion, she pulled it out to see the name Michael Thoms on the screen. It took her a few seconds for the association to click—the reservoir project.

Her pulse rocketed. She could use a timely miracle.

"Excuse me, I need to take this," she said to Kendall, then stepped away and connected the call. "Amy Bradshaw."

"Amy. Michael Thoms from the Greater Michigan Water Commission."

"Hello, Mr. Thoms. What can I do for you?"

"Tell me you're still interested in managing the Peninsula Reservoir project."

She suppressed a squeal. "Yes, I'm still interested. Did something change?"

"The first applicant didn't work out, so we're looking for a new project manager. I'm making preliminary calls on behalf of the search committee to check availability."

"I could start in one week," she said.

"I'll make a note of it. Meanwhile, if you've completed recent projects you'd like for us to know about, you can email me an updated resume."

Amy glanced up at the covered bridge looming over her, doubtful that anyone else being considered would have such a unique project on their resume. "Yes, I'll do that right away, thank you."

"I'll be in touch soon," he said.

Amy disconnected the call and pumped her fist.

"Good news?" Kendall asked mildly, as if to remind her he was still there.

"Very. The project manager position over the reservoir project I mentioned earlier is available again."

"And you're back in the running?"

She nodded. "It would be a great job for me to spend time with Tony—good hours and an easy commute."

He gave her a flat smile. "Sounds…ideal."

Except she feared if she took Tony away while things between Tony and Kendall were unresolved, once they returned to Michigan, Tony would act out even more.

"I'll talk to Tony about his attitude," she said. "But I can't make any promises."

"If you're offered the job, can you postpone your start date and stay a few more weeks, to give me and Tony a chance to connect?"

So she could be tortured every day by Kendall's presence? And there was no guarantee that Tony would warm up to him, no matter how long they stayed. Actually, some distance might improve their relationship. "I'm sorry, but I can't. I have to get home."

His mouth twitched downward at her mention of the word *home*. "Then would you consider leaving him with me for a while?" he asked.

"No," she said bluntly. She knew her son well enough to know that would alienate him—from them both.

"You're not leaving me very many choices here," he said quietly.

She gave him a little smile. "I'm sorry, because I know what that's like." She let her words settle in, then she gestured to the bridge. "I need to get back to work. I have a lot to do before I leave this place for good."

His jaw hardened and his eyes impeached her.

With her heart languishing in her chest, Amy turned and drank in the splendid lines of Evermore Bridge, knowing that when the project ended, she'd have an emotional bridge to cross, too.

30

Kendall tried to concentrate on the spreadsheet on his laptop screen, but his mind kept wandering to—as usual—Amy. Had a day passed in the past twelve years that he hadn't thought about her?

He pushed to his feet and paced the construction office, trying to work off nervous energy. His mind and heart raced and he hadn't slept well in days.

A two-year calendar crawled around the office walls. On it, Marcus had circled the federal deadline with a red marker. But Kendall was focused on another date, three days from now—the date that Amy was planning to leave Sweetness and take his son with her. The ribbon-cutting ceremony for the bridge was Saturday afternoon. She and Tony were leaving Sunday morning.

Time was running out.

He glanced at the black chalkboard next to the door that read "Sweetness Population, 536." He wanted so much to officially bump that number by two, for Amy and Tony to be here and become part of the community. Maybe she could learn to love him again and they would have a chance to be a family.

Kendall leaned over to grip the sides of the desk. He was accustomed to being able to mediate situations, but not only did this one seem beyond his capabilities, everything he did made things worse. Losing Amy again alone was bad enough, but losing Tony, too—he didn't think he could stand it, even if the boy had made it clear he didn't want to be around him. Kendall tightened his hold on the desk until the wood bit into his hands, feeling very close to losing control.

A sharp rap on the door made him straighten. "Come in," he called, trying to rein in his emotions.

The door opened and Dr. Cross stood there. "A word, Mr. Armstrong?"

Kendall closed his eyes briefly, but he felt like hitting something—maybe this was a fortuitous visit. "If you're spoiling for another fight, Doc, then you came to the right place."

The man stabbed at his glasses, which Kendall now noticed had been taped at the bridge. "I don't want to fight you again, Mr. Armstrong. I came to ask your advice."

Kendall squinted. "Is that a shiner?"

The man looked miserable and lifted a hand to his black eye. "Yes. Rachel has many talents, including an impressive right hook."

Kendall sighed, then gestured. "Come on in."

The doctor entered the trailer, closing the door behind him. "Thank you."

"What can I do for you, Doc?"

"I was hoping you could tell me how I might woo Ms. Hutchins."

"Woo?"

"Yes. What did you do to attract her interest?"

Kendall lifted his hands. "I don't know...I...was nice to her, I guess."

"I've tried to be nice to her, but as you can see," he said, removing his glasses to reveal the swollen eye, "she doesn't respond positively to my niceness. And now that grotesquely deformed Dr. Devine seems to have captured her attention."

Kendall surveyed the short, slender man, feeling a wave of sympathy for him. "Yes, I've met Dr. Devine."

Cross snorted. "He's not a real doctor, you know—not a physician. He's an academic."

"Yeah, well, I suspect the title doesn't have as much to do with it as..." He trailed off, perusing the man's thin frame and pale countenance.

The man jammed his glasses back on his face. "What?"

Kendall pursed his mouth. "Maybe he's handy."

"Pardon me?"

"Women love a handy man, you know, a guy who can fix things."

"I'm handy. I fix people."

"Uh, right. Well, I mean things around the house.

You know, things that let you use tools and flex your mus—" He stopped, again surveying the man, who probably couldn't lift Kendall's tool belt. Then he had an idea and snapped his fingers.

"I happen to know Rachel has a hole in her bedroom wall that needs to be patched. I'll bet if you offered to fix it for her, she'd take you up on it. Then she could see how handy you are."

"Her bedroom?" The doctor's eyes lit up, then his shoulders fell. "But I don't know how to do that."

"I'll teach you," Kendall said. He went over to a supply closet and rummaged for a container of spackle and a putty knife. Then he scanned the office walls for a good place to demonstrate, settling on the closet exterior wall. Picturing his own face as the target, he took aim, then rammed his fist into the drywall with a grunt, leaving a dent.

"Well done, Mr. Armstrong. How is your hand?"

"You don't know how good that felt," Kendall muttered, flexing his fingers. "Okay, so to patch the hole, all you do is dip the putty knife into the spackle, dab it into the hole, then smooth it over in one swipe." He demonstrated, then stood back. "See?"

"It's a bit like wound filler," Dr. Cross noted, then smiled. "During residency, I did a rotation with a medical examiner."

"Er…okay." The office phone rang. Kendall wondered fleetingly if it was the results of the D.O.E.

report they were still waiting for. "Excuse me." He picked up the receiver. "Kendall Armstrong."

"Mr. Armstrong, my name is Michael Thoms, calling on behalf of the Greater Michigan Water Commission. I'd like to speak with someone about the engineer on the Evermore Bridge project, Ms. Amy Bradshaw."

Kendall frowned. "What kind of information do you need?"

"General feedback on Ms. Bradshaw's performance. She's being considered for the managing position on a sizable municipal project. We're just performing due diligence with former employers."

Kendall's mind churned. The man was asking for an endorsement that would ensure he would be separated from Amy and Tony.

"I should add, of course, that your comments will be confidential. Ms. Bradshaw won't know what was said about her or her performance."

"Mr. Thoms, I'm afraid I'm in the middle of something right now. Can I get back to you?" After a few moments more conversation, Kendall took down the man's contact information, then replaced the receiver.

"Bad news, Mr. Armstrong?"

He looked up at Dr. Cross. "I'm sorry?"

"I don't mean to intrude, but Dr. Salinger mentioned you're waiting for a government report that could be a setback for our fair town. I hope that wasn't the call."

"No, it wasn't," Kendall said, coming around the desk.

"Are you okay, Mr. Armstrong? You look distressed."

"I'm fine." Maybe if he kept saying he was fine, he would be. "Where were we? Oh, right." He rammed his fist into the wall again, relishing the flash of pain.

"Well done again, Mr. Armstrong. Shall I try to patch the hole this time?"

"Go for it."

"Ah, the things men will do to win a woman's love," Dr. Cross said, tackling the hole with gusto.

Kendall nursed his hand, which still didn't hurt as much as his heart. "You said it, Doc."

A few minutes later, armed with a bucket of spackle, a putty knife and newfound confidence as a handy man, Dr. Cross left smiling. "Thank you, Mr. Armstrong, for the advice."

Kendall waved and closed the door, thinking he could use some advice himself. Porter was too busy making sure Dr. Devine kept his distance from Nikki, and Marcus…well, he thought the world of his brother, but Marcus had never been in love, and didn't understand matters of the heart.

But he knew someone who did.

He reached for the phone to make a long overdue call. After a few rings, an angelic voice came on the line.

"Hello?"

"Hi, Mom, it's Kendall."

"Oh, hello, dear. How's my favorite boy?"

He smiled into the phone. He happened to know that Emily Armstrong called all three of her sons her favorite. "I'm fine."

"Are you?" she asked, her voice shaded with concern. "You haven't sounded like yourself lately... and I can't remember the last time you called. Your brothers have been making excuses for you, but I know something's amiss."

He gave a rueful laugh. Mothers held the weight of the world on their shoulders. "You're right, Mom, as always." He sighed. "I really messed up."

"I'm listening."

"Do you remember Amy Bradshaw?"

"Of course I remember Amy. She was a lovely girl, and you were so smitten with her."

"Yes, I was," he admitted. "She's a structural engineer now, and she's back in Sweetness rebuilding the Evermore Bridge."

"That's wonderful for the town, and for Amy. It sounds as if she's done well for herself."

"She has."

"Is she single?"

"She is...and she has a child." He wet his lips. "My child."

He knew what was going through his mother's mind. Of her three sons, she least expected Kendall, the even-keeled, levelheaded one, to father a child out of wedlock. "You didn't know?"

"No."

"How old is the child? Is it a boy or a girl? Is it healthy?"

He smiled. "I have a son. He's twelve years old, and yes, he's healthy, if a little moody."

"Sweetheart, even you, my best child, were moody at that age. What's his name?"

"Anthony Alton. He goes by Tony."

She was quiet for a while, then said, "That was kind of Amy to name him after your father. Is the boy like you?"

"Maybe too much. I'm not his favorite person right now."

"And how is the situation between you and Amy?"

Kendall massaged the bridge of his nose. "I'm not Amy's favorite person, either. I know now why I never heard from her again. She hasn't forgiven me for not taking her away from here. She hated this town."

"She had a rough go of it, poor girl. So there are no feelings left between the two of you?"

"I wouldn't say that," he said carefully. "I've asked her to stay so we can try to work things out, but she doesn't want to live here, and I can't leave because of the commitment I made to Marcus and Porter." He sighed. "Meanwhile, I'm in the position of doing something that would force her to stay here for a while, and I don't know what to do." He told her about the job offer waiting for Amy in Broadway, and how much he desperately wanted to spend more time with Tony.

"So you want my opinion on whether the end justifies the means."

"I suppose."

"Kendall, darling, do you love her?"

Leave it to his mother to get straight to the point. "Yes."

"Are you sure? Because if you really love someone, you put their needs before your own. Just like Amy did for that baby when she left Sweetness. Her life would've been simpler if she'd stayed, but she obviously felt strongly about not raising her child there, about getting out and making something of herself to build a life for the two of them."

Kendall swallowed hard. He'd assumed that Tony's life would've been better if he'd been involved from the start. Amy's, too. But what if that wasn't true? What if they truly were better off without him?

"Are you there, dear?"

"Yeah, just thinking, Mom."

"Thinking is good. You're more like your father than your brothers. Alton was a thinking man, too. Everything will be fine, dear, even if it isn't fine. Do you understand?"

"Yes, ma'am." Things and people couldn't always be neat and well-ordered the way he liked them. Yeah, he got it.

"Good. Now, when do I get to meet my grandson?"

31

Amy turned in the mirror to check her appearance—a brown skirt suit, pink blouse and high-heeled leather boots in deference to the more chilly temperatures that had descended the past couple of days. It was typical spring weather in the North Georgia mountains, too-chilly one day, too-warm the next. The humidity was lower today, so she hoped her blown-out, ironed-down hairstyle would last through the picture-taking.

She'd been to lots of ribbon-cutting ceremonies, but she had to admit, none of them had ever been as personal as this one. She'd never been so proud of a project…and never before had the end of a project signaled the end of a phase of her life, and the beginning of a new one.

She moved and something crackled in her pocket. She withdrew the letter she'd received by express mail—the postmaster at the window inside the General Store had been atwitter about the arrival of the town's first time-sensitive letter. It was the formal offer of the project manager position of the Peninsula Reservoir repair, the position she had accepted verbally two days ago.

Good money, great hours, job security.

She walked over to her bedroom window and looked down on the only street of the almost-town of Sweetness. So why did the idea of creating sidewalks for this place suddenly seem more appealing than the job she'd jumped through hoops to get?

A knock sounded. She pushed the letter back into her jacket pocket and walked over to open the door. Tony stood there, dressed in the nicest clothes he had with him—his school uniform.

He walked inside, holding up a striped tie. "I wasn't at the stupid school long enough to learn how to tie this thing."

She smiled. "You don't have to wear a tie."

"Yeah, I do. This thing today is for you, Mom."

"The ribbon-cutting ceremony is for the bridge and the whole town," she corrected gently, but her chest infused with pleasure as she looped the tie over his neck and tied it. "But thank you. And your grandmother will be impressed to see you wearing a tie."

His brow furrowed. "Will she like me?"

"Like you? I'll have to keep my eye on her to make sure she doesn't spirit you away." She leaned forward to kiss the end of his nose.

He smiled, then he said, "But remember, you can't do that in public."

"Got it."

"Or clean my face."

"Right."

"Or fuss with my hair."

"Okay." She laughed. "You realize your grandmother is going to do all those things, right?"

He shrugged. "Is that what grandmothers do?"

His question stopped her, crowded her heart. When she'd decided not to tell Kendall about his child, she'd deprived Tony of the only grandmother he had, the only uncles.

"Yes," she said, her voice thick. "Grandmothers are required to embarrass you in public."

He looked like he wouldn't mind much. Obviously, he was curious about this grandmother person. "Can we go? Betsy asked me to sit next to her."

Amy lifted an eyebrow. "Betsy?"

"Mom."

"I didn't say anything. I'm almost ready." But as she walked over to the dresser, she knew her days of worrying about him getting his heart broken were numbered. She picked up the gold necklace with the mother-child pendant.

"What's that?" Tony asked.

"It was my mother's," she said, showing it to him. "It's a mother and a baby. It represents her and me, and now, me and you."

"I've never seen you wear it before."

"Betsy helped to find it for me. She works in the Lost and Found warehouse."

"For things that people found after the tornado?"

"Right. Someone came across this necklace and Betsy and Molly traced it back to me." She leaned down. "Will you fasten the clasp for me?"

He nodded and took it in his awkward hands. She was prepared for it to take a while. "You don't talk about your mother," he mumbled.

"That's because I don't remember her."

"Dad, I mean, Kendall, showed me where your parents are buried."

She noticed the slip, but didn't let on. "He's been taking care of the graves."

"Why?"

"Out of respect."

"Got it," he said of the clasp, proud of himself. She wasn't sure if he caught that last part, or just chose to ignore it. Things between him and Kendall continued to be rocky.

She arranged the pendant, then smoothed a hand over her hair. It would have to do.

"You look kind of hot, Mom."

She laughed. "Okay, let's go. We wouldn't want to keep Betsy waiting."

"Mom."

They drove to the bridge site in her SUV and parked alongside the road behind other vehicles, then walked the rest of the way. Folding chairs were lined up in rows in front of the bridge that was draped with a large red bow over the eastern portal. Enormous white tents had been erected over food tables for a celebratory meal after the ceremony. Everyone was dressed up. When Amy caught sight of Kendall in a gray suit, her heart stuttered. He was so handsome, it left her breathless. Regrets flashed through her mind, but she promised herself today would be a day of celebration.

He caught sight of her and waved. Next to him stood Emily Armstrong, as cherubic as ever in a powder-blue coat and hat, if a little more gray-headed. Amy steered Tony in their direction and gave Emily a warm hug.

"So good to see you, my dear," said Emily. "Aren't you a beauty?"

"Thank you, Emily. It's wonderful to see you, too."

Emily then turned her attention to Tony. "And this handsome lad must be my grandson."

"Hi," Tony said awkwardly, and stuck out his hand.

But Emily gathered him up in a bear hug that Amy thought he might never emerge from.

She caught Kendall's gaze over their embrace, could see the moment moved him. When he looked at her, it was if he were asking, "Do you see what he missed out on?"

Amy had to look away. The day was already feeling way too emotional.

When Emily finally released Tony, she tweaked his cheeks and brushed his bangs with her fingers.

"You look so much like your father. Except I don't think he was quite as tall at your age."

"Really?" Tony said, his eyes big.

"Really. I think you're going to be taller."

Amy bit back a smile. Emily couldn't have told him anything to make him happier than that he might grow up to be bigger and stronger than his father.

Emily opened her purse and pulled out a camera. "How about a family photo?"

"I'll take it," Amy offered. She sighted the three of them in the frame and took a couple of shots.

"Now one of Mom and Tony," Kendall suggested, then stood aside while Amy took it.

"And one of Kendall and Tony," Emily suggested, then stood aside while Amy took that one. They didn't touch, and both of them looked wary.

"Will you take one of me and Mom?" Tony asked his grandmother.

"Of course."

Amy handed over the camera, then stood next to Tony and smiled until Emily had taken the shots. Then Emily gestured to Kendall. "Get in with them, son."

Kendall started to protest. "Mom—"

"It's for Tony," Emily said. "A picture of him with his mom and his dad. I can't get you all in the frame, you're going to have to crowd in a little. That's it."

Amy swallowed when Kendall's body came up behind hers. It was as close as they'd been since he left her bed that awful morning in the boardinghouse.

His sandalwood aftershave reached her nostrils. She inhaled him into her lungs.

"You look nice," he whispered in her ear.

"So do you," she whispered back.

"There," Emily said. "Amy, dear, I'll make sure you get a copy of these. Are you and Tony staying in Sweetness for a while, I hope?"

"No," Amy said, putting her hand on Tony's shoulder. "We're heading home tomorrow morning."

"So soon?"

"We were only visiting."

"Mom got a big fancy job," Tony said. "She's building a dam."

Amy smiled. "It's a reservoir…and it's not so fancy, but I'm pleased."

Tony looked up and cupped his hand over his mouth. "Mom, over there's Betsy! Can I go?"

"Yes, but find us again after the ceremony, please."

"Okay."

"Say goodbye to your grandmother."

"Bye, Grandma!" he shouted as he ran off.

Porter and Marcus appeared, also wearing suits, to give their mother hugs and to accept her kisses. But their faces seemed concerned as Marcus handed Kendall a piece of paper.

"The D.O.E. report from Richardson," Marcus said.

"Give me the highlights," Kendall said, taking the paper.

"We passed—barely. But we have to overhaul the cafeteria right away," Porter said. "No one will eat the food. The waste is bankrupting us...and Richardson threatened to bring the Health Department down on our heads."

"We might as well convert it into a diner, like we planned," Kendall said.

Porter scoffed. "Can you see Colonel Molly running a diner?"

"No," Marcus said. "I'm tired of this nonsense. I'll find someone else to take over."

"Remember, the manager of the dining hall is a position designated 'female specific' in our new bylaws," Kendall warned. It was one of the mandates the Broadway women had put in place to ensure key positions in the community didn't become male-dominated, at least not within the first five years of the town's inception.

"So?" Marcus said with a frown. "I'll find someone, a woman who can cook, someone I can work with."

"A woman you can work with?" Porter said. "I have to see this."

"Me, too," Kendall said.

"Me, three," Emily said, giving her eldest a pointed look.

Amy bit back a smile.

Marcus frowned. "Isn't it about time to get this show on the road?" He marched toward the front of the bridge, and Porter followed.

"We have seats for both of you up front," Kendall said.

Emily patted his arm. "Thank you, dear…we're right behind you."

It was Emily's way, Amy noted nervously, of saying she wanted to have some time alone with Amy.

Emily walked slowly through the crowd. "The bridge is beautiful, Amy. You should be so proud."

Amy fell in step next to her. "Thank you, Emily. I am."

"As for Tony, well, I couldn't be more pleased. What a wonderful surprise for our family."

"I'm glad you feel that way."

"Has my son been a bear to deal with?"

"At times," Amy admitted. "Although I'm sure he feels as if he has his reasons to be angry with me."

"My son has committed himself to rebuilding this town on an environmentally friendly platform," Emily said. "But there's nothing on earth more wasteful than anger directed at something that happened in the past. People have to be concerned with 'now' and 'next.'"

Amy nodded as they arrived at the reserved-seats section. "That's a good philosophy."

"One we all should take to heart," Emily said with a pat to Amy's hand as they took their seats.

Amy maintained a tight smile. Emily Armstrong had to be a durable woman to raise the sons that she'd raised, and there was more than enough wisdom in that head of hers to run this entire town. But the reason Amy didn't want to remain in Sweetness was for the precise reason Emily explained—it was impossible to forget the past when you lived in a place that wouldn't let you.

Nikki came by and gave Emily a hug. Apparently, they were friends. She sat on the other side of Porter's mother and they were soon chatting. A news crew from Atlanta was setting up a camera nearby—the Armstrong brothers had secured impressive coverage of the event.

Amy glanced around to locate Tony and found him sitting several rows back, next to Betsy. They were duly ignoring each other. Among the crowd she saw Colonel Molly who looked stoic in her dress Army uniform. Amy wondered if Marcus knew what he was up against, and could only guess at what kind of steel magnolia would be able to take Molly's place. Dr. Devine was still in town. He waved as he sat next to Rachel Hutchins. No surprise, there. They made a stunning couple, her Barbie to his Ken. One row back and studying the golden duo like a hawk was Dr. Cross with—Amy squinted—*two* black eyes?

Several people, including her foremen and so many other workers, came by to congratulate her. Amy reciprocated, surprised at how many of them she knew by name. Women from the boardinghouse, too—another surprise. She was wary, her guard up, watching for people who talked about her behind her back, but were friendly to her face. But she detected no falseness, only genuine appreciation for the work she'd done for the town.

"You certainly know a lot of people to only be visiting," Emily observed.

Amy didn't respond.

"Lovely necklace, by the way," Emily said, nodding to the pendant that Amy didn't realize she was playing with.

"Thank you," Amy said, feeling oddly comforted by the weight of the smooth pendant. She had no reason to be nervous. The Armstrong brothers would be giving the talks and cutting the ribbon. She would, at most, have to stand if introduced.

But the crush of the crowd was getting to her, the congratulatory smiles and the hands pressed against hers. It was too...invasive.

She was glad when Marcus approached the podium and called for everyone to take a seat. He began by talking about the original Evermore Bridge and why it had always been an important landmark in Sweetness. He touched on the devastation of the tornado. Then he explained the reasons they felt it was necessary to rebuild the bridge to connect the land on the other side, as well as mentioned some proposed uses of the land. Dr. Devine was introduced, which triggered much female twittering.

Then Marcus handed the podium over to Kendall.

Her heart stirred to see this side of him, the ambassador for the town. His town.

"When we decided rebuilding Evermore Bridge

was our next priority," Kendall began, "we couldn't think of anyone more appropriate to oversee the design and construction than our very own Amy Bradshaw, who grew up in Sweetness."

Amy's skin tingled as eyes turned in her direction, including Kendall's. She willed him to hurry.

"As you can see, Amy delivered a structure as elegant as the original, but stronger and more functional, while still maintaining the historical integrity of the design. As you walk through the bridge tonight after the ribbon is cut, notice the unpainted timbers on the inside—those timbers are original to the first bridge and represent our commitment to reclaiming pieces of history and using them to make the future stronger." He looked at her and smiled. "Ladies and gentlemen, I'd like to ask Amy Bradshaw to come up for a special presentation by Rachel Hutchins."

Amy's skin prickled from the attention—and the applause. What was this all about?

She walked up, feeling self-conscious, and Rachel appeared, holding a slim package.

"I'll keep this short," Rachel said. "We wanted to give Amy something to remember us by, a little piece of Sweetness to take home with her." She tore off the brown paper wrapping.

It was a framed photograph of the original Evermore Bridge, caught in the full glory of a fall day. How many times had she seen it just this way? So many that even with the new bridge in front of her,

Amy would always remember it like this. She was touched.

"Thank you," she said to Rachel, remorseful for the way she'd treated the woman, suddenly struck by the realization that she'd come back to this place with a chip on her shoulder, expecting to be treated like trashy little Amy Bradshaw. But instead, she'd received nothing but fairness and tolerance.

She looked out over the audience at the rapt faces of the men, women and children. She'd bet her last dollar that every single person who lived in the town was at this gathering, communing with friends and expressing their sense of pride in the endeavor they'd all undertaken…together. She felt humbled. And un-worthy.

Amy blinked back tears and looked to Kendall for help, to save her from losing it in front of everyone.

He must have understood because he stepped back to the microphone. "And while we have Amy up here, we'd like to ask her to do the honors of cutting the ribbon."

Another surprise, but this one she could do be-cause it kept her moving. Marcus handed her a large pair of ceremonial scissors and, on cue, she sliced the ribbon across the portal. Cameras flashed and clicked by the dozens. Cheers went up and the tiny band from the school started playing something lively but unrecognizable. It was, Amy realized, small-town America at its best.

She stood aside as residents flooded the bridge,

all of them eager for a glimpse inside. The dining tents were instantly filled, too. At Marcus's request, she did a brief interview with the news crew to talk about the project. Then she tried to make her way toward where Tony and Emily were eating, but kept getting waylaid by well-wishers.

An hour passed, then another, and dusk began to fall, as well as the temperatures. The crowd began to wane, and Amy found herself alone. She scanned the dissipating crowd for Tony, but she didn't see him.

"He's with Mom," Kendall said behind her, answering her unspoken question.

There went her heart again. Amy turned. "She's good with him."

"Lots of practice," he said.

"You were good up there tonight," she said. "Impressive."

"Porter's better at speaking to a crowd, but I wanted to be the one to talk about you."

"It was all nice," she said, then held up the picture. "Your idea?"

"No. Rachel wanted to do something special."

She was probably eager to get Amy out of town, Amy thought wryly. But if Rachel had a thing for Kendall, she couldn't blame her.

"I have a favor to ask," Amy said.

"Name it."

"I ordered a headstone for my aunt Heddy's grave. When it arrives at the General Store, will you see that it gets set?"

"No problem."

"Thank you." She saw Tony and Emily nearby. "I guess I'd better get Tony and head back. We still have to pack."

"Why don't we take a walk and let them have a little more time together?" He nodded toward the covered bridge. "For old times' sake?"

Amy wavered, then nodded. "For old times' sake."

32

Kendall reached for the framed picture Amy was holding. "Let me carry that." He needed to fill his hands with something so he didn't reach for her.

She let him take it and pushed her hands into her jacket pockets against the cold air. "The camera crew from Atlanta was a nice touch."

"We're hoping it'll bring visitors up here to see the bridge."

They walked under the eastern portal and slowly made their way across the wooden floor treads, now dusty from hundreds of pairs of feet traveling back and forth to explore the solemn structure. The quiet coziness of it was churchlike, almost spiritual. The clean scents of wood and paint enveloped them. Small lights in the ceiling illuminated the intricate truss design and cast a warm glow below. Sprinkled throughout the structure were the unpainted and aged timbers of the original bridge. They were alone, their footsteps echoing as they walked. It was warmer inside because the massive pieces of wood retained the heat they'd absorbed during the day.

He glanced at Amy's lovely profile, wondering what she was thinking. He could tell earlier that the events of the day had gotten to her. He could always tell when she was on the verge of tears. Her bottom lip trembled and her nose twitched. But were they happy tears or sad tears? He'd been away from her too long to read her that well.

"So what do *you* think of the bridge?" he asked.

She smiled. "Is that a trick question? I wouldn't be much of a designer if I said I wasn't pleased with my own design."

"Okay, what do you think of this bridge compared to the old one?"

"I don't think anything is ever as good as the original."

He got the distinct feeling she wasn't talking about bridges anymore. "How can you say that? This bridge is more beautiful than the original and it's stronger."

"Aesthetically and logically, I see that," she said. "I guess I mean a new version is never as grand as the *idea* of the original. I have the old covered bridge so romanticized in my head, I don't think anything could come close to it."

"I know what you mean," he said. "But you can't let the fantasy of the original overshadow the beauty of what's right in front of you."

She stopped and moved to the side under the guise

of examining something on the wall. But he knew that she was aware of every knothole in this structure. She was withdrawing. He leaned the picture against the wall and moved behind her.

"Amy, I know I hurt you all those years ago, and I'm sorry."

Her shoulders started to shake and he realized she was crying.

He touched her arm gingerly. When she didn't pull away, he turned her in his arms, lifted her face to the golden light and caressed away the tears with his thumbs. Then he kissed her. He was always so much better at showing Amy how he felt about her rather than telling her.

He foraged her mouth hungrily, desperate to express how much he needed her. The thought that she could be gone tomorrow increased his intensity. He crushed her body to his, molding her soft curves to his hard frame. Desire whipped through him like an electric current. He pressed her back, into the wall, remembering all the times they'd made love like this in the old bridge. They would tuck into the hidden corners and get as naked as they dared, then slide over each other, timing their release for when an unsuspecting farmer would come lumbering through with a harvest loaded on the back of his truck, sending a vibration through the bridge and their bodies that left them gasping for breath.

He broke the kiss, then drove his hands into her

hair. "Do you remember, baby? Do you remember how good it was? God, I just look at you and want you."

She moaned and undulated into him. "Mmm." Then she froze. "Stop. We can't do this."

He released her, then pulled a hand down his face. His heart and his body were raging. "Amy, I wish I could go back in time and do things differently."

She shook her head. "We can't go back, Kendall."

"But we can start from *this*. We have Tony now, and—"

"I can't, Kendall." Her voice was choked. "I can't let you hurt me anymore. I'm going back home—"

"*This* is your home!"

"No," she said through her tears. "Home is more than the place where you're born, Kendall. I'm going back to my home to forget about you…again."

Hurt reeled through his chest. "You're going to have to deal with me, Amy, because I intend to be a part of Tony's life."

"We'll see," she said.

"No, that's a fact," he said, barely managing to keep his voice level. "I will be with my son!"

Amy hugged herself and started to walk away.

Kendall felt helpless watching her go. Then he spotted the framed photograph. "Wait!" he called. "Your picture."

Amy turned back, but kept walking. "You keep it. I don't want it."

Then she turned and walked out of the bridge and out of his life.

Again.

Amy had managed to dry her tears by the time she reached Tony and Emily, who were walking along the ridge of the creek, looking at rocks.

"Mom, look, Grandma found a real fossil!" He ran over and showed her a red rock with the shell of some ancient (or not so ancient) animal imprinted in it.

"Wow, that's exciting stuff. I'd forgotten that the clay around here is good for forming fossils."

"Grandma said I could come visit her in Calhoun, Georgia."

"Yes, we'll talk about that," Amy said. "Meanwhile, you should go say goodbye to your father."

He frowned. "I don't want to."

Amy tamped down a spike of irritation. "We're leaving early in the morning, and you won't have time to say goodbye then."

"I said I don't want to!" He turned to Emily and gave her a brief hug. "Goodbye, Grandma." Then he took off running down the road toward where their SUV was parked.

Amy looked at Emily and lifted her hands.

"We could hear you arguing," Emily said.

Amy closed her eyes. "Oh. Okay, will you tell Kendall that we're leaving in the morning at seven.

If he's in front of the boardinghouse, I'll make sure he gets to say goodbye to Tony."

"I will," Emily said. "Goodbye, Amy. And good luck."

Amy accepted her warm hug. "When are you going back to Calhoun?"

"Tonight. Marcus is coming by in a few minutes to pick me up."

"I'll make sure Tony calls you often, Emily."

"Thank you, dear."

Amy hurried to the SUV where Tony was waiting, his face sullen. When she climbed in, she said, "Are you sure you don't want to say goodbye to your father?"

"I'm sure."

"Okay. Maybe you'll feel differently in the morning."

33

Between thinking about Kendall and worrying about the trip home, Amy didn't sleep a wink. When daylight began to bleed through the window, she gave up all pretense of trying and got up to take a cold shower to get her awake enough to drive.

Her stomach muscles and her chest ached from crying. All night she'd replayed everything that Kendall had ever said to her…*I need you…I want you…I admire you…we have Tony.*

Not once had he ever told her that he loved her, or made her feel as if she had input into their future plans. Or heaven forbid, suggest that they mold their life around her career or her needs. She realized Kendall's seeming fixation on Sweetness was a big reason she had developed such an aversion to the place. It wasn't so much the town as much as what it represented.

Dominance. Power. Control.

She'd fought hard to be independent, to show her son that with hard work, anything was possible. She wasn't going to be absorbed into Kendall's life, not now. It was his strength that had drawn her to Kendall, but now his strength was driving her away.

She toweled off and dressed in comfortable driving clothes, then packed her toiletries and tucked her robe and gown into her suitcase. She glanced at her watch. They still had a few minutes. She glanced around the room thinking she would miss some aspects of being here.

Kendall.

From the dresser her cell phone rang. She glanced at the caller ID, surprised to see Michael Thoms calling so early on a weekend. She connected the call. "This is Amy."

"Amy, hi, it's Michael Thoms. Sorry to call so early, I thought I'd get your voice mail. I'm going to be out most of this week, so I just wanted to leave a couple of admin items for you to take care of when you get in the office."

She wrote down the names of the people in Human Resources she needed to report to, and where to call to get the copies of the files she needed to bring her up to speed on the project.

"That's it," he said. "I'm looking forward to working with you."

"Same here. I really appreciate the opportunity to show you what I can do."

"Hey, with the glowing report your last employer gave you I was almost afraid not to hire you. The guy told me I'd be an idiot if I didn't snap you up."

She raised an eyebrow. "Really?"

"Yeah. I normally don't tell applicants about their reference comments, but this guy was adamant that I hire you. Armstrong, I think was his name, Kendall Armstrong."

Kendall? "Oh…okay, good to know."

"I'll see you later in the week."

Amy disconnected the call, and sat holding the phone, not sure what to make of Kendall's aggressive recommendation. Maybe it was his way of saving face. He'd asked her to stay in Sweetness but was he secretly hoping she'd leave? Because he realized he didn't want to have a life with her, or because being a father to a belligerent boy was too daunting?

Or both?

Amy puffed out her cheeks. At least she could feel good about her decision to go. When tears threatened, she sniffed them back. There would be plenty of time for crying later. She'd been through this before.

She walked to the window and looked down to find Kendall's black extended-cab pickup sitting there, waiting. Emily had given him the message. Now Amy wished she hadn't offered because no matter what, it meant she had to talk to him again.

She wheeled her suitcases to the door, hoping she'd catch Nikki downstairs to say goodbye. She left her room and quietly made her way down the hall to Tony's. She hoped he'd gotten more sleep than she had, or he'd be cranky all the way home.

She knocked on his door lightly, waited a few seconds and knocked again. When he didn't answer, she made a rueful noise. He'd probably overslept. She tamped down irritation. If they got started a little late, it wasn't the end of the world. It was just that right now, she felt like she couldn't get out of Sweetness fast enough.

She tried the knob and realized it wasn't locked. Chiding his carelessness, she opened the door, knocking again.

"Tony?" she whispered. His room was dark. "Time to get up."

She felt for the light switch and turned it on. He was buried under the covers. "Hey, get up sleepy-head," she said, giving him a poke.

But she didn't hit flesh—only fluff. She flung back the covers to discover his bed had been stuffed with pillows. "Tony?"

She ran for the bathroom. It was empty. She yanked open the closet door to look for his back-pack, but his closet was empty, and his backpack was gone.

Tony was gone.

Frantic, she ran back to the door, then saw the note taped to it.

Mom, don't worry about me. I know you don't want to be around Dad and if I'm not around, you won't have to. I'll be okay. Love, Tony

Amy closed her eyes. Dear God, where had he gone this time? And how much of a head start had he gotten? Her mind spun and her stomach rolled. She ran back to her room and grabbed up her cell phone, then dialed his number. He didn't answer.

"This is Tony. At the beep, well, you know what to do."

"Tony," she said, not bothering to keep the panic out of her voice, "wherever you are, stop, get to a safe place and call me." She disconnected the call and sent him a text, which he didn't answer.

She needed help. She needed Kendall. Amy tore out of the room and down the stairs, heedless of the noise she made. She ran down the hallway, through the great room and burst out the front door.

Kendall spotted her and got out, then ran to her, cupping her face. "What's wrong?"

She was crying. "Tony's gone! He ran away again."

He looked anguished. "Do you know when?"

"No. I just found this," she said, extending the note.

Kendall scanned the note, then he crushed it into a ball. "Get in. Did you try calling him?"

"And texting him," she said, climbing in, then closing the door. "It rolled to voice mail and he didn't respond."

"Can you think of where he'd go?"

"Back to Broadway, maybe. What if he made it out to the highway and he's hitchhiking again?"

"Do you think he would've stolen a car?"

"No, he doesn't know how to drive yet. But what if he took off on a four-wheeler?"

Kendall put the truck back in Park, then jumped out and sprinted down the side path where the ATVs were usually parked.

He came running back. "One's missing—he could've taken it… I didn't see anyone else take it out while I was sitting outside. If he's heading for the interstate, maybe he was planning to ditch it there and hitchhike."

"Hitchhike where?" she shrieked. "From the note, it sounds like he's not going home."

Then they looked at each other.

"Mom's," he said.

"Your mother's," she said at the same time.

Kendall pulled out his phone. "I'll call Mom to alert her. You call 911 and let the state police know to be looking for a hitchhiker on Interstate 75 South-bound between the exit for Route 7 and Calhoun, Georgia."

While she recited details about Tony's age and de-scription over the phone to the 911 operator, Kendall snapped his phone closed.

"He's not there," he said quietly, "but Mom is call-ing the local police and they'll be on the lookout."

As he steered the pickup out of town and toward the interstate, Amy kept her eyes peeled for any sight of Tony on a four-wheeler. Her heart was pounding. She couldn't keep the tears at bay.

Kendall reached over to squeeze her knee. "We'll find him. This is all my fault. He did this to protect you from me."

"He's confused," she said.

"If I hadn't been such an ass about everything, he wouldn't feel like he needed to do this. I've been angry and bitter, and it stops now. I'm so sorry. I love you, Amy, but if you or Tony don't want anything to do with me, then I'll just back away and leave you alone."

Amy blinked. "What did you say?"

"I said I'll just back away if that's what you want."

"Before that."

He frowned. "I love you?"

Her eyebrows when up. "Is that a question?"

"No...I love you."

Amy lifted her hands. "When did you decide that you loved me?"

He frowned. "Is this a joke? I've always loved you."

She was incredulous. "You've never said those words."

"But...you knew. Didn't you?"

"How would I know, Kendall, if you didn't tell me?"

"By the way I kissed you? Held you? Made love to you?"

"No, I never knew, not for sure. You said everything but I love you, so I just thought that meant you didn't. And when you didn't come after me—"

"You told me not to. I found out what city you lived in, but that's as far as I dug."

"You knew where I lived, but you didn't try to contact me?"

"Not directly, but why do you think I posted that ad in your paper?"

She frowned. "You posted it? I thought Marcus did."

"No. He told me to handle the ad. I put it in the Broadway newspaper because…I was hoping to lure you back home."

"You did?" Amy could scarcely believe her ears.

"But now I know that home is wherever you and Tony are. I told Marcus and Porter last night that I'm pulling out of the Sweetness partnership. I'll move anywhere to be close to you."

Amy's mind reeled. It was too much to process. She couldn't think straight until they found Tony.

"There's the four-wheeler," Kendall said, pointing to the right and slowing down.

Her heart skipped a beat. "He's not on it?"

"Probably ran out of gas. He's on foot." He looked over to her. "Let's hope no one's picked him up yet."

She scanned both sides of the road, terrified now that she knew he intended to hitchhike again. She looked over at Kendall, so grateful he was with her.

"Look, over there. There's something," he said, pointing and leaning forward. "Yes, that's him. That's Tony."

34

At the sight of his son on the side of the road, Kendall was almost weak with relief.

Amy started crying in earnest.

He reached over to squeeze her again. "Told you we'd find him."

She covered his hand with hers. "Thank you."

Kendall swallowed hard. Why was she thanking him when it was his fault in the first place that Tony had run? But for the moment, he just wanted to let her enjoy the fact that her son was okay.

And let his own heart rate get back to normal. Even though he'd been in some jams, various overseas skirmishes that he'd had to shoot himself out of, this was the most terrified he'd ever been. The fact that Amy dealt with this kind of parental stress day in and day out proved how amazing she was.

And he was ready to help shoulder that burden if she would let him. The talk with his brothers hadn't been nearly as hard as he thought it would be. They were disappointed that he was pulling out of the

Sweetness project, but they understood the fact that he had higher priorities now.

As they drove closer, Tony turned toward them and stuck out his thumb. Kendall put on his signal and slowed. At first Tony smiled, but when he realized who was driving, his smile faded.

Kendall pulled the truck alongside him. Amy zoomed down the window, then jerked her thumb toward the extended-cab seat. "Get in."

"Mom, I—"

"Get in the vehicle...*now*."

He frowned, his mouth jutting. "How long am I grounded for this time?"

"Your children are now grounded," she said.

Kendall had to turn his head to smother a smile.

Tony climbed in and settled in the seat behind them, still not making eye contact with Kendall. "I was trying to do you a favor," he said to his mother, then cut his gaze to Kendall.

"Don't you do me any favors," she said. "I raised you, remember? I can take care of myself."

"But he makes you cry!" Tony said, lurching forward in his seat.

"Your father can make me cry because..." Amy said, looking at Kendall. "Because I love him."

Kendall's heart swelled with hope that maybe he hadn't burned every bridge with Amy.

"But I heard you tell him you were going back to Broadway and you wanted to forget about him."

"I tried that once before," Amy said. "It didn't work."

Tony grunted. "I don't know what that means."

"It means," Amy said, "that I've changed my mind. How would you feel about you and I staying in Sweetness with your dad and being a family?"

Kendall was so happy, he had to slow down to take it all in. But he was holding his breath for Tony's answer.

"What about your big job?" Tony asked Amy.

"I have a job in Sweetness—sidewalks. And whatever else needs to be done."

Tony frowned, finally looking at Kendall. "Are you going to marry her?"

"I don't know," Kendall said, then he looked at Amy. "Will you marry me?"

"Yes."

Kendall grinned, then looked back to Tony. "Yes, I'm going to marry her."

"When?"

"As soon as your uncle Porter gets a church built."

Tony stuck his head between their seats. "Does this mean you're going to start having sex again?"

Kendall glanced at Amy, then back to Tony. "It looks that way."

"Can I have two brothers? No sisters, just brothers."

"We'll take that under advisement," Amy said.

Tony looked back and forth between them. "And does this mean we can all be Armstrongs now?"

Kendall decided to let Amy take that one.

"Yes," Amy said. "After we're married, I think we should all be Armstrongs."

"Tony Armstrong," Tony said, testing the sound of it. He nodded. "I like it."

They were on the long approach back into town, when they came up on a sign that read, Welcome to Sweetness, Georgia.

Kendall reached over to squeeze her hand. "Welcome home, baby."

She leaned over and kissed him. Kendall didn't think it was possible to be so happy. He made a vow at that moment that he would do his best to make her that happy, too.

* * * * *

Don't miss book three in the
SOUTHERN ROADS *trilogy,*
BABY, DON'T GO.
Marcus Armstrong is the last and the
biggest of the Armstrong brothers.
But the bigger they are, the harder they fall.
And Marcus falls hard for a sweet, shy,
home-cookin' Southern belle...who isn't
quite what she seems!

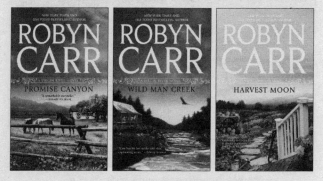

REQUEST YOUR FREE BOOKS!

2 FREE NOVELS
FROM THE ROMANCE COLLECTION
PLUS 2 FREE GIFTS!

YES! Please send me 2 FREE novels from the Romance Collection and my 2 FREE gifts (gifts are worth about $10). After receiving them, if I don't wish to receive any more books, I can return the shipping statement marked "cancel." If I don't cancel, I will receive 4 brand-new novels every month and be billed just $5.99 per book in the U.S. or $6.49 per book in Canada. That's a saving of at least 25% off the cover price. It's quite a bargain! Shipping and handling is just 50¢ per book in the U.S. and 75¢ per book in Canada.* I understand that accepting the 2 free books and gifts places me under no obligation to buy anything. I can always return a shipment and cancel at any time. Even if I never buy another book, the two free books and gifts are mine to keep forever.

194/394 MDN FELQ

Name	(PLEASE PRINT)	
Address		Apt. #
City	State/Prov.	Zip/Postal Code

Signature (if under 18, a parent or guardian must sign)

Mail to the **Reader Service:**
IN U.S.A.: P.O. Box 1867, Buffalo, NY 14240-1867
IN CANADA: P.O. Box 609, Fort Erie, Ontario L2A 5X3

Not valid for current subscribers to the Romance Collection
or the Romance/Suspense Collection.

Want to try two free books from another line?
Call 1-800-873-8635 or visit www.ReaderService.com.

* Terms and prices subject to change without notice. Prices do not include applicable taxes. Sales tax applicable in N.Y. Canadian residents will be charged applicable taxes. Offer not valid in Quebec. This offer is limited to one order per household. All orders subject to credit approval. Credit or debit balances in a customer's account(s) may be offset by any other outstanding balance owed by or to the customer. Please allow 4 to 6 weeks for delivery. Offer available while quantities last.

Your Privacy—The Reader Service is committed to protecting your privacy. Our Privacy Policy is available online at www.ReaderService.com or upon request from the Reader Service.

We make a portion of our mailing list available to reputable third parties that offer products we believe may interest you. If you prefer that we not exchange your name with third parties, or if you wish to clarify or modify your communication preferences, please visit us at www.ReaderService.com/consumerschoice or write to us at Reader Service Preference Service, P.O. Box 9062, Buffalo, NY 14269. Include your complete name and address.